THE STREET OF SEVEN STARS

By

Mary Roberts Rinehart

CHAPTER I

The old stucco house sat back in a garden, or what must once have been a garden, when that part of the Austrian city had been a royal game preserve. Tradition had it that the Empress Maria Theresa had used the building as a hunting-lodge, and undoubtedly there was something royal in the proportions of the salon. With all the candles lighted in the great glass chandelier, and no sidelights, so that the broken paneling was mercifully obscured by gloom, it was easy to believe that the great empress herself had sat in one of the tall old chairs and listened to anecdotes of questionable character; even, if tradition may be believed, related not a few herself.

The chandelier was not lighted on this rainy November night. Outside in the garden the trees creaked and bent before the wind, and the heavy barred gate, left open by the last comer, a piano student named Scatchett and dubbed "Scatch"— the gate slammed to and fro monotonously, giving now and then just enough pause for a hope that it had latched itself, a hope that was always destroyed by the next gust.

One candle burned in the salon. Originally lighted for the purpose of enabling Miss Scatchett to locate the score of a Tschaikowsky concerto, it had been moved to the small center table, and had served to give light if not festivity to the afternoon coffee and cakes. It still burned, a gnarled and stubby fragment, in its china holder; round it the disorder of the recent refreshment, three empty cups, a half of a small cake, a crumpled napkin or two,—there were never enough to go round,—and on the floor the score of the concerto, clearly abandoned for the things of the flesh.

The room was cold. The long casement windows creaked in time with the slamming of the gate and the candle flickered in response to a draft under the doors. The concerto flapped and slid along the uneven old floor. At the sound a girl in a black dress, who had been huddled near the tile stove, rose impatiently and picked it up. There was no impatience, however, in the way she handled the loose sheets. She put them together carefully, almost tenderly, and placed them on the top of the grand piano, anchoring them against the draft with a china dog from the stand.

The room was very bare—a long mirror between two of the windows, half a dozen chairs, a stand or two, and in a corner the grand piano. There were no rugs —the bare floor stretched bleakly into dim corners and was lost. The crystal pendants of the great chandelier looked like stalactites in a cave. The girl touched the piano keys; they were ice under her fingers.

In a sort of desperation she drew a chair underneath the chandelier, and armed with a handful of matches proceeded to the unheard-of extravagance of lighting it, not here and there, but throughout as high as she could reach, standing perilously on her tiptoes on the chair.

The resulting illumination revealed a number of things: It showed that the girl was young and comely and that she had been crying; it revealed the fact that the coal-pail was empty and the stove almost so; it let the initiated into the secret that the blackish fluid in the cups had been made with coffee extract that had been made of Heaven knows what; and it revealed in the cavernous corner near the door a number of trunks. The girl, having lighted all the candles, stood on the chair and looked at the trunks. She was very young, very tragic, very feminine. A door slammed down the hall and she stopped crying instantly. Diving into one of those receptacles that are a part of the mystery of the sex, she rubbed a chamois skin over her nose and her reddened eyelids.

The situation was a difficult one, but hardly, except to Harmony Wells, a tragedy. Few of us are so constructed that the Suite "Arlesienne" will serve as a luncheon, or a faulty fingering of the Waldweben from "Siegfried" will keep us awake at night. Harmony had lain awake more than once over some crime against her namesake, had paid penances of early rising and two hours of scales before breakfast, working with stiffened fingers in her cold little room where there was no room for a stove, and sitting on the edge of the bed in a faded kimono where once pink butterflies sported in a once blue-silk garden. Then coffee, rolls, and honey, and back again to work, with little Scatchett at the piano in the salon beyond the partition, wearing a sweater and fingerless gloves and holding a hot-water bottle on her knees. Three rooms beyond, down the stone hall, the Big Soprano, doing Madama Butterfly in bad German, helped to make an encircling wall of sound in the center of which one might practice peacefully.

Only the Portier objected. Morning after morning, crawling out at dawn from under his featherbed in the lodge below, he opened his door and listened to Harmony doing penance above; and morning after morning he shook his fist up the stone staircase.

"Gott im Himmel!" he would say to his wife, fumbling with the knot of his mustache bandage, "what a people, these Americans! So much noise and no music!"

"And mad!" grumbled his wife. "All the day coal, coal to heat; and at night the windows open! Karl the milkboy has seen it."

And now the little colony was breaking up. The Big Soprano was going back to her church, grand opera having found no place for her. Scatch was returning to be married, her heart full, indeed, of music, but her head much occupied with the trousseau in her trunks. The Harmar sisters had gone two weeks before, their funds having given out. Indeed, funds were very low with all of them. The "Bitte zum speisen" of the little German maid often called them to nothing more opulent than a stew of beef and carrots.

Not that all had been sordid. The butter had gone for opera tickets, and never was butter better spent. And there had been gala days—a fruitcake from Harmony's mother, a venison steak at Christmas, and once or twice on birthdays real American ice cream at a fabulous price and worth it. Harmony had bought a suit, too, a marvel of tailoring and cheapness, and a willow plume that would have cost treble its price in New York. Oh, yes, gala days, indeed, to offset the butter and the rainy winter and the faltering technic and the anxiety about money. For that they all had always, the old tragedy of the American music student abroad—

4

the expensive lessons, the delays in getting to the Master himself, the contention against German greed or Austrian whim. And always back in one's mind the home people, to whom one dares not confess that after nine months of waiting, or a year, one has seen the Master once or not at all.

Or—and one of the Harmar girls had carried back this scar in her soul—to go back rejected, as one of the unfit, on whom even the undermasters refuse to waste time. That has been, and often. Harmony stood on her chair and looked at the trunks. The Big Soprano was calling down the hall.

"Scatch," she was shouting briskly, "where is my hairbrush?"

A wail from Scatch from behind a closed door.

"I packed it, Heaven knows where! Do you need it really? Haven't you got a comb?"

"As soon as I get something on I'm coming to shake you. Half the teeth are out of my comb. I don't believe you packed it. Look under the bed."

Silence for a moment, while Scatch obeyed for the next moment.

"Here it is," she called joyously. "And here are Harmony's bedroom slippers. Oh, Harry, I found your slippers!" The girl got down off the chair and went to the door.

"Thanks, dear," she said. "I'm coming in a minute."

She went to the mirror, which had reflected the Empress Maria Theresa, and looked at her eyes. They were still red. Perhaps if she opened the window the air would brighten them.

Armed with the brush, little Scatchett hurried to the Big Soprano's room. She flung the brush on the bed and closed the door. She held her shabby wrapper about her and listened just inside the door. There were no footsteps, only the banging of the gate in the wind. She turned to the Big Soprano, heating a curling iron in the flame of a candle, and held out her hand.

"Look!" she said. "Under my bed! Ten kronen!"

Without a word the Big Soprano put down her curling-iron, and ponderously getting down on her knees, candle in hand, inspected the dusty floor beneath her bed. It revealed nothing but a cigarette, on which she pounced. Still squatting, she lighted the cigarette in the candle flame and sat solemnly puffing it.

"The first for a week," she said. "Pull out the wardrobe, Scatch; there may be another relic of my prosperous days."

But little Scatchett was not interested in Austrian cigarettes with a government monopoly and gilt tips. She was looking at the ten-kronen piece.

"Where is the other?" she asked in a whisper.

"In my powder-box."

Little Scatchett lifted the china lid and dropped the tiny gold-piece.

"Every little bit," she said flippantly, but still in a whisper, "added to what she's got, makes just a little bit more."

"Have you thought of a place to leave it for her? If Rosa finds it, it's good-bye. Heaven knows it was hard enough to get together, without losing it now. I'll have to jump overboard and swim ashore at New York—I haven't even a dollar for tips."

"New York!" said little Scatchett with her eyes glowing. "If Henry meets me I know he will—"

"Tut!" The Big Soprano got up cumbrously and stood looking down. "You and your Henry! Scatchy, child, has it occurred to your maudlin young mind that money isn't the only thing Harmony is going to need? She's going to be alone— and this is a bad town to be alone in. And she is not like us. You have your Henry. I'm a beefy person who has a stomach, and I'm thankful for it. But she is different —she's got the thing that you are as well without, the thing that my lack of is sending me back to fight in a church choir instead of grand opera."

Little Scatchett was rather puzzled.

"Temperament?" she asked. It had always been accepted in the little colony that Harmony was a real musician, a star in their lesser firmament.

The Big Soprano sniffed.

"If you like," she said. "Soul is a better word. Only the rich ought to have souls, Scatchy, dear."

This was over the younger girl's head, and anyhow Harmony was coming down the hall.

"I thought, under her pillow," she whispered. "She'll find it—"

Harmony came in, to find the Big Soprano heating a curler in the flame of a candle.

CHAPTER II

Harmony found the little hoard under her pillow that night when, having seen Scatch and the Big Soprano off at the station, she had come back alone to the apartment on the Siebensternstrasse. The trunks were gone now. Only the concerto score still lay on the piano, where little Scatchett, mentally on the dock at New York with Henry's arms about her, had forgotten it. The candles in the great chandelier had died in tears of paraffin that spattered the floor beneath. One or two of the sockets were still smoking, and the sharp odor of burning wickends filled the room.

Harmony had come through the garden quickly. She had had an uneasy sense of being followed, and the garden, with its moaning trees and slamming gate and the great dark house in the background, was a forbidding place at best. She had rung the bell and had stood, her back against the door, eyes and ears strained in the darkness. She had fancied that a figure had stopped outside the gate and stood looking in, but the next moment the gate had swung to and the Portier was fumbling at the lock behind her.

The Portier had put on his trousers over his night garments, and his mustache bandage gave him a sinister expression, rather augmented when he smiled at her. The Portier liked Harmony in spite of the early morning practicing; she looked like a singer at the opera for whom he cherished a hidden attachment. The singer had never seen him, but it was for her he wore the mustache bandage. Perhaps some day—hopefully! One must be ready!

The Portier gave Harmony a tiny candle and Harmony held out his tip, the five Hellers of custom. But the Portier was keen, and Rosa was a niece of his wife and talked more than she should. He refused the tip with a gesture.

"Bitte, Fraulein!" he said through the bandage. "It is for me a pleasure to admit you. And perhaps if the Fraulein is cold, a basin of soup."

The Portier was not pleasant to the eye. His nightshirt was open over his hairy chest and his feet were bare to the stone floor. But to Harmony that lonely night he was beautiful. She tried to speak and could not but she held out her hand in impulsive gratitude, and the Portier in his best manner bent over and kissed it. As she reached the curve of the stone staircase, carrying her tiny candle, the Portier was following her with his eyes. She was very like the girl of the opera.

The clang of the door below and the rattle of the chain were comforting to Harmony's ears. From the safety of the darkened salon she peered out into the garden again, but no skulking figure detached itself from the shadows, and the gate remained, for a marvel, closed.

It was when—having picked up her violin in a very passion of loneliness, only to put it down when she found that the familiar sounds echoed and reechoed sadly through the silent rooms—it was when she was ready for bed that she found the money under her pillow, and a scrawl from Scatchy, a breathless, apologetic scrawl, little Scatchett having adored her from afar, as the plain adore the beautiful, the mediocre the gifted:—

DEAREST HARRY [here a large blot, Scatchy being addicted to blots]: I am honestly frightened when I think what we are doing. But, oh, my dear, if you could know how pleased we are with ourselves you'd not deny us this pleasure. Harry, you have it—the real thing, you know, whatever it is—and I haven't. None of the rest of us had. And you must stay. To go now, just when lessons would mean everything—well, you must not think of it. We have scads to take us home, more than we need, both of us, or at least—well, I'm lying, and you know it. But we have enough, by being careful, and we want you to have this. It isn't much, but it may help. Ten Kronen of it I found to-night under my bed, and it may be yours anyhow.

"Sadie [Sadie was the Big Soprano] keeps saying awful things about our leaving you here, and she has rather terrified me. You are so beautiful, Harry,—although you never let us tell you so. And Sadie says you have a soul and I haven't, and that souls are deadly things to have. I feel to-night that in urging you to stay I am taking the burden of your soul on me! Do be careful, Harry. If any one you do not know speaks to you call a policeman. And be sure you get into a respectable pension. There are queer ones.

"Sadie and I think that if you can get along on what you get from home—you said your mother would get insurance, didn't you?—and will keep this as a sort of fund to take you home if anything should go wrong—. But perhaps we are needlessly worried. In any case, of course it's a loan, and you can preserve that magnificent independence of yours by sending it back when you get to work to make your fortune. And if you are doubtful at all, just remember that hopeful little mother of yours who sent you over to get what she had never been able to have for herself, and who planned this for you from the time you were a kiddy and she named you Harmony.

"I'm not saying good-bye. I can't.

"SCATCH."

That night, while the Portier and his wife slept under their crimson feather beds and the crystals of the chandelier in the salon shook in the draft as if the old Austrian court still danced beneath, Harmony fought her battle. And a battle it was. Scatchy and the Big Soprano had not known everything. There had been no insurance on her father's life; the little mother was penniless. A married sister would care for her, but what then? Harmony had enough remaining of her letter of credit to take her home, and she had—the hoard under the pillow. To go back and teach the violin; or to stay and finish under the master, be presented, as he had promised her, at a special concert in Vienna, with all the prestige at home that that would mean, and its resulting possibility of fame and fortune—which?

She decided to stay. There might be a concert or so, and she could teach English. The Viennese were crazy about English. Some of the stores advertised "English Spoken." That would be something to fall back on, a clerkship during the day.

Toward dawn she discovered that she was very cold, and she went into the Big Soprano's deserted and disordered room. The tile stove was warm and comfortable, but on the toilet table there lay a disreputable comb with most of the teeth gone. Harmony kissed this unromantic object! Which reveals the fact that, genius or not, she was only a young and rather frightened girl, and that every atom of her ached with loneliness.

She did not sleep at all, but sat curled up on the bed with her feet under her and thought things out. At dawn the Portier, crawling out into the cold from under his feathers, opened the door into the hall and listened. She was playing, not practicing, and the music was the barcarolle from the "Tales" of Hoffmann. Standing in the doorway in his night attire, his chest open to the frigid morning air, his face upraised to the floor above, he hummed the melody in a throaty tenor.

When the music had died away he went in and closed the door sheepishly. His wife stood over the stove, a stick of firewood in her hand. She eyed him.

"So! It is the American Fraulein now!"

"I did but hum a little. She drags out my heart with her music." He fumbled with his mustache bandage, which was knotted behind, keeping one eye on his wife, whose morning pleasure it was to untie it for him.

"She leaves to-day," she announced, ignoring the knot.

"Why? She is alone. Rosa says—"

"She leaves to-day!"

The knot was hopeless now, double-tied and pulled to smooth compactness. The Portier jerked at it.

"No Fraulein stays here alone. It is not respectable. And what saw I last night, after she entered and you stood moon-gazing up the stair after her! A man in the gateway!"

The Portier was angry. He snarled something through the bandage, which had slipped down over his mouth, and picked up a great knife.

"She will stay if she so desire," he muttered furiously, and, raising the knife, he cut the knotted string. His mustache, faintly gray and sweetly up-curled, stood revealed.

"She will stay!" he repeated. "And when you see men at the gate, let me know. She is an angel!"

"And she looks like the angel at the opera, hein?"

This was a crushing blow. The Portier wilted. Such things come from telling one's cousin, who keeps a brushshop, what is in one's heart. Yesterday his wife had needed a brush, and to-day—Himmel, the girl must go!

Harmony knew also that she must go. The apartment was large and expensive; Rosa ate much and wasted more. She must find somewhere a tiny room with board, a humble little room but with a stove. It is folly to practice with stiffened fingers. A room where her playing would not annoy people, that was important.

She paid Rosa off that morning out of money left for that purpose. Rosa wept. She said she would stay with the Fraulein for her keep, because it was not the custom for young ladies to be alone in the city—young girls of the people, of course; but beautiful young ladies, no!

Harmony gave her an extra krone or two out of sheer gratitude, but she could not keep her. And at noon, having packed her trunk, she went down to interview the Portier and his wife, who were agents under the owner for the old house.

The Portier, entirely subdued, was sweeping out the hallway. He looked past the girl, not at her, and observed impassively that the lease was up and it was her privilege to go. In the daylight she was not so like the angel, and after all she could only play the violin. The angel had a voice, such a voice! And besides, there was an eye at the crack of the door.

The bit of cheer of the night before was gone; it was with a heavy heart that Harmony started on her quest for cheaper quarters.

Winter, which had threatened for a month, had come at last. The cobblestones glittered with ice and the small puddles in the gutters were frozen. Across the street a spotted deer, shot in the mountains the day before and hanging from a hook before a wild-game shop, was frozen quite stiff. It was a pretty creature. The girl turned her eyes away. A young man, buying cheese and tinned fish in the shop, watched after her.

"That's an American girl, isn't it?" he asked in American-German.

The shopkeeper was voluble. Also Rosa had bought much from him, and Rosa talked. When the American left the shop he knew everything of Harmony that Rosa knew except her name. Rosa called her "The Beautiful One." Also he was short one krone four beliers in his change, which is readily done when a customer is plainly thinking of a "beautiful one."

9

Harmony searched all day for the little room with board and a stove and no objection to practicing. There were plenty—but the rates! The willow plume looked prosperous, and she had a way of making the plainest garments appear costly. Landladies looked at the plume and the suit and heard the soft swish of silk beneath, which marks only self-respect in the American woman but is extravagance in Europe, and added to their regular terms until poor Harmony's heart almost stood still. And then at last toward evening she happened on a gloomy little pension near the corner of the Alserstrasse, and it being dark and the plume not showing, and the landlady missing the rustle owing to cotton in her ears for earache, Harmony found terms that she could meet for a time.

A mean little room enough, but with a stove. The bed sagged in the center, and the toilet table had a mirror that made one eye appear higher than the other and twisted one's nose. But there was an odor of stewing cabbage in the air. Also, alas, there was the odor of many previous stewed cabbages, and of dusty carpets and stale tobacco. Harmony had had no lunch; she turned rather faint.

She arranged to come at once, and got out into the comparative purity of the staircase atmosphere and felt her way down. She reeled once or twice. At the bottom of the dark stairs she stood for a moment with her eyes closed, to the dismay of a young man who had just come in with a cheese and some tinned fish under his arm.

He put down his packages on the stone floor and caught her arm.

"Not ill, are you?" he asked in English, and then remembering. "Bist du krank?" He colored violently at that, recalling too late the familiarity of the "du."

Harmony smiled faintly.

"Only tired," she said in English. "And the odor of cabbage—".

Her color had come back and she freed herself from his supporting hand. He whistled softly. He had recognized her.

"Cabbage, of course!" he said. "The pension upstairs is full of it. I live there, and I've eaten so much of it I could be served up with pork."

"I am going to live there. Is it as bad as that?"

He waved a hand toward the parcels on the floor.

"So bad," he observed, "that I keep body and soul together by buying strong and odorous food at the delicatessens—odorous, because only rugged flavors rise above the atmosphere up there. Cheese is the only thing that really knocks out the cabbage, and once or twice even cheese has retired defeated."

"But I don't like cheese." In sheer relief from the loneliness of the day her spirits were rising.

"Then coffee! But not there. Coffee at the coffee-house on the corner. I say—" He hesitated.

"Yes?"

"Would you—don't you think a cup of coffee would set you up a bit?"

"It sounds attractive,"—uncertainly.

"Coffee with whipped cream and some little cakes?"

Harmony hesitated. In the gloom of the hall she could hardly see this brisk

10

young American—young, she knew by his voice, tall by his silhouette, strong by the way he had caught her. She could not see his face, but she liked his voice.

"Do you mean—with you?"

"I'm a doctor. I am going to fill my own prescription."

That sounded reassuring. Doctors were not as other men; they were legitimate friends in need.

"I am sure it is not proper, but—"

"Proper! Of course it is. I shall send you a bill for professional services. Besides, won't we be formally introduced to-night by the landlady? Come now—to the coffee-house and the Paris edition of the 'Herald'!" But the next moment he paused and ran his hand over his chin. "I'm pretty disreputable," he explained. "I have been in a clinic all day, and, hang it all, I'm not shaved."

"What difference does that make?"

"My dear young lady," he explained gravely, picking up the cheese and the tinned fish, "it makes a difference in me that I wish you to realize before you see me in a strong light."

He rapped at the Portier's door, with the intention of leaving his parcels there, but receiving no reply tucked them under his arm. A moment later Harmony was in the open air, rather dazed, a bit excited, and lovely with the color the adventure brought into her face. Her companion walked beside her, tall, slightly stooped. She essayed a fugitive little side-glance up at him, and meeting his eyes hastily averted hers.

They passed a policeman, and suddenly there flashed into the girl's mind little Scatchett's letter.

"Do be careful, Harry. If any one you do not know speaks to you, call a policeman."

CHAPTER III

The coffee-house was warm and bright. Round its small tables were gathered miscellaneous groups, here and there a woman, but mostly men—uniformed officers, who made of the neighborhood coffee-house a sort of club, where under their breath they criticized the Government and retailed small regimental gossip; professors from the university, still wearing under the beards of middle life the fine horizontal scars of student days; elderly doctors from the general hospital across the street; even a Hofrath or two, drinking beer and reading the "Fliegende Blaetter" and "Simplicissimus"; and in an alcove round a billiard table a group of noisy Korps students. Over all a permeating odor of coffee, strong black coffee, made with a fig or two to give it color. It rose even above the blue tobacco haze and dominated the atmosphere with its spicy and stimulating richness. A bustle of waiters, a hum of conversation, the rattle of newspapers and the click of billiard balls—this was the coffee-house.

Harmony had never been inside one before. The little music colony had been a tight-closed corporation, retaining its American integrity, in spite of the salon of Maria Theresa and three expensive lessons a week in German. Harmony knew the art galleries and the churches, which were free, and the opera, thanks to no butter at supper. But of that backbone of Austrian life, the coffee-house, she was profoundly ignorant.

Her companion found her a seat in a corner near a heater and disappeared for an instant on the search for the Paris edition of the "Herald." The girl followed him with her eyes. Seen under the bright electric lights, he was not handsome, hardly good-looking. His mouth was wide, his nose irregular, his hair a nondescript brown,—but the mouth had humor, the nose character, and, thank Heaven, there was plenty of hair. Not that Harmony saw all this at once. As he tacked to and fro round the tables, with a nod here and a word there, she got a sort of ensemble effect—a tall man, possibly thirty, broadshouldered, somewhat stooped, as tall men are apt to be. And shabby, undeniably shabby!

The shabbiness was a shock. A much-braided officer, trim from the points of his mustache to the points of his shoes, rose to speak to him. The shabbiness was accentuated by the contrast. Possibly the revelation was an easement to the girl's nervousness. This smiling and unpressed individual, blithely waving aloft the Paris edition of the "Herald" and equally blithely ignoring the maledictions of the student from whom he had taken it—even Scatchy could not have called him a vulture or threatened him with the police.

He placed the paper before her and sat down at her side, not to interfere with her outlook over the room.

"Warmer?" he asked.

"Very much."

"Coffee is coming. And cinnamon cakes with plenty of sugar. They know me here and they know where I live. They save the sugariest cakes for me. Don't let me bother you; go on and read. See which of the smart set is getting a divorce— or is it always the same one? And who's President back home."

"I'd rather look round. It's curious, isn't it?"

"Curious? It's heavenly! It's the one thing I am going to take back to America with me—one coffee-house, one dozen military men for local color, one dozen students ditto, and one proprietor's wife to sit in the cage and shortchange the unsuspecting. I'll grow wealthy."

"But what about the medical practice?"

He leaned over toward her; his dark-gray eyes fulfilled the humorous promise of his mouth.

"Why, it will work out perfectly," he said whimsically. "The great American public will eat cinnamon cakes and drink coffee until the feeble American nervous system will be shattered. I shall have an office across the street!"

After that, having seen how tired she looked, he forbade conversation until she had had her coffee. She ate the cakes, too, and he watched her with comfortable satisfaction.

"Nod your head but don't speak," he said. "Remember, I am prescribing, and there's to be no conversation until the coffee is down. Shall I or shall I not open the cheese?"

But Harmony did not wish the cheese, and so signified. Something inherently delicate in the unknown kept him from more than an occasional swift glance at her. He read aloud, as she ate, bits of news from the paper, pausing to sip his own coffee and to cast an eye over the crowded room. Here and there an officer, gazing with too open admiration on Harmony's lovely face, found himself fixed by a pair of steel-gray eyes that were anything but humorous at that instant, and thought best to shift his gaze.

The coffee finished, the girl began to gather up her wraps. But the unknown protested.

"The function of a coffee-house," he explained gravely, "is twofold. Coffee is only the first half. The second half is conversation."

"I converse very badly."

"So do I. Suppose we talk about ourselves. We are sure to do that well. Shall I commence?"

Harmony was in no mood to protest. Having swallowed coffee, why choke over conversation? Besides, she was very comfortable. It was warm there, with the heater at her back; better than the little room with the sagging bed and the doors covered with wall paper. Her feet had stopped aching, too, She could have sat there for hours. And—why evade it?—she was interested. This whimsical and respectful young man with his absurd talk and his shabby clothes had roused her curiosity.

"Please," she assented.

"Then, first of all, my name. I'm getting that over early, because it isn't much, as names go. Peter Byrne it is. Don't shudder."

"Certainly I'm not shuddering."

"I have another name, put in by my Irish father to conciliate a German uncle of my mother's. Augustus! It's rather a mess. What shall I put on my professional brassplate? If I put P. Augustus Byrne nobody's fooled. They know my wretched first name is Peter."

"Or Patrick."

"I rather like Patrick—if I thought it might pass as Patrick! Patrick has possibilities. The diminutive is Pat, and that's not bad. But Peter!"

"Do you know," Harmony confessed half shyly, "I like Peter as a name."

"Peter it shall be, then. I go down to posterity and fame as Peter Byrne. The rest doesn't amount to much, but I want you to know it, since you have been good enough to accept me on faith. I'm here alone, from a little town in eastern Ohio; worked my way through a coeducational college in the West and escaped unmarried; did two years in a drygoods store until, by saving and working in my vacations, I got through medical college and tried general practice. Didn't like it—always wanted to do surgery. A little legacy from the German uncle, trying to atone for the 'Augustus,' gave me enough money to come here. I've got a chance with the Days—surgeons, you know—when I go back, if I can hang on long

13

enough. That's all. Here's a traveler's check with my name on it, to vouch for the truth of this thrilling narrative. Gaze on it with awe; there are only a few of them left!"

Harmony was as delicately strung, as vibratingly responsive as the strings of her own violin, and under the even lightness of his tone she felt many things that met a response in her—loneliness and struggle, and the ever-present anxiety about money, grim determination, hope and fear, and even occasional despair. He was still young, but there were lines in his face and a hint of gray in his hair. Even had he been less frank, she would have known soon enough—the dingy little pension, the shabby clothes—

She held out her hand.

"Thank you for telling me," she said simply. "I think I understand very well because—it's music with me: violin. And my friends have gone, so I am alone, too."

He leaned his elbows on the table and looked out over the crowd without seeing it.

"It's curious, isn't it?" he said. "Here we are, you and I, meeting in the center of Europe, both lonely as the mischief, both working our heads off for an idea that may never pan out! Why aren't you at home to-night, eating a civilized beefsteak and running upstairs to get ready for a nice young man to bring you a box of chocolates? Why am I not measuring out calico in Shipley & West's? Instead, we are going to Frau Schwarz', to listen to cold ham and scorched compote eaten in six different languages."

Harmony made no immediate reply. He seemed to expect none. She was drawing on her gloves, her eyes, like his, roving over the crowd.

Far back among the tables a young man rose and yawned. Then, seeing Byrne, he waved a greeting to him. Byrne's eyes, from being introspective, became watchful.

The young man was handsome in a florid, red-checked way, with black hair and blue eyes. Unlike Byrne, he was foppishly neat. He was not alone. A slim little Austrian girl, exceedingly chic, rose when he did and threw away the end of a cigarette.

"Why do we go so soon?" she demanded fretfully in German. "It is early still."

He replied in English. It was a curious way they had, and eminently satisfactory, each understanding better than he spoke the other's language.

"Because, my beloved," he said lightly, "you are smoking a great many poisonous and highly expensive cigarettes. Also I wish to speak to Peter."

The girl followed his eyes and stiffened jealously.

"Who is that with Peter?"

"We are going over to find out, little one. Old Peter with a woman at last!"

The little Austrian walked delicately, swaying her slim body with a slow and sensuous grace. She touched an officer as she passed him, and paused to apologize, to the officer's delight and her escort's irritation. And Peter Byrne watched and waited, a line of annoyance between his brows. The girl was ahead;

14

that complicated things.

When she was within a dozen feet of the table he rose hastily, with a word of apology, and met the couple. It was adroitly done. He had taken the little Austrian's arm and led her by the table while he was still greeting her. He held her in conversation in his absurd German until they had reached the swinging doors, while her companion followed helplessly. And he bowed her out, protesting his undying admiration for her eyes, while the florid youth alternately raged behind him and stared back at Harmony, interested and unconscious behind her table.

The little Austrian was on the pavement when Byrne turned, unsmiling, to the other man.

"That won't do, you know, Stewart," he said, grave but not unfriendly.

"The Kid wouldn't bite her."

"We'll not argue about it."

After a second's awkward pause Stewart smiled.

"Certainly not," he agreed cheerfully. "That is up to you, of course. I didn't know. We're looking for you to-night."

A sudden repulsion for the evening's engagement rose in Byrne, but the situation following his ungraciousness was delicate.

"I'll be round," he said. "I have a lecture and I may be late, but I'll come."

The "Kid" was not stupid. She moved off into the night, chin in air, angrily flushed.

"You saw!" she choked, when Stewart had overtaken her and slipped a hand through her arm. "He protects her from me! It is because of you. Before I knew you—"

"Before you knew me, little one," he said cheerfully, "you were exactly what you are now."

She paused on the curb and raised her voice.

"So! And what is that?"

"Beautiful as the stars, only—not so remote."

In their curious bi-lingual talk there was little room for subtlety. The "beautiful" calmed her, but the second part of the sentence roused her suspicion.

"Remote? What is that?"

"I was thinking of Worthington."

The name was a signal for war. Stewart repented, but too late.

In the cold evening air, to the amusement of a passing detail of soldiers trundling a breadwagon by a rope, Stewart stood on the pavement and dodged verbal brickbats of Viennese idioms and German epithets. He drew his chin into the up-turned collar of his overcoat and waited, an absurdly patient figure, until the hail of consonants had subsided into a rain of tears. Then he took the girl's elbow again and led her, childishly weeping, into a narrow side street beyond the prying ears and eyes of the Alserstrasse.

Byrne went back to Harmony. The incident of Stewart and the girl was closed and he dismissed it instantly. That situation was not his, or of his making. But here in the coffee-house, lovely, alluring, rather puzzled at this moment, was also a

15

situation. For there was a situation. He had suspected it that morning, listening to the delicatessen-seller's narrative of Rosa's account of the disrupted colony across in the old lodge; he had been certain of it that evening, finding Harmony in the dark entrance to his own rather sordid pension. Now, in the bright light of the coffee-house, surmising her poverty, seeing her beauty, the emotional coming and going of her color, her frank loneliness, and God save the mark!—her trust in him, he accepted the situation and adopted it: his responsibility, if you please.

He straightened under it. He knew the old city fairly well—enough to love it and to loathe it in one breath. He had seen its tragedies and passed them by, or had, in his haphazard way, thrown a greeting to them, or even a glass of native wine. And he knew the musical temperament; the all or nothing of its insistent demands; its heights that are higher than others, its wretchednesses that are hell. Once in the Hofstadt Theater, where he had bought standing room, he had seen a girl he had known in Berlin, where he was taking clinics and where she was cooking her own meals. She had been studying singing. In the Hofstadt Theater she had worn a sable coat and had avoided his eyes.

Perhaps the old coffee-house had seen nothing more absurd, in its years of coffee and billiards and Munchener beer, than Peter's new resolution that night: this poverty adopting poverty, this youth adopting youth, with the altruistic purpose of saving it from itself.

And this, mind you, before Peter Byrne had heard Harmony's story or knew her name, Rosa having called her "The Beautiful One" in her narrative, and the delicatessen-seller being literal in his repetition.

Back to "The Beautiful One" went Peter Byrne, and, true to his new part of protector and guardian, squared his shoulders and tried to look much older than he really was, and responsible. The result was a grimness that alarmed Harmony back to the forgotten proprieties.

"I think I must go," she said hurriedly, after a glance at his determinedly altruistic profile. "I must finish packing my things. The Portier has promised—"

"Go! Why, you haven't even told me your name!"

"Frau Schwarz will present you to-night," primly and rising.

Peter Byrne rose, too.

"I am going back with you. You should not go through that lonely yard alone after dark."

"Yard! How do you know that?"

Byrne was picking up the cheese, which he had thoughtlessly set on the heater, and which proved to be in an alarming state of dissolution. It took a moment to rewrap, and incidentally furnished an inspiration. He indicated it airily.

"Saw you this morning coming out—delicatessen shop across the street," he said glibly. And then, in an outburst of honesty which the girl's eyes seemed somehow to compel: "That's true, but it's not all the truth. I was on the bus last night, and when you got off alone I—I saw you were an American, and that's not a good neighborhood. I took the liberty of following you to your gate!"

He need not have been alarmed. Harmony was only grateful, and said so. And in her gratitude she made no objection to his suggestion that he see her safely to the old lodge and help her carry her hand-luggage and her violin to the pension. He paid the trifling score, and followed by many eyes in the room they went out into the crisp night together.

At the lodge the doors stood wide, and a vigorous sound of scrubbing showed that the Portier's wife was preparing for the inspection of possible new tenants. She was cleaning down the stairs by the light of a candle, and the steam of the hot water on the cold marble invested her like an aura. She stood aside to let them pass, and then went cumbrously down the stairs to where, a fork in one hand and a pipe in the other, the Portier was frying chops for the evening meal.

"What have I said?" she demanded from the doorway. "Your angel is here."

"So!"

"She with whom you sing, old cracked voice! Whose money you refuse, because she reminds you of your opera singer! She is again here, and with a man!"

"It is the way of the young and beautiful—there is always a man," said the Portier, turning a chop.

His wife wiped her steaming hands on her apron and turned away, exasperated.

"It is the same man whom I last night saw at the gate," she threw back over her shoulder. "I knew it from the first; but you, great booby, can see nothing but red lips. Bah!"

Upstairs in the salon of Maria Theresa, lighted by one candle and freezing cold, in a stiff chair under the great chandelier Peter Byrne sat and waited and blew on his fingers. Down below, in the Street of Seven Stars, the arc lights swung in the wind.

CHAPTER IV

The supper that evening was even unusually bad. Frau Schwarz, much crimped and clad in frayed black satin, presided at the head of the long table. There were few, almost no Americans, the Americans flocking to good food at reckless prices in more fashionable pensions; to the Frau Gallitzenstein's, for instance, in the Kochgasse, where there was to be had real beefsteak, where turkeys were served at Thanksgiving and Christmas, and where, were one so minded, one might revel in whipped cream.

The Pension Schwarz, however, was not without adornment. In the center of the table was a large bunch of red cotton roses with wire stems and green paper leaves, and over the side-table, with its luxury of compote in tall glass dishes and its wealth of small hard cakes, there hung a framed motto which said, "Nicht Rauchen," "No Smoking,"—and which looked suspiciously as if it had once adorned a compartment of a railroad train.

Peter Byrne was early in the dining-room. He had made, for him, a careful toilet, which consisted of a shave and clean linen. But he had gone further: He had discovered, for the first time in the three months of its defection, a button

17

missing from his coat, and had set about to replace it. He had cut a button from another coat, by the easy method of amputating it with a surgical bistoury, and had sewed it in its new position with a curved surgical needle and a few inches of sterilized catgut. The operation was slow and painful, and accomplished only with the aid of two cigarettes and an artery clip. When it was over he tied the ends in a surgeon's knot underneath and stood back to consider the result. It seemed neat enough, but conspicuous. After a moment or two of troubled thought he blacked the white catgut with a dot of ink and went on his way rejoicing.

Peter Byrne was entirely untroubled as to the wisdom of the course he had laid out for himself. He followed no consecutive line of thought as he dressed. When he was not smoking he was whistling, and when he was doing neither, and the needle proved refractory in his cold fingers, he was swearing to himself. For there was no fire in the room. The materials for a fire were there, and a white tile stove, as cozy as an obelisk in a cemetery, stood in the corner. But fires are expensive, and hardly necessary when one sleeps with all one's windows open—one window, to be exact, the room being very small—and spends most of the day in a warm and comfortable shambles called a hospital.

To tell the truth he was not thinking of Harmony at all, except subconsciously, as instance the button. He was going over, step by step, the technic of an operation he had seen that afternoon, weighing, considering, even criticizing. His conclusion, reached as he brushed back his hair and put away his sewing implements, was somewhat to the effect that he could have done a better piece of work with his eyes shut and his hands tied behind his back; and that if it were not for the wealth of material to work on he'd pack up and go home. Which brought him back to Harmony and his new responsibility. He took off the necktie he had absently put on and hunted out a better one.

He was late at supper—an offense that brought a scowl from the head of the table, a scowl that he met with a cheerful smile. Harmony was already in her place. Seated between a little Bulgarian and a Jewish student from Galicia, she was almost immediately struggling in a sea of language, into which she struck out now and then tentatively, only to be again submerged. Byrne had bowed to her conventionally, even coldly, aware of the sharp eyes and tongues round the table, but Harmony did not understand. She had expected moral support from his presence, and failing that she sank back into the loneliness and depression of the day. Her bright color faded; her eyes looked tragic and rather aloof. She ate almost nothing, and left the table before the others had finished.

What curious little dramas of the table are played under unseeing eyes! What small tragedies begin with the soup and end with dessert! What heartaches with a salad! Small tragedies of averted eyes, looking away from appealing ones; lips that tremble with wretchedness nibbling daintily at a morsel; smiles that sear; foolish bits of talk that mean nothing except to one, and to that one everything! Harmony, freezing at Peter's formal bow and gazing obstinately ahead during the rest of the meal, or no nearer Peter than the red-paper roses, and Peter, showering the little Bulgarian next to her with detestable German in the hope of a glance.

18

And over all the odor of cabbage salad, and the "Nicht Rauchen" sign, and an acrimonious discussion on eugenics between an American woman doctor named Gates and a German matron who had had fifteen children, and who reduced every general statement to a personal insult.

Peter followed Harmony as soon as he dared. Her door was closed, and she was playing very softly, so as to disturb no one. Defiantly, too, had he only known it, her small chin up and her color high again; playing the "Humoresque," of all things, in the hope, of course, that he would hear it and guess from her choice the wild merriment of her mood. Peter rapped once or twice, but obtained no answer, save that the "Humoresque" rose a bit higher; and, Dr. Gates coming along the hall just then, he was forced to light a cigarette to cover his pausing.

Dr. Gates, however, was not suspicious. She was a smallish woman of forty or thereabout, with keen eyes behind glasses and a masculine disregard of clothes, and she paused by Byrne to let him help her into her ulster.

"New girl, eh?" she said, with a birdlike nod toward the door. "Very gay, isn't she, to have just finished a supper like that! Honestly, Peter, what are we going to do?"

"Growl and stay on, as we have for six months. There is better food, but not for our terms."

Dr. Gates sighed, and picking a soft felt hat from the table put it on with a single jerk down over her hair.

"Oh, darn money, anyhow!" she said. "Come and walk to the corner with me. I have a lecture."

Peter promised to follow in a moment, and hurried back to his room. There, on a page from one of his lecture notebooks, he wrote—

"Are you ill? Or have I done anything?"

"P. B."

This with great care he was pushing under Harmony's door when the little Bulgarian came along and stopped, smiling. He said nothing, nor did Peter, who rose and dusted his knees. The little Bulgarian spoke no English and little German. Between them was the wall of language. But higher than this barrier was the understanding of their common sex. He held out his hand, still smiling, and Peter, grinning sheepishly, took it. Then he followed the woman doctor down the stairs.

To say that Peter Byrne was already in love with Harmony would be absurd. She attracted him, as any beautiful and helpless girl attracts an unattracted man. He was much more concerned, now that he feared he had offended her, than he would have been without this fillip to his interest. But even his concern did not prevent his taking copious and intelligent notes at his lecture that night, or interfere with his enjoyment of the Stein of beer with which, after it was over, he washed down its involved German.

The engagement at Stewart's irked him somewhat. He did not approve of Stewart exactly, not from any dislike of the man, but from a lack of fineness in the man himself—an intangible thing that seems to be a matter of that

19

unfashionable essence, the soul, as against the clay; of the thing contained, by an inverse metonymy, for the container.

Boyer, a nerve man from Texas, met him on the street, and they walked to Stewart's apartment together. The frosty air and the rapid exercise combined to drive away Byrne's irritation; that, and the recollection that it was Saturday night and that to-morrow there would be no clinics, no lectures, no operations; that the great shambles would be closed down and that priests would read mass to convalescents in the chapels. He was whistling as he walked along.

Boyer, a much older man, whose wife had come over with him, stopped under a street light to consult his watch.

"Almost ten!" he said. "I hope you don't mind, Byrne; but I told Jennie I was going to your pension. She detests Stewart."

"Oh, that's all right. She knows you're playing poker?"

"Yes. She doesn't object to poker. It's the other. You can't make a good woman understand that sort of thing."

"Thank God for that!"

After a moment of silence Byrne took up his whistling again. It was the "Humoresque."

Stewart's apartment was on the third floor. Admission at that hour was to be gained only by ringing, and Boyer touched the bell. The lights were still on, however, in the hallways, revealing not overclean stairs and, for a wonder, an electric elevator. This, however, a card announced as out of order. Boyer stopped and examined the card grimly.

"'Out of order'!" he observed. "Out of order since last spring, judging by that card. Vorwarts!"

They climbed easily, deliberately. At home in God's country Boyer played golf, as became the leading specialist of his county. Byrne, with a driving-arm like the rod of a locomotive, had been obliged to forswear the more expensive game for tennis, with a resulting muscular development that his slight stoop belied. He was as hard as nails, without an ounce of fat, and he climbed the long steep flights with an elasticity that left even Boyer a step or so behind.

Stewart opened the door himself, long German pipe in hand, his coat replaced by a worn smoking-jacket. The little apartment was thick with smoke, and from a room on the right came the click of chips and the sound of beer mugs on wood.

Marie, restored to good humor, came out to greet them, and both men bowed ceremoniously over her hand, clicking their heels together and bowing from the waist. Byrne sniffed.

"What do I smell, Marie?" he demanded. "Surely not sausages!"

Marie dimpled. It was an old joke, to be greeted as one greets an old friend. It was always sausages.

"Sausages, of a truth—fat ones.'

"But surely not with mustard?"

"Ach, ja—englisch mustard."

Stewart and Boyer had gone on ahead. Marie laid a detaining hand on Byrne's

20

arm.

"I was very angry with you to-day."

"With me?"

Like the others who occasionally gathered in Stewart's unconventional menage, Byrne had adopted Stewart's custom of addressing Marie in English, while she replied in her own tongue.

"Ja. I wished but to see nearer the American Fraulein's hat, and you—She is rich, so?"

"I really don't know. I think not."

"And good?"

"Yes, of course."

Marie was small; she stood, her head back, her eyes narrowed, looking up at Byrne. There was nothing evil in her face, it was not even hard. Rather, there was a sort of weariness, as of age and experience. She had put on a white dress, cut out at the neck, and above her collarbones were small, cuplike hollows. She was very thin.

"I was sad to-night," she said plaintively. "I wished to jump out the window."

Byrne was startled, but the girl was smiling at the recollection.

"And I made you feel like that?"

"Not you—the other Fraulein. I was dirt to her. I—" She stopped tragically, then sniffled.

"The sausages!" she cried, and gathering up her skirts ran toward the kitchen. Byrne went on into the sitting-room.

Stewart was a single man spending two years in post-graduate work in Germany and Austria, not so much because the Germans and Austrians could teach what could not be taught at home, but because of the wealth of clinical material. The great European hospitals, filled to overflowing, offered unlimited choice of cases. The contempt for human life of overpopulated cities, coupled with the extreme poverty and helplessness of the masses, combined to form that tragic part of the world which dies that others may live.

Stewart, like Byrne, was doing surgery, and the very lack of fineness which Byrne felt in the man promised something in his work, a sort of ruthlessness, a singleness of purpose, good or bad, an overwhelming egotism that in his profession might only be a necessary self-reliance.

His singleness of purpose had, at the beginning of his residence in Vienna, devoted itself to making him comfortable. With the narrow means at his control he had the choice of two alternatives: To live, as Byrne was living, in a third-class pension, stewing in summer, freezing in winter, starving always; or the alternative he had chosen.

The Stewart apartment had only three rooms, but it possessed that luxury of luxuries, a bath. It was not a bath in the usual sense of water on tap, and shining nickel plate, but a bath for all that, where with premeditation and forethought one might bathe. The room had once been a fuel and store room, but now boasted a tin tub and a stove with a reservoir on top, where water might be heated to the boiling point, at the same time bringing up the atmosphere to a point where the tin tub sizzled if one touched it.

Behind the bathroom a tiny kitchen with a brick stove; next, a bedroom; the whole incredibly neat. Along one side of the wall a clothespress, which the combined wardrobes of two did not fill. And beyond that again, opening through an arch with a dingy chenille curtain, the sitting-room, now in chaotic disorder.

Byrne went directly to the sitting-room. There were four men already there: Stewart and Boyer, a pathology man named Wallace Hunter, doing research work at the general hospital, and a young piano student from Tennessee named MacLean. The cards had been already dealt, and Byrne stood by waiting for the hand to be played.

The game was a small one, as befitted the means of the majority. It was a regular Saturday night affair, as much a custom as the beer that sat in Steins on the floor beside each man, or as Marie's boiled Wiener sausages.

The blue chips represented a Krone, the white ones five Hellers. MacLean, who was hardly more than a boy, was winning, drawing in chips with quick gestures of his long pianist's fingers.

Byrne sat down and picked up his cards. Stewart was staying out, and so, after a glance, did he. The other three drew cards and fell to betting. Stewart leaned back and filled his long pipe, and after a second's hesitation Byrne turned to him.

"I don't know just what to say, Stewart," he began in an undertone. "I'm sorry. I didn't want to hurt Marie, but—"

"Oh, that's all right." Stewart drew at his pipe and bent forward to watch the game with an air of ending the discussion.

"Not at all. I did hurt her and I want to explain. Marie has been kind to me, and I like her. You know that."

"Don't be an ass!" Stewart turned on him sharply. "Marie is a little fool, that's all. I didn't know it was an American girl."

Byrne played in bad luck. His mind was not on the cards. He stayed out of the last hand, and with a cigarette wandered about the room. He glanced into the tidy bedroom and beyond, to where Marie hovered over the stove.

She turned and saw him.

"Come," she called. "Watch the supper for me while I go down for more beer."

"But no," he replied, imitating her tone. "Watch the supper for me while I go down for more beer."

"I love thee," she called merrily. "Tell the Herr Doktor I love thee. And here is the pitcher."

When he returned the supper was already laid in the little kitchen. The cards were put away, and young MacLean and Wallace Hunter were replacing the cover and the lamp on the card-table. Stewart was orating from a pinnacle of proprietorship.

"Exactly," he was saying, in reply to something gone before; "I used to come here Saturday nights—used to come early and take a bath. Worthington had rented it furnished for a song. Used to sit in a corner and envy Worthington his

22

bathtub, and that lamp there, and decent food, and a bed that didn't suffer from necrosis in the center. Then when he was called home I took it."

"Girl and all, wasn't it?"

"Girl and all. Old Worth said she was straight, and, by Jove, she is. He came back last fall on his wedding trip—he married a wealthy girl and came to see us. I was out, but Marie was here. There was the deuce to pay."

He lowered his voice. The men had gathered about him in a group.

"Jealous, eh?" from Hunter.

"Jealous? No! He tried to kiss her and she hit him—said he didn't respect her!"

"It's a curious code of honor," said Boyer thoughtfully. And indeed to none but Stewart did it seem amusing. This little girl of the streets, driven by God knows what necessity to make her own code and, having made it, living up to it with every fiber of her.

"Bitte zum speisen!" called Marie gayly from her brick stove, and the men trooped out to the kitchen.

The supper was spread on the table, with the pitcher of beer in the center. There were Swiss cheese and cold ham and rolls, and above all sausages and mustard. Peter drank a great deal of beer, as did the others, and sang German songs with a frightful accent and much vigor and sentiment, as also did the others.

Then he went back to the cold room in the Pension Schwarz, and told himself he was a fool to live alone when one could live like a prince for the same sum properly laid out. He dropped into the hollow center of his bed, where his big figure fitted as comfortably as though it lay in a washtub, and before his eyes there came a vision of Stewart's flat and the slippers by the fire—which was eminently human.

However, a moment later he yawned, and said aloud, with considerable vigor, that he'd be damned if he would—which was eminently Peter Byrne. Almost immediately, with the bed coverings, augmented by his overcoat, drawn snug to his chin, and the better necktie swinging from the gasjet in the air from the opened window, Peter was asleep. For four hours he had entirely forgotten Harmony.

CHAPTER V

The peace of a gray Sunday morning hung like a cloud over the little Pension Schwarz. In the kitchen the elderly maid, with a shawl over her shoulders and stiffened fingers, made the fire, while in the dining-room the little chambermaid cut butter and divided it sparingly among a dozen breakfast trays—on each tray two hard rolls, a butter pat, a plate, a cup. On two trays Olga, with a glance over her shoulder, placed two butter pats. The mistress yet slept, but in the kitchen Katrina had a keen eye for butter—and a hard heart.

Katrina came to the door.

"The hot water is ready," she announced. "And the coffee also. Hast thou been

23

to mass?"

"Ja."

"That is a lie." This quite on general principle, it being one of the cook's small tyrannies to exact religious observance from her underling, and one of Olga's Sunday morning's indulgences to oversleep and avoid the mass. Olga took the accusation meekly and without reply, being occupied at that moment in standing between Katrina and the extra pats of butter.

"For the lie," said Katrina calmly, "thou shalt have no butter this morning. There, the Herr Doktor rings for water. Get it, wicked one!"

Katrina turned slowly in the doorway.

"The new Fraulein is American?"

"Ja."

Katrina shrugged her shoulders.

"Then I shall put more water to heat," she said resignedly. "The Americans use much water. God knows it cannot be healthy!"

Olga filled her pitcher from the great copper kettle and stood with it poised in her thin young arms.

"The new Fraulein is very beautiful," she continued aloud. "Thinkest thou it is the hot water?"

"Is an egg more beautiful for being boiled?" demanded Katrina. "Go, and be less foolish. See, it is not the Herr Doktor who rings, but the new American."

Olga carried her pitcher to Harmony's door, and being bidden, entered. The room was frigid and Harmony, at the window in her nightgown, was closing the outer casement. The inner still swung open. Olga, having put down her pitcher, shivered.

"Surely the Fraulein has not slept with open windows?"

"Always with open windows." Harmony having secured the inner casement, was wrapping herself in the blue silk kimono with the faded butterflies. Merely to look at it made Olga shiver afresh. She shook her head.

"But the air of the night," she said, "it is full of mists and illnesses! Will you have breakfast now?"

"In ten minutes, after I have bathed."

Olga having put a match to the stove went back to the kitchen, shaking her head.

"They are strange, the Americans!" she said to latrine. "And if to be lovely one must bathe daily, and sleep with open windows—"

Harmony had slept soundly after all. Her pique at Byrne had passed with the reading of his note, and the sensation of his protection and nearness had been almost physical. In the virginal little apartment in the lodge of Maria Theresa the only masculine presence had been that of the Portier, carrying up coals at ninety Hellers a bucket, or of the accompanist who each alternate day had played for the Big Soprano to practice. And they had felt no deprivation, except for those occasional times when Scatchy developed a reckless wish to see the interior of a dancing-hall or one of the little theaters that opened after the opera.

24

But, as calmly as though she had never argued alone with a cabman or disputed the bill at the delicatessen shop, Harmony had thrown herself on the protection of this shabby big American whom she had met but once, and, having done so, slept like a baby. Not, of course, that she realized her dependence. She had felt very old and experienced and exceedingly courageous as she put out her light the night before and took a flying leap into the bed. She was still old and experienced, if a trifle less courageous, that Sunday morning.

Promptly in ten minutes Olga brought the breakfast, two rolls, two pats of butter—shades of the sleeping mistress and Katrina the thrifty—and a cup of coffee. On the tray was a bit of paper torn from a notebook:—

"Part of the prescription is an occasional walk in good company. Will you walk with me this afternoon? I would come in person to ask you, but am spending the morning in my bathrobe, while my one remaining American suit is being pressed.

"P. B."

Harmony got the ink and her pen from her trunk and wrote below:—

"You are very kind to me. Yes, indeed.

"H. W."

When frequent slamming of doors and steps along the passageway told Harmony that the pension was fully awake, she got out her violin. The idea of work obsessed her. To-morrow there would be the hunt for something to do to supplement her resources, this afternoon she had rashly promised to walk. The morning, then, must be given up to work. But after all she did little.

For an hour, perhaps, she practiced. The little Bulgarian paused outside her door and listened, rapt, his eyes closed. Peter Byrne, listening while he sorted lecture memoranda at his little table in bathrobe and slippers, absently filed the little note with the others—where he came across it months later—next to a lecture on McBurney's Point, and spent a sad hour or so over it. Over all the sordid little pension, with its odors of food and stale air, its spotted napery and dusty artificial flowers, the music hovered, and made for the time all things lovely.

In her room across from Harmony's, Anna Gates was sewing, or preparing to sew. Her hair in a knob, her sleeves rolled up, the room in violent disorder, she was bending over the bed, cutting savagely at a roll of pink flannel. Because she was working with curved surgeon's scissors, borrowed from Peter, the cut edges were strangely scalloped. Her method as well as her tools was unique. Clearly she was intent on a body garment, for now and then she picked up the flannel and held it to her. Having thus, as one may say, got the line of the thing, she proceeded to cut again, jaw tight set, small veins on her forehead swelling, a small replica of Peter Byrne sewing a button on his coat.

After a time it became clear to her that her method was wrong. She rolled up the flannel viciously and flung it into a corner, and proceeded to her Sunday morning occupation of putting away the garments she had worn during the week, a vast and motley collection.

On the irritability of her mood Harmony's music had a late but certain effect. She made a toilet, a trifle less casual than usual, seeing that she put on her stays, and rather sheepishly picked up the bundle from the corner. She hunted about for a thimble, being certain she had brought one from home a year before, but failed to find it. And finally, bundle under her arm and smiling, she knocked at Harmony's door.

"Would you mind letting me sit with you?" she asked. "I'll not stir. I want to sew, and my room is such a mess!"

Harmony threw the door wide. "You will make me very happy, if only my practicing does not disturb you."

Dr. Gates came in and closed the door.

"I'll probably be the disturbing element," she said. "I'm a noisy sewer."

Harmony's immaculate room and radiant person put her in good humor immediately. She borrowed a thimble—not because she cared whether she had one or not, but because she knew a thimble was a part of the game—and settled herself in a corner, her ragged pieces in her lap. For an hour she plodded along and Harmony played. Then the girl put down her bow and turned to the corner. The little doctor was jerking at a knot in her thread.

"It's in the most damnable knot!" she said, and Harmony was suddenly aware that she was crying, and heartily ashamed of it.

"Please don't pay any attention to me," she implored. "I hate to sew. That's the trouble. Or perhaps it's not all the trouble. I'm a fool about music."

"Perhaps, if you hate to sew—"

"I hate a good many things, my dear, when you play like that. I hate being over here in this place, and I hate fleas and German cooking and clinics, and I hate being forty years old and as poor as a church-mouse and as ugly as sin, and I hate never having had any children!"

Harmony was very uncomfortable and just a little shocked. But the next moment Dr. Gates had wiped her eyes with a scrap of the flannel and was smiling up through her glasses.

"The plain truth really is that I have indigestion. I dare say I'm really weeping in anticipation over the Sunday dinner! The food's bad and I can't afford to live anywhere else. I'd take a room and do my own cooking, but what time have I?" She spread out the pieces of flannel on her knee. "Does this look like anything to you?"

"A petticoat, isn't it?"

"I didn't intend it as a petticoat."

"I thought, on account of the scallops—"

"Scallops!" Dr. Gates gazed at the painfully cut pink edges and from them to Harmony. Then she laughed, peal after peal of joyous mirth.

"Scallops!" she gasped at last. "Oh, my dear, if you'd seen me cutting 'em! And with Peter Byrne's scissors!"

Now here at last they were on common ground. Harmony, delicately flushed, repeated the name, clung to it conversationally, using little adroitnesses to bring the talk back to him. All roads of talk led to Peter—Peter's future, Peter's poverty, Peter's refusing to have his hair cut, Peter's encounter with a major of the guards, and the duel Peter almost fought. It developed that Peter, as the challenged, had had the choice of weapons, and had chosen fists, and that the major had been carried away. Dr. Gates grew rather weary of Peter at last and fell back on the pink flannel. She confided to Harmony that the various pieces, united, were to make a dressing-gown for a little American boy at the hospital. "Although," she commented, "it looks more like a chair cover."

Harmony offered to help her, and got out a sewing-box that was lined with a piece of her mother's wedding dress. And as she straightened the crooked edges she told the doctor about the wedding dress, and about the mother who had called her Harmony because of the hope in her heart. And soon, by dint of skillful listening, which is always better than questioning, the faded little woman doctor knew all the story.

She was rather aghast.

"But suppose you cannot find anything to do?"

"I must," simply.

"It's such a terrible city for a girl alone."

"I'm not really alone. I know you now."

"An impoverished spinster! Much help I shall be!"

"And there is Peter Byrne."

"Peter!" Dr. Gates sniffed. "Peter is poorer than I am, if there is any comparison in destitution!"

Harmony stiffened a trifle.

"Of course I do not mean money," she said. "There are such things as encouragement, and—and friendliness."

"One cannot eat encouragement," retorted Dr. Gates sagely. "And friendliness between you and any man—bah! Even Peter is only human, my dear."

"I am sure he is very good."

"So he is. He is very poor. But you are very attractive. There, I'm a skeptic about men, but you can trust Peter. Only don't fall in love with him. It will be years before he can marry. And don't let him fall in love with you. He probably will."

Whereupon Dr. Gates taking herself and her pink flannel off to prepare for lunch, Harmony sent a formal note to Peter Byrne, regretting that a headache kept her from taking the afternoon walk as she had promised. Also, to avoid meeting him, she did without dinner, and spent the afternoon crying herself into a headache that was real enough.

Anna Gates was no fool. While she made her few preparations for dinner she repented bitterly what she had said to Harmony. It is difficult for the sophistry of forty to remember and cherish the innocence of twenty. For illusions it is apt to substitute facts, the material for the spiritual, the body against the soul. Dr. Gates, from her school of general practice, had come to view life along physiological lines.

With her customary frankness she approached Peter after the meal.

"I've been making mischief, Peter. I been talking too much, as usual."

"Certainly not about me, Doctor. Out of my blameless life—"

27

"About you, as a representative member of your sex. I'm a fool."

Peter looked serious. He had put on the newly pressed suit and his best tie, and was looking distinguished and just now rather stern.

"To whom?"

"To the young Wells person. Frankly, Peter, I dare say at this moment she thinks you are everything you shouldn't be, because I said you were only human. Why it should be evil to be human, or human to be evil—"

"I cannot imagine," said Peter slowly, "the reason for any conversation about me."

"Nor I, when I look back. We seemed to talk about other things, but it always ended with you. Perhaps you were our one subject in common. Then she irritated me by her calm confidence. The world was good, everybody was good. She would find a safe occupation and all would be well."

"So you warned her against me," said Peter grimly.

"I told her you were human and that she was attractive. Shall I make 'way with myself?"

"Cui bono?" demanded Peter, smiling in spite of himself. "The mischief is done."

Dr. Gates looked up at him.

"I'm in love with you myself, Peter!" she said gratefully. "Perhaps it is the tie. Did you ever eat such a meal?"

CHAPTER VI

A very pale and dispirited Harmony it was who bathed her eyes in cold water that evening and obeyed little Olga's "Bitte sum speisen." The chairs round the dining-table were only half occupied—a free concert had taken some, Sunday excursions others. The little Bulgarian, secretly considered to be a political spy, was never about on this one evening of the week. Rumor had it that on these evenings, secreted in an attic room far off in the sixteenth district, he wrote and sent off reports of what he had learned during the week—his gleanings from near-by tables in coffee-houses or from the indiscreet hours after midnight in the cafe, where the Austrian military was wont to gather and drink.

Into the empty chair beside Harmony Peter slid his long figure, and met a tremulous bow and silence. From the head of the table Frau Schwarz was talking volubly—as if, by mere sound, to distract attention from the scantiness of the meal. Under cover of the Babel Peter spoke to the girl. Having had his warning his tone was friendly, without a hint of the intimacy of the day before.

"Better?"

"Not entirely. Somewhat."

"I wish you had sent Olga to me for some tablets. No one needs to suffer from headache, when five grains or so of powder will help them."

"I am afraid of headache tablets."

"Not when your physician prescribes them, I hope!"

This was the right note. Harmony brightened a little. After all, what had she to do with the man himself? He had constituted himself her physician. That was all.

"The next time I shall send Olga."

"Good!" he responded heartily; and proceeded to make such a meal as he might, talking little, and nursing, by a careful indifference, her new-growing confidence.

It was when he had pushed his plate away and lighted a cigarette—according to the custom of the pension, which accorded the "Nicht Rauchen" sign the same attention that it did to the portrait of the deceased Herr Schwarz—that he turned to her again.

"I am sorry you are not able to walk. It promises a nice night."

Peter was clever. Harmony, expecting an invitation to walk, had nerved herself to a cool refusal. This took her off guard.

"Then you do not prescribe air?"

"That's up to how you feel. If you care to go out and don't mind my going along as a sort of Old Dog Tray I haven't anything else to do."

Dr. Gates, eating stewed fruit across the table, gave Peter a swift glance of admiration, which he caught and acknowledged. He was rather exultant himself; certainly he had been adroit.

"I'd rather like a short walk. It will make me sleep," said Harmony, who had missed the by-play. "And Old Dog Tray would be a very nice companion, I'm sure."

It is doubtful, however, if Anna Gates would have applauded Peter had she followed the two in their rambling walk that night. Direction mattering little and companionship everything, they wandered on, talking of immaterial things—of the rough pavements, of the shop windows, of the gray medieval buildings. They came to a full stop in front of the Votivkirche, and discussed gravely the twin Gothic spires and the Benk sculptures on the facade. And there in the open square, casting diplomacy to the winds, Peter Byrne turned to Harmony and blurted out what was in his heart.

"Look here," he said, "you don't care a rap about spires. I don't believe you know anything about them. I don't. What did that idiot of a woman doctor say to you to-day?"

"I don't know what you mean."

"You do very well. And I'm going to set you right. She starts out with two premises: I'm a man, and you're young and attractive. Then she draws some sort of fool deduction. You know what I mean?"

"I don't see why we need discuss it," said poor Harmony. "Or how you know —"

"I know because she told me. She knew she had been a fool, and she came to me. I don't know whether it makes any difference to you or not, but—we'd started out so well, and then to have it spoiled! My dear girl, you are beautiful and I know it. That's all the more reason why, if you'll stand for it, you need some one to look after you—I'll not say like a brother, because all the ones I ever knew were

29

darned poor brothers to their sisters, but some one who will keep an eye on you and who isn't going to fall in love with you."

"I didn't think you were falling in love with me; nor did I wish you to."

"Certainly not. Besides, I—" Here Peter Byrne had another inspiration, not so good as the first—"Besides, there is somebody at home, you understand? That makes it all right, doesn't it?"

"A girl at home?"

"A girl," said Peter, lying manfully.

"How very nice!" said Harmony, and put out her hand. Peter, feeling all sorts of a cheat, took it, and got his reward in a complete restoral of their former comradely relations. From abstractions of church towers and street paving they went, with the directness of the young, to themselves. Thereafter, during that memorable walk, they talked blissful personalities, Harmony's future, Peter's career, money—or its lack—their ambitions, their hopes, even—and here was intimacy, indeed!—their disappointments, their failures of courage, their occasional loss of faith in themselves.

The first real snow of the year was falling as they turned back toward the Pension Schwarz, a damp snow that stuck fast and melted with a chilly cold that had in it nothing but depression. The upper spires of the Votivkirche were hidden in a gray mist; the trees in the park took on, against the gloom of the city hall, a snowy luminosity. Save for an occasional pedestrian, making his way home under an umbrella, the streets were deserted. Byrne and Harmony had no umbrella, but the girl rejected his offer of a taxicab.

"We should be home too quickly," she observed naively. "And we have so much to say about me. Now I thought that perhaps by giving English lessons in the afternoon and working all morning at my music—"

And so on and on, square after square, with Peter listening gravely, his head bent. And square after square it was borne in on him what a precarious future stretched before this girl beside him, how very slender her resources, how more than dubious the outcome.

Poverty, which had only stimulated Peter Byrne in the past, ate deep into his soul that night.

Epochmaking as the walk had been, seeing that it had reestablished a friendship and made a working basis for future comradely relations, they were back at the corner of the Alserstrasse before ten. As they turned in at the little street, a man, lurching somewhat, almost collided with Harmony. He was a short, heavy-set person with a carefully curled mustache, and he was singing, not loudly, but with all his maudlin heart in his voice, the barcarolle from the "Tales" of Hoffmann. He saw Harmony, and still singing planted himself in her path. When Byrne would have pushed him aside Harmony caught his arm.

"It is only the Portier from the lodge," she said.

The Portier, having come to rest on a throaty and rather wavering note, stood before Harmony, bowing.

"The Fraulein has gone and I am very sad," he said thickly. "There is no more music, and Rosa has run away with a soldier from Salzburg who has only one lung."

"But think!" Harmony said in German. "No more practicing in the early dawn, no young ladies bringing mud into your newscrubbed hall! It is better, is it not? All day you may rest and smoke!"

Byrne led Harmony past the drunken Portier, who turned with caution and bowed after them.

"Gute Nacht," he called. "Kuss die Hand, Fraulein. Four rooms and the salon and a bath of the finest."

As they went up the Hirschengasse they could hear him pursuing his unsteady way down the street and singing lustily. At the door of the Pension Schwarz Harmony paused.

"Do you mind if I ask one question?"

"You honor me, madam."

"Then—what is the name of the girl back home?"

Peter Byrne was suddenly conscious of a complete void as to feminine names. He offered, in a sort of panic, the first one he recalled:—

"Emma."

"Emma! What a nice, old-fashioned name!" But there was a touch of disappointment in her voice.

Harmony had a lesson the next day. She was a favorite pupil with the master. Out of so much musical chaff he winnowed only now and then a grain of real ability. And Harmony had that. Scatchy and the Big Soprano had been right—she had the real thing.

The short half-hour lesson had a way with Harmony of lengthening itself to an hour or more, much to the disgust of the lady secretary in the anteroom. On that Monday Harmony had pleased the old man to one of his rare enthusiasms.

"Six months," he said, "and you will go back to your America and show them how over here we teach violin. I will a letter—letters—give you, and you shall put on the programme, of your concerts that you are my pupil, is it not so?"

Harmony was drawing on her worn gloves; her hands trembled a little with the praise and excitement.

"If I can stay so long," she answered unsteadily.

"You must stay. Have I so long labored, and now before it is finished you talk of going! Gott im Himmel!"

"It is a matter of money. My father is dead. And unless I find something to do I shall have to go back."

The master had heard many such statements. They never ceased to rouse his ire against a world that had money for everything but music. He spent five minutes in indignant protest, then:—

"But you are clever and young, child. You will find a way to stay. Perhaps I can now and then find a concert for you." It was a lure he had thrown out before, a hook without a bait. It needed no bait, being always eagerly swallowed. "And no more talk of going away. I refuse to allow. You shall not go."

Harmony paid the lady secretary on her way out. The master was interested. He liked Harmony and he believed in her. But fifty Kronen is fifty Kronen, and South American beef is high of price. He followed Harmony into the outer room and bowed her out of his studio.

"The Fraulein has paid?" he demanded, turning sharply to the lady secretary.

"Always."

"After the lesson?"

"Ja, Herr Professor."

"It is better," said the master, "that she pay hereafter before the lesson."

"Ja, Herr Professor."

Whereupon the lady secretary put a red-ink cross before Harmony's name. There were many such crosses on the ledger.

CHAPTER VII

For three days Byrne hardly saw Harmony. He was off early in the morning, hurried back to the midday meal and was gone again the moment it was over. He had lectures in the evenings, too, and although he lingered for an hour or so after supper it was to find Harmony taken possession of by the little Bulgarian, seized with a sudden thirst for things American.

On the evening of the second day he had left Harmony, enmeshed and helpless in a tangle of language, trying to explain to the little Bulgarian the reason American women wished to vote. Byrne flung down the stairs and out into the street, almost colliding with Stewart.

They walked on together, Stewart with the comfortably rolling gait of the man who has just dined well, Byrne with his heavy, rather solid tread. The two men were not congenial, and the frequent intervals without speech between them were rather for lack of understanding than for that completeness of it which often fathers long silences. Byrne was the first to speak after their greeting.

"Marie all right?"

"Fine. Said if I saw you to ask you to supper some night this week."

"Thanks. Does it matter which night?"

"Any but Thursday. We're hearing 'La Boheme.'"

"Say Friday, then."

Byrne's tone lacked enthusiasm, but Stewart in his after-dinner mood failed to notice it.

"Have you thought any more about our conversation of the other night?"

"What was that?"

Stewart poked him playfully in the ribs.

"Wake up, Byrne!" he said. "You remember well enough. Neither the Days nor any one else is going to have the benefit of your assistance if you go on living the way you have been. I was at Schwarz's. It is the double drain there that tells on one—eating little and being eaten much. Those old walls are full of vermin. Why don't you take our apartment?"

"Yours?"

"Yes, for a couple of months. I'm through with Schleich and Breidau can't take me for two months. It's Marie's off season and we're going to Semmering for the winter sports. We're ahead enough to take a holiday. And if you want the flat for the same amount you are spending now, or less, you can have it, and—a home, old man."

Byrne was irritated, the more so that he realized that the offer tempted him. To his resentment was added a contempt of himself.

"Thanks," he said. "I think not."

"Oh, all right." Stewart was rather offended. "I can't do more than give you a chance."

They separated shortly after and Byrne went on alone. The snow of Sunday had turned to a fine rain which had lasted all of Monday and Tuesday. The sidewalks were slimy; wagons slid in the ooze of the streets; and the smoke from the little stoves in the street-cars followed them in depressing horizontal clouds. Cabmen sat and smoked in the interior of musty cabs. The women hod-carriers on a new building steamed like horses as they worked.

Byrne walked along, his head thrust down into his up-turned collar; moisture gathered on his face like dew, condensed rather than precipitated. And as he walked there came before him a vision of the little flat on the Hochgasse, with the lamp on the table, and the general air of warmth and cheer, and a figure presiding over the brick stove in the kitchen. Byrne shook himself like a great dog and turned in at the gate of the hospital. He was thoroughly ashamed of himself.

That week was full of disappointments for Harmony. Wherever she turned she faced a wall of indifference or, what was worse, an interest that frightened her. Like a bird in a cage she beat helplessly against barriers of language, of strange customs, of stolidity that were not far from absolute cruelty.

She held to her determination, however, at first with hope, then, as the pension in advance and the lessons at fifty Kronen—also in advance,—went on, recklessly. She played marvelously those days, crying out through her violin the despair she had sealed her lips against. On Thursday, playing for the master, she turned to find him flourishing his handkerchief, and went home in a sort of daze, incredulous that she could have moved him to tears.

The little Bulgarian was frankly her slave now. He had given up the coffee-houses that he might spend that hour near her, on the chance of seeing her or, failing that, of hearing her play. At night in the Cafe Hungaria he sat for hours at a time, his elbows on the table, a bottle of native wine before him, and dreamed of her. He was very fat, the little Georgiev, very swarthy, very pathetic. The Balkan kettle was simmering in those days, and he had been set to watch the fire. But instead he had kindled a flame of his own, and was feeding it with stray words, odd glances, a bit of music, the curve of a woman's hair behind her ears. For reports he wrote verses in modern Greek, and through one of those inadvertences which make tragedy, the Minister of War down in troubled Bulgaria once received between the pages of a report in cipher on the fortifications of the Danube a verse in fervid hexameter that made even that grim official smile.

Harmony was quite unconscious. She went on her way methodically: so many hours of work, so many lessons at fifty Kronen, so many afternoons searching for something to do, making rounds of shops where her English might be valuable.

And after a few weeks Peter Byrne found time to help. After one experience, when Harmony left a shop with flaming face and tears in her eyes, he had thought it best to go with her. The first interview, under Peter's grim eyes, was a failure. The shopkeeper was obviously suspicious of Peter. After that, whenever he could escape from clinics, Peter went along, but stayed outside, smoking his eternal cigarette, and keeping a watchful eye on things inside the shop.

Only once was he needed. At that time, suspecting that all was not well, from the girl's eyes and the leer on the shopkeeper's face, he had opened the door in time to hear enough. He had lifted the proprietor bodily and flung him with a crash into a glass showcase of ornaments for the hair. Then, entirely cheerful and happy, and unmolested by the frightened clerks, he led Harmony outside and in a sort of atavistic triumph bought her a bunch of valley lilies.

Nevertheless, in his sane moments, Peter knew that things were very bad, indeed. He was still not in love with the girl. He analyzed his own feeling very carefully, and that was his conclusion. Nevertheless he did a quixotic thing— which was Peter, of course, all over.

He took supper with Stewart and Marie on Friday, and the idea came to him there. Hardly came to him, being Marie's originally. The little flat was cozy and bright. Marie, having straightened her kitchen, brought in a waist she was making and sat sewing while the two men talked. Their conversation was technical, a new extirpation of the thyroid gland, a recent nephrectomy.

In her curious way Marie liked Peter and respected him. She struggled with the technicalities of their talk as she sewed, finding here and there a comprehensive bit. At those times she sat, needle poised, intelligent eyes on the speakers, until she lost herself again in the mazes of their English.

At ten o'clock she rose and put away her sewing. Peter saw her get the stone pitcher and knew she was on her way for the evening beer. He took advantage of her absence to broach the matter of Harmony.

"She's up against it, as a matter of fact," he finished. "It ought to be easy enough for her to find something, but it isn't."

"I hardly saw her that day in the coffee-house; but she's rather handsome, isn't she?"

"That's one of the difficulties. Yes."

Stewart smoked and reflected. "No friends here at all?"

"None. There were three girls at first. Two have gone home."

"Could she teach violin?"

"I should think so."

"Aren't there any kids in the American colony who want lessons? There's usually some sort of infant prodigy ready to play at any entertainments of the Doctors'

34

Club."

"They don't want an American teacher, I fancy; but I suppose I could put a card up in the club rooms. Damn it all!" cried Peter with a burst of honest resentment, "why do I have to be poor?"

"If you were rolling in gold you could hardly offer her money, could you?"

Peter had not thought of that before. It was the only comfort he found in his poverty. Marie had brought in the beer and was carefully filling the mugs. "Why do you not marry her?" she asked unexpectedly. "Then you could take this flat. We are going to Semmering for the winter sports. I would show her about the stove."

"Marry her, of course!" said Peter gravely. "Just pick her up and carry her to church! The trifling fact that she does not wish to marry me need have nothing to do with it."

"Ah, but does she not wish it?" demanded Marie. "Are you so certain, stupid big one? Do not women always love you?"

Ridiculous as the thought was, Peter pondered it as he went back to the Pension Schwarz. About himself he was absurdly modest, almost humble. It had never occurred to him that women might care for him for himself. In his struggling life there had been little time for women. But about himself as the solution of a problem—that was different.

He argued the thing over. In the unlikely contingency of the girl's being willing, was Stewart right—could two people live as cheaply as one? Marie was an Austrian and knew how to manage—that was different. And another thing troubled him. He dreaded to disturb the delicate adjustment of their relationship; the terra incognita of a young girl's mind daunted him. There was another consideration which he put resolutely in the back of his mind—his career. He had seen many a promising one killed by early marriage, men driven to the hack work of the profession by the scourge of financial necessity. But that was a matter of the future; the necessity was immediate.

The night was very cold. Gusts of wind from the snow-covered Schneeberg drove along the streets, making each corner a fortress defended by the elements, a battlement to be seized, lost, seized again. Peter Byrne battled valiantly but mechanically. And as he fought he made his decision.

He acted with characteristic promptness. Possibly, too, he was afraid of the strength of his own resolution. By morning sanity might prevail, and in cold daylight he would see the absurdity of his position. He almost ran up the winding staircase. At the top his cold fingers fumbled the key and he swore under his breath. He slammed the door behind him. Peter always slammed doors, and had an apologetic way of opening the door again and closing it gently, as if to show that he could. Harmony's room was dark, but he had surprised her once into a confession that when she was very downhearted she liked to sit in the dark and be very blue indeed. So he stopped and knocked. There was no reply, but from Dr. Gates's room across there came a hum of conversation. He knew at once that Harmony was there.

Peter hardly hesitated. He took off his soft hat and ran a hand over his hair, and he straightened his tie. These preliminaries to a proposal of marriage being disposed of, he rapped at the door.

Anna Gates opened it. She wore a hideous red-flannel wrapper, and in deference to Harmony a thimble. Her flat breast was stuck with pins, and pinkish threads revealed the fact that the bathrobe was still under way.

"Peter!" she cried. "Come in and get warm."

Harmony, in the blue kimono, gave a little gasp, and flung round her shoulders the mass of pink on which she had been working.

"Please go out!" she said. "I am not dressed."

"You are covered," returned Anna Gates. "That's all that any sort of clothing can do. Don't mind her, Peter, and sit on the bed. Look out for pins!"

Peter, however, did not sit down. He stood just inside the closed door and stared at Harmony—Harmony in the red light from the little open door of the stove; Harmony in blue and pink and a bit of white petticoat; Harmony with her hair over her shoulders and tied out of her eyes with an encircling band of rosy flannel.

"Do sit!" cried Anna Gates. "You fill the room so. Bless you, Peter, what a collar!"

No man likes to know his collar is soiled, especially on the eve of proposing marriage to a pink and blue and white vision. Peter, seated now on the bed, writhed.

"I rapped at Miss Wells's door," he said. "You were not there."

This last, of course, to Harmony.

Anna Gates sniffed.

"Naturally!"

"I had something to say to you. I—I dare say it is hardly pension etiquette for you to go over to your room and let me say it there?"

Harmony smiled above the flannel.

"Could you call it through the door?"

"Hardly."

"Fiddlesticks!" said Dr. Gates, rising. "I'll go over, of course, but not for long. There's no fire."

With her hand on the knob, however, Harmony interfered.

"Please!" she implored. "I am not dressed and I'd rather not." She turned to Peter. "You can say it before her, can't you? She—I have told her all about things."

Peter hesitated. He felt ridiculous for the second time that night. Then:—

"It was merely an idea I had. I saw a little apartment furnished—you could learn to use the stove, unless, of course, you don't like housekeeping—and food is really awfully cheap. Why, at these delicatessen places and bakeshops—"

Here he paused for breath and found Dr. Gates's quizzical glance fixed on him, and Harmony's startled eyes.

"What I am trying to say," he exploded, "is that I believe if you would marry me it would solve some of your troubles anyhow." He was talking for time now,

36

against Harmony's incredulous face. "You'd be taking on others, of course. I'm not much and I'm as poor—well, you know. It—it was the apartment that gave me the idea—"

"And the stove!" said Harmony; and suddenly burst into joyous laughter. After a rather shocked instant Dr. Gates joined her. It was real mirth with Harmony, the first laugh of days, that curious laughter of women that is not far from tears.

Peter sat on the bed uncomfortably. He grinned sheepishly and made a last feeble attempt to stick to his guns.

"I mean it. You know I'm not in love with you or you with me, of course. But we are such a pair of waifs, and I thought we might get along. Lord knows I need some one to look after me!"

"And Emma?"

"There is no Emma. I made her up."

Harmony sobered at that.

"It is only"—she gasped a little for breath—"it is only your—your transparency, Peter." It was the first time she had called him Peter. "You know how things are with me and you want to help me, and out of your generosity you are willing to take on another burden. Oh, Peter!"

And here, Harmony being an emotional young person, the tears beat the laughter to the surface and had to be wiped away under the cover of mirth.

Anna Gates, having recovered herself, sat back and surveyed them both sternly through her glasses.

"Once for all," she said brusquely, "let such foolishness end. Peter, I am ashamed of you. Marriage is not for you—not yet, not for a dozen years. Any man can saddle himself with a wife; not every man can be what you may be if you keep your senses and stay single. And the same is true for you, girl. To tide over a bad six months you would sacrifice the very thing you are both struggling for?"

"I'm sure we don't intend to do it," replied Harmony meekly.

"Not now. Some day you may be tempted. When that time comes, remember what I say. Matrimonially speaking, each of you is fatal to the other. Now go away and let me alone. I'm not accustomed to proposals of marriage."

It was in some confusion of mind that Peter Byrne took himself off to the bedroom with the cold tiled stove and the bed that was as comfortable as a washtub. Undeniably he was relieved. Also Harmony's problem was yet unsolved. Also she had called him Peter.

Also he had said he was not in love with her. Was he so sure of that?

At midnight, just as Peter, rolled in the bedclothing, had managed to warm the cold concavity of his bed and had dozed off, Anna Gates knocked at his door.

"Yes?" said Peter, still comfortably asleep.

"It is Dr. Gates."

"Sorry, Doctor—have to 'xcuse me," mumbled Peter from the blanket.

"Peter!"

Peter roused to a chilled and indignant consciousness and sat up in bed.

"Well?"

"Open the door just a crack."

Resignedly Peter crawled out of bed, carefully turning the coverings up to retain as much heat as possible. An icy blast from the open window blew round him, setting everything movable in the little room to quivering. He fumbled in the dark for his slippers, failed to find them, and yawning noisily went to the door.

Anna Gates, with a candle, was outside. Her short, graying hair was out of its hard knot, and hung in an equally uncompromising six-inch plait down her back. She had no glasses, and over the candle-frame she peered shortsightedly at Peter.

"It's about Jimmy," she said. "I don't know what's got into me, but I've forgotten for three days. It's a good bit more than time for a letter."

"Great Scott!"

"Both yesterday and to-day he asked for it and to-day he fretted a little. The nurse found him crying."

"The poor little devil!" said Peter contritely. "Overdue, is it? I'll fix it to-night."

"Leave it under the door where I can get it in the morning. I'm off at seven."

"The envelope?"

"Here it is. And take my candle. I'm going to bed."

That was at midnight or shortly after. Half after one struck from the twin clocks of the Votivkirche and echoed from the Stephansplatz across the city. It found Peter with the window closed, sitting up in bed, a candle balanced on one knee, a writing-tablet on the other.

He was writing a spirited narrative of a chamois hunt in which he had taken part that day, including a detailed description of the quarry, which weighed, according to Peter, two hundred and fifty pounds, Peter being strong on imagination and short on facts as regards the Alpine chamois. Then, trying to read the letter from a small boy's point of view and deciding that it lacked snap, he added by way of postscript a harrowing incident of avalanche, rope, guide, and ice axe. He ended in a sort of glow of authorship, and after some thought took fifty pounds off the chamois.

The letter finished, he put it in a much-used envelope addressed to Jimmy Conroy—an envelope that stamped the whole episode as authentic, bearing as it did an undecipherable date and the postmark of a tiny village in the Austrian Tyrol.

It was almost two when Peter put out the candle and settled himself to sleep.

It was just two o'clock when the night nurse, making rounds in her ward in the general hospital, found a small boy very much awake on his pillow, and taking off her felt slipper shook it at him in pretended fury.

"Now, thou bad one!" she said. "Awake, when the Herr Doktor orders sleep! Shall I use the slipper?"

The boy replied in German with a strong English accent.

"I cannot sleep. Yesterday the Fraulein Elisabet said that in the mountains there are accidents, and that sometimes—"

"The Fraulein Elisabet is a great fool. Tomorrow comes thy letter of a certainty. The post has been delayed with great snows. Thy father has perhaps captured a great boar, or a—a chamois, and he writes of it."

"Do chamois have horns?"

"Ja. Great horns—so."

"He will send them to me! And there are no accidents?"

"None. Now sleep, or—the slipper."

CHAPTER VIII

So far Harmony's small world in the old city had consisted of Scatchy and the Big Soprano, Peter, and Anna Gates, with far off in the firmament the master. Scatchy and the Big Soprano had gone, weeping anxious postcards from every way station it is true, but nevertheless gone. Peter and Anna Gates remained, and the master as long as her funds held out. To them now she was about to add Jimmy.

The bathrobe was finished. Out of the little doctor's chaos of pink flannel Harmony had brought order. The result, masculine and complete even to its tassels and cord of pink yarn, was ready to be presented. It was with mingled emotions that Anna Gates wrapped it up and gave it to Harmony the next morning.

"He hasn't been so well the last day or two," she said. "He doesn't sleep much— that's the worst of those heart conditions. Sometimes, while I've been working on this thing, I've wondered—Well, we're making a fight anyhow. And better take the letter, too, Harry. I might forget and make lecture notes on it, and if I spoil that envelope—"

Harmony had arranged to carry the bathrobe to the hospital, meeting the doctor there after her early clinic. She knew Jimmy's little story quite well. Anna Gates had told it to her in detail.

"Just one of the tragedies of the world, my dear," she had finished. "You think you have a tragedy, but you have youth and hope; I think I have my own little tragedy, because I have to go through the rest of life alone, when taken in time I'd have been a good wife and mother. Still I have my work. But this little chap, brought over here by a father who hoped to see him cured, and spent all he had to bring him here, and then—died. It gets me by the throat."

"And the boy does not know?" Harmony had asked, her eyes wide.

"No, thanks to Peter. He thinks his father is still in the mountains. When we heard about it Peter went up and saw that he was buried. It took about all the money there was. He wrote home about it, too, to the place they came from. There has never been any reply. Then ever since Peter has written these letters. Jimmy lives for them."

Peter! It was always Peter. Peter did this. Peter said that. Peter thought thus. A very large part of Harmony's life was Peter in those days.

She was thinking of him as she waited at the gate of the hospital for Anna Gates, thinking of his shabby gray suit and unkempt hair, of his letter that she carried to Jimmy Conroy, of his quixotic proposal of the night before. Of the proposal, most of all—it was so eminently characteristic of Peter, from the conception of the plan to its execution. Harmony's thought of Peter was very tender that morning as she stood in the arched gateway out of reach of the wind from the Schneeberg. The tenderness and the bright color brought by the wind made her very beautiful. Little Marie, waiting across the Alserstrasse for a bus, and stamping from one foot to the other to keep warm, recognized and admired her. After all, the American women were chic, she decided, although some of the doctors had wives of a dowdiness—Himmel! And she could copy the Fraulein's hat for two Kronen and a bit of ribbon she possessed.

The presentation of the bathrobe was a success. Six nurses and a Dozent with a red beard stood about and watched Jimmy put into it, and the Dozent, who had been engaged for five years and could not marry because the hospital board forbade it, made a speech for Jimmy in awe-inspiring German, ending up with a poem that was intended to be funny, but that made the nurses cry. From which it will be seen that Jimmy was a great favorite.

During the ceremony, for such it was, the Germans loving a ceremony, Jimmy kept his eyes on the letter in Anna Gates's hand and waited. That the letter had come was enough. He lay back in anticipatory joy, and let himself be talked over, and bathrobed, and his hair parted Austrian fashion and turned up over a finger, which is very Austrian indeed. He liked Harmony. The girl caught his eyes on her more than once. He interrupted the speech once to ask her just what part of the robe she had made, and whether she had made the tassel. When she admitted the tassel, his admiration became mixed with respect.

It was a bright day, for a marvel. Sunlight came through the barred window behind Jimmy's bed, and brought into dazzling radiance the pink bathrobe, and Harmony's eyes, and fat Nurse Elisabet's white apron. It lay on the bedspread in great squares, outlined by the shadows of the window bars. Now and then the sentry, pacing outside, would advance as far as Jimmy's window, and a warlike silhouette of military cap and the upper end of a carbine would appear on the coverlet. These events, however, were rare, the sentry preferring the shelter of the gateway and the odor of boiling onions from the lodge just inside.

The Dozent retired to his room for the second breakfast; the nurses went about the business of the ward; Dr. Anna Gates drew a hairpin from her hair and made a great show of opening the many times opened envelope.

"The letter at last!" she said. "Shall I read it or will you?"

"You read it. It takes me so long. I'll read it all day, after you are gone. I always do."

Anna Gates read the letter. She read aloud poor Peter's first halting lines, when he was struggling against sleep and cold. They were mainly an apology for the delay. Then forgetting discomfort in the joy of creation, he became more comfortable. The account of the near-accident was wonderfully graphic; the description of the chamois was fervid, if not accurate. But consternation came with the end.

The letter apparently finished, there was yet another sheet. The doctor read on.

"For Heaven's sake," said Peter's frantic postscript, "find out how much a medium-sized chamois—"

Dr. Gates stopped "—ought to weigh," was the rest of it, "and fix it right in the letter. The kid's too smart to be fooled and I never saw a chamois outside of a drug store. They have horns, haven't they?"

"That's funny!" said Jimmy Conway.

"That was one of my papers slipped in by mistake," remarked Dr. Gates, with dignity, and flashing a wild appeal for help to Harmony.

"How did one of your papers get in when it was sealed?"

"I think," observed Harmony, leaning forward, "that little boys must not ask too many questions, especially when Christmas is only six weeks off."

"I know! He wants to send me the horns the way he sent me the boar's tusks."

For Peter, having in one letter unwisely recorded the slaughter of a boar, had been obliged to ransack Vienna for a pair of tusks. The tusks had not been so difficult. But horns!

Jimmy was contented with his solution and asked no more questions. The morning's excitement had tired him, and he lay back. Dr. Gates went to hold a whispered consultation with the nurse, and came back, looking grave.

The boy was asleep, holding the letter in his thin hands.

The visit to the hospital was a good thing for Harmony—to find some one worse off than she was, to satisfy that eternal desire of women to do something, however small, for some one else. Her own troubles looked very small to her that day as she left the hospital and stepped out into the bright sunshine.

She passed the impassive sentry, then turned and went back to him.

"Do you wish to do a very kind thing?" she asked in German.

Now the conversation of an Austrian sentry consists of yea, yea, and nay, nay, and not always that. But Harmony was lovely and the sun was moderating the wind. The sentry looked round; no one was near.

"What do you wish?"

"Inside that third window is a small boy and he is very ill. I do not think—perhaps he will never be well again. Could you not, now and then, pass the window? It pleases him."

"Pass the window! But why?"

"In America we see few of our soldiers. He likes to see you and the gun."

"Ah, the gun!" He smiled and nodded in comprehension, then, as an officer appeared in the door of a coffee-house across the street, he stiffened into immobility and stared past Harmony into space. But the girl knew he would do as she had desired.

That day brought good luck to Harmony. The wife of one of the professors at the hospital desired English conversation at two Kronen an hour.

Peter brought the news home at noon, and that afternoon Harmony was engaged. It was little enough, but it was something. It did much more than offer her two Kronen an hour; it gave her back her self-confidence, although the

41

immediate result was rather tragic.

The Frau Professor Bergmeister, infatuated with English and with Harmony, engaged her, and took her first two Kronen worth that afternoon. It was the day for a music-lesson. Harmony arrived five minutes late, panting, hat awry, and so full of the Frau Professor Bergmeister that she could think of nothing else.

Obedient to orders she had placed the envelope containing her fifty Kronen before the secretary as she went in. The master was out of humor. Should he, the teacher of the great Koert, be kept waiting for a chit of a girl—only, of course, he said "das Kindchen" or some other German equivalent for chit—and then have her come into the sacred presence breathless, and salute him between gasps as the Frau Professor Bergmeister?

Being excited and now confused by her error, and being also rather tremulous with three flights of stairs at top speed, Harmony dropped her bow. In point of heinousness this classes with dropping one's infant child from an upper window, or sitting on the wrong side of a carriage when with a lady.

The master, thus thrice outraged, rose slowly and glared at Harmony. Then with a lordly gesture to her to follow he stalked to the outer room, and picking up the envelope with the fifty Kronen held it out to her without a word.

Harmony's world came crashing about her ears. She stared stupidly at the envelope in her hand, at the master's retreating back.

Two girl students waiting their turn, envelopes in hand, giggled together. Harmony saw them and flushed scarlet. But the lady secretary touched her arm.

"It does not matter, Fraulein. He does so sometimes. Always he is sorry. You will come for your next lesson, not so? and all will be well. You are his well-beloved pupil. To-night he will not eat for grief that he has hurt you."

The ring of sincerity in the shabby secretary's voice was unmistakable. Her tense throat relaxed. She looked across at the two students who had laughed. They were not laughing now. Something of fellowship and understanding passed between them in the glance. After all, it was in the day's work—would come to one of them next, perhaps. And they had much in common—the struggle, their faith, the everlasting loneliness, the little white envelopes, each with its fifty Kronen.

Vaguely comforted, but with the light gone out of her day of days, Harmony went down the three long flights and out into the brightness of the winter day.

On the Ring she almost ran into Peter. He was striding toward her, giving a definite impression of being bound for some particular destination and of being behind time. That this was not the case was shown by the celerity with which, when he saw Harmony, he turned about and walked with her.

"I had an hour or two," he explained, "and I thought I'd walk. But walking is a social habit, like drinking. I hate to walk alone. How about the Frau Professor?"

"She has taken me on. I'm very happy. But, Dr. Byrne—"

"You called me Peter last night."

"That was different. You had just proposed to me."

"Oh, if that's all that's necessary—" He stopped in the center of the busy Ring with every evident intention of proposing again.

"Please, Peter!"

"Aha! Victory! Well, what about the Frau Professor Bergmeister?"

"She asks so many questions about America; and I cannot answer them."

"For instance?"

"Well, taxes now. She's very much interested in taxes."

"Never owned anything taxable except a dog—and that wasn't a tax anyhow; it was a license. Can't you switch her on to medicine or surgery, where I'd be of some use?"

"She says to-morrow we'll talk of the tariff and customs duties."

"Well, I've got something to say on that." He pulled from his overcoat pocket a largish bundle—Peter always bulged with packages—and held it out for her to see. "Tell the Frau Professor Bergmeister with my compliments," he said, "that because some idiot at home sent me five pounds of tobacco, hearing from afar my groans over the tobacco here, I have passed from mere financial stress to destitution. The Austrian customs have taken from me to-day the equivalent of ten dollars in duty. I offered them the tobacco on bended knee, but they scorned it."

"Really, Peter?"

"Really."

Under this lightness Harmony sensed the real anxiety. Ten dollars was fifty Kronen, and fifty Kronen was a great deal of money. She reached over and patted his arm.

"You'll make it up in some way. Can't you cut off some little extravagance?"

"I might cut down on my tailor bills." He looked down at himself whimsically. "Or on ties. I'm positively reckless about ties!"

They walked on in silence. A detachment of soldiery, busy with that eternal military activity that seems to get nowhere, passed on a dog-trot. Peter looked at them critically.

"Bosnians," he observed. "Raw, half-fed troops from Bosnia, nine out of ten of them tubercular. It's a rotten game, this military play of Europe. How's Jimmy?"

"We left him very happy with your letter."

Peter flushed. "I expect it was pretty poor stuff," he apologized. "I've never seen the Alps except from a train window, and as for a chamois—"

"He says his father will surely send him the horns."

Peter groaned.

"Of course!" he said. "Why, in Heaven's name, didn't I make it an eagle? One can always buy a feather or two. But horns? He really liked the letter?"

"He adored it. He went to sleep almost at once with it in his hands."

Peter glowed. The small irritation of the custom-house forgotten, he talked of Jimmy; of what had been done and might still be done, if only there were money; and from Jimmy he talked boy. He had had a boys' club at home during his short experience in general practice. Boys were his hobby.

"Scum of the earth, most of them," he said, his plain face glowing. "Dirty little beggars off the street. At first they stole my tobacco; and one of them pawned a medical book or two! Then they got to playing the game right. By Jove, Harmony, I wish you could have seen them! Used to line 'em up and make 'em spell, and the two best spellers were allowed to fight it out with gloves—my own method, and it worked. Spell! They'd spell their heads off to get a chance at the gloves. Gee, how I hated to give them up!"

This was a new Peter, a boyish individual Harmony had never met before. For the first time it struck her that Peter was young. He had always seemed rather old, solid and dependable, the fault of his elder brother attitude to her, no doubt. She was suddenly rather shy, a bit aloof. Peter felt the change and thought she was bored. He talked of other things.

A surprise was waiting for them in the cold lower hallway of the Pension Schwarz. A trunk was there, locked and roped, and on the trunk, in ulster and hat, sat Dr. Gates. Olga, looking rather frightened, was coming down with a traveling-bag. She put down the bag and scuttled up the staircase like a scared rabbit. The little doctor was grim. She eyed Peter and Harmony with an impersonal hostility, referable to her humor.

"I've been waiting for you two," she flung at them. "I've had a terrific row upstairs and I'm going. That woman's a devil!"

It had been a bad day for Harmony, and this new development, after everything else, assumed the proportions of a crisis. She had clung, at first out of sheer loneliness and recently out of affection, to the sharp little doctor with her mannish affectations, her soft and womanly heart.

"Sit down, child." Anna Gates moved over on the trunk. "You are fagged out. Peter, will you stop looking murderous and listen to me? How much did it cost the three of us to live in this abode of virtue?"

It was simple addition. The total was rather appalling.

"I thought so. Now this is my plan. It may not be conventional, but it will be respectable enough to satisfy anybody. And it will be cheaper, I'm sure of that: We are all going out to the hunting-lodge of Maria Theresa, and Harmony shall keep house for us!"

CHAPTER IX

It was the middle of November when Anna Gates, sitting on her trunk in the cold entrance hall on the Hirschengasse, flung the conversational bomb that left empty three rooms in the Pension Schwarz.

Mid-December found Harmony back and fully established in the lodge of Maria Theresa on the Street of Seven Stars—back, but with a difference. True, the gate still swung back and forward on rusty hinges, obedient to every whim of the December gales; but the casement windows in the salon no longer creaked or admitted drafts, thanks to Peter and a roll of rubber weather-casing. The grand piano, which had been Scatchy's rented extravagance, had gone never to return, and in its corner stood a battered but still usable upright. Under the great chandelier sat a table with an oil lamp, and evening and morning the white-tiled stove gleamed warm with fire. On the table by the lamp were the combined medical books of Peter and Anna Gates, and an ash-tray which also they used in common.

Shabby still, of course, bare, almost denuded, the salon of Maria Theresa. But at night, with the lamp lighted and the little door of the stove open, and perhaps, when the dishes from supper had been washed, with Harmony playing softly, it took resolution on Peter's part to put on his overcoat and face a lecture on the resection of a rib or a discussion of the function of the pituitary body.

The new arrangement had proved itself in more ways than one not only greater in comfort, but in economy. Food was amazingly cheap. Coal, which had cost ninety Hellers a bucket at the Pension Schwarz, they bought in quantity and could afford to use lavishly. Oil for the lamp was a trifle. They dined on venison now and then, when the shop across boasted a deer from the mountains. They had other game occasionally, when Peter, carrying home a mysterious package, would make them guess what it might contain. Always on such occasions Harmony guessed rabbits. She knew how to cook rabbits, and some of the other game worried her.

For Harmony was the cook. It had taken many arguments and much coaxing to make Peter see it that way. In vain Harmony argued the extravagance of Rosa, now married to the soldier from Salzburg with one lung, or the tendency of the delicatessen seller to weigh short if one did not watch him. Peter was firm.

It was Dr. Gates, after all, who found the solution.

"Don't be too obstinate, Peter," she admonished him. "The child needs occupation; she can't practice all day. You and I can keep up the financial end well enough, reduced as it is. Let her keep house to her heart's content. That can be her contribution to the general fund."

And that eventually was the way it settled itself, not without demur from Harmony, who feared her part was too small, and who irritated Anna almost to a frenzy by cleaning the apartment from end to end to make certain of her usefulness.

A curious little household surely, one that made the wife of the Portier shake her head, and speak much beneath her breath with the wife of the brushmaker about the Americans having queer ways and not as the Austrians.

The short month had seen a change in all of them. Peter showed it least of all, perhaps. Men feel physical discomfort less keenly than women, and Peter had been only subconsciously wretched. He had gained a pound or two in flesh, perhaps, and he was unmistakably tidier. Anna Gates was growing round and rosy, and Harmony had trimmed her a hat. But the real change was in Harmony herself.

The girl had become a woman. Who knows the curious psychology by which such changes come—not in a month or a year; but in an hour, a breath. One moment Harmony was a shy, tender young creature, all emotion, quivering at a word, aloof at a glance, prone to occasional introspection and mysterious daydreams; the next she was a young woman, tender but not shyly so, incredibly poised, almost formidably dignified on occasion, but with little girlish lapses into frolic and high spirits.

The transition moment with Harmony came about in this wise: They had been settled for three weeks. The odor of stewing cabbages at the Pension Schwarz had retired into the oblivion of lost scents, to be recalled, along with its accompanying memory of discomfort, with every odor of stewing cabbages for years to come. At the hospital Jimmy had had a bad week again. It had been an anxious time for all of them. In vain the sentry had stopped outside the third window and smiled and nodded through it; in vain—when the street was deserted and there was none to notice—he went through a bit of the manual of arms on the pavement outside, ending by setting his gun down with a martial and ringing clang.

In vain had Peter exhausted himself in literary efforts, climbing unheard-of peaks, taking walking-tours through such a Switzerland as never was, shooting animals of various sorts, but all hornless, as he carefully emphasized.

And now Jimmy was better again. He was propped up in bed, and with the aid of Nurse Elisabet he had cut out a paper sentry and set it in the barred window. The real sentry had been very much astonished; he had almost fallen over backward. On recovering he went entirely through the manual of arms, and was almost seen by an Oberst-lieutenant. It was all most exciting.

Harmony had been to see Jimmy on the day in question. She had taken him some gelatin, not without apprehension, it being her first essay in jelly and Jimmy being frank with the candor of childhood. The jelly had been a great success.

It was when she was about to go that Jimmy broached a matter very near his heart.

"The horns haven't come, have they?" he asked wistfully.

"No, not yet."

"Do you think he got my letter about them?"

"He answered it, didn't he?"

Jimmy drew a long breath. "It's very funny. He's mostly so quick. If I had the horns, Sister Elisabet would tie them there at the foot of the bed. And I could pretend I was hunting."

Harmony had a great piece of luck that day. As she went home she saw hanging in front of the wild-game shop next to the delicatessen store a fresh deer, and this time it was a stag. Like the others it hung head down, and as it swayed on its hook its great antlers tapped against the shop door as if mutely begging admission.

She could not buy the antlers. In vain she pleaded, explained, implored. Harmony enlisted the Portier, and took him across with her. The wild-game seller was obdurate. He would sell the deer entire, or he would mount head and antlers for his wife's cousin in Galicia as a Christmas gift.

Harmony went back to the lodge and climbed the stairs. She was profoundly depressed. Even the discovery that Peter had come home early and was building a fire in the kitchen brought only a fleeting smile. Anna was not yet home.

Peter built the fire. The winter dusk was falling and Harmony made a movement to light the candles. Peter stopped her.

"Can't we have the firelight for a little while? You are always beautiful, but—you are lovely in the firelight, Harmony."

"That is because you like me. We always think our friends are beautiful."

"I am fond of Anna, but I have never thought her beautiful."

The kitchen was small. Harmony, rolling up her sleeves by the table, and Peter before the stove were very close together. The dusk was fast fading into darkness; to this tiny room at the back of the old house few street sounds penetrated. Round them, shutting them off together from the world of shops with lighted windows, rumbling busses and hurrying humanity, lay the old lodge with its dingy gardens, its whitewashed halls, its dark and twisting staircases.

Peter had been very careful. He had cultivated a comradely manner with the girl that had kept her entirely at her ease with him. But it had been growing increasingly hard. He was only human after all. And he was very comfortable. Love, healthy human love, thrives on physical ease. Indigestion is a greater foe to it than poverty. Great love songs are written, not by poets starving in hall bedrooms, with insistent hunger gnawing and undermining all that is of the spirit, but by full-fed gentlemen who sing out of an overflowing of content and wide fellowship, and who write, no doubt, just after dinner. Love, being a hunger, does not thrive on hunger.

Thus Peter. He had never found women essential, being occupied in the struggle for other essentials. Women had had little part in his busy life. Once or twice he had seen visions, dreamed dreams, to waken himself savagely to the fact that not for many years could he afford the luxury of tender eyes looking up into his, of soft arms about his neck. So he had kept away from women with almost ferocious determination. And now!

He drew a chair before the stove and sat down. Standing or sitting, he was much too large for the kitchen. He sat in the chair, with his hands hanging, fingers interlaced between his knees.

The firelight glowed over his strong, rather irregular features. Harmony, knife poised over the evening's potatoes, looked at him.

"I think you are sad to-night, Peter."

"Depressed a bit. That's all."

"It isn't money again?"

It was generally money with any of the three, and only the week before Peter had found an error in his bank balance which meant that he was a hundred Kronen or so poorer than he had thought. This discovery had been very upsetting.

"Not more than usual. Don't mind me. I'll probably end in a roaring bad temper and smash something. My moody spells often break up that way!"

Harmony put down the paring-knife, and going over to where he sat rested a hand on his shoulder. Peter drew away from it.

"I have hurt you in some way?"

"Of course not."

47

"Could—could you talk about whatever it is? That helps sometimes."

"You wouldn't understand."

"You haven't quarreled with Anna?" Harmony asked, real concern in her voice.

"No. Good Lord, Harmony, don't ask me what's wrong! I don't know myself."

He got up almost violently and set the little chair back against the wall. Hurt and astonished, Harmony went back to the table. The kitchen was entirely dark, save for the firelight, which gleamed on the bare floor and the red legs of the table. She was fumbling with a match and the candle when she realized that Peter was just behind her, very close.

"Dearest," he said huskily. The next moment he had caught her to him, was kissing her lips, her hair.

Harmony's heart beat wildly. There was no use struggling against him. The gates of his self-control were down: all his loneliness, his starved senses rushed forth in tardy assertion.

After a moment Peter kissed her eyelids very gently and let her go. Harmony was trembling, but with shock and alarm only. The storm that had torn him root and branch from his firm ground of self-restraint left her only shaken. He was still very close to her; she could hear him breathing. He did not attempt to speak. With every atom of strength that was left in him he was fighting a mad desire to take her in his arms again and keep her there.

That was the moment when Harmony became a woman.

She lighted the candle with the match she still held. Then she turned and faced him.

"That sort of thing is not for you and me, Peter," she said quietly.

"Why not?"

"There isn't any question about it."

He was still reckless, even argumentative; the crying need of her still obsessed him. "Why not? Why should I not take you in my arms? If there is a moment of happiness to be had in this grind of work and loneliness—"

"It has not made me happy."

Perhaps nothing else she could have said would have been so effectual. Love demands reciprocation; he could read no passion in her voice. He knew then that he had left her unstirred. He dropped his outstretched arms.

"I'm sorry. I didn't mean to do it."

"I would rather not talk about it, please."

The banging of a door far off told them that Anna Gates had arrived and was taking off her galoshes in the entry. Peter drew a long breath, and, after his habit, shook himself.

"Very well, we'll not talk of it. But, for Heaven's sake, Harmony, don't avoid me. I'm not a cad. I'll let you alone."

There was only time for a glance of understanding between them, of promise from Peter, of acceptance from the girl. When Anna Gates entered the kitchen she found Harmony peeling potatoes and Peter filling up an already overfed stove.

That night, during that darkest hour before the dawn when the thrifty city

48

fathers of the old town had shut off the street lights because two hours later the sun would rise and furnish light that cost the taxpayers nothing, the Portier's wife awakened.

The room was very silent, too silent. On those rare occasions when the Portier's wife awakened in the night and heard the twin clocks of the Votivkirche strike three, and listened, perhaps, while the delicatessen seller ambled home from the Schubert Society, singing beerily as he ambled, she was wont to hear from the bed beside hers the rhythmic respiration that told her how safe from Schubert Societies and such like evils was her lord. There was no sound at all.

The Portier's wife raised herself on her elbow and reached over. Owing to the width of the table that stood between the beds and to a sweeping that day which had left the beds far apart she met nothing but empty air. Words had small effect on the Portier, who slept fathoms deep in unconsciousness. Also she did not wish to get up—the floor was cold and a wind blowing. Could she not hear it and the creaking of the deer across the street, as it swung on its hook?

The wife of the Portier was a person of resource. She took the iron candlestick from the table and flung it into the darkness at the Portier's pillow. No startled yell followed.

Suspicion thus confirmed, the Portier's wife forgot the cold floor and the wind, and barefoot felt her way into the hall.

Suspicion was doubly confirmed. The chain was off the door; it even stood open an inch or two.

Armed with a second candlestick she stationed herself inside the door and waited. The stone floor was icy, but the fury of a woman scorned kept her warm. The Votivkirche struck one, two, three quarters of an hour. The candlestick in her hand changed from iron to ice, from ice to red-hot fire. Still the Portier had not come back and the door chain swung in the wind.

At four o'clock she retired to the bedroom again. Indignation had changed to fear, coupled with sneezing. Surely even the Schubert Society—What was that?

From the Portier's bed was coming a rhythmic respiration!

She roused him, standing over him with the iron candlestick, now lighted, and gazing at him with eyes in which alarm struggled with suspicion.

"Thou hast been out of thy bed!"

"But no!"

"An hour since the bed was empty."

"Thou dreamest."

"The chain is off the door."

"Let it remain so and sleep. What have we to steal or the Americans above? Sleep and keep peace."

He yawned and was instantly asleep again. The Portier's wife crawled into her bed and warmed her aching feet under the crimson feather comfort. But her soul was shaken.

The Devil had been known to come at night and take innocent ones out to do his evil. The innocent ones knew it not, but it might be told by the soles of the feet, which were always soiled.

At dawn the Portier's wife cautiously uncovered the soles of her sleeping lord's feet, and fell back gasping. They were quite black, as of one who had tramped in garden mould.

Early the next morning Harmony, after a restless night, opened the door from the salon of Maria Theresa into the hall and set out a pitcher for the milk.

On the floor, just outside, lay the antlers from the deer across the street. Tied to them was a bit of paper, and on it was written the one word, "Still!"

CHAPTER X

In looking back after a catastrophe it is easy to trace the steps by which the inevitable advanced. Destiny marches, not by great leaps but with a thousand small and painful steps, and here and there it leaves its mark, a footprint on a naked soul. We trace a life by its scars, as a tree by its rings.

Anna Gates was not the best possible companion for Harmony, and this with every allowance for her real kindliness, her genuine affection for the girl. Life had destroyed her illusions, and it was of illusions that Harmony's veil had been woven. To Anna Gates, worn with a thousand sleepless nights, a thousand thankless days, withered before her time with the struggling routine of medical practice, sapped with endless calls for sympathy and aid, existence ceased to be spiritual and became physiological.

Life and birth and death had lost their mysteries. The veil was rent.

To fit this existence of hers she had built herself a curious creed, a philosophy of individualism, from behind which she flung strange bombshells of theories, shafts of distorted moralities, personal liberties, irresponsibilities, a supreme scorn for modern law and the prophets. Nature, she claimed, was her law and her prophet.

In her hard-working, virginal life her theories had wrought no mischief. Temptation had been lacking to exploit them, and even in the event of the opportunity it was doubtful whether she would have had the strength of her convictions. Men love theories, but seldom have the courage of them, and Anna Gates was largely masculine. Women, being literal, are apt to absorb dangerous doctrine and put it to the test. When it is false doctrine they discover it too late.

Harmony was now a woman.

Anna would have cut off her hand sooner than have brought the girl to harm; but she loved to generalize. It amused her to see Harmony's eyes widen with horror at one of her radical beliefs. Nothing pleased her more than to pit her individualism against the girl's rigid and conventional morality, and down her by some apparently unanswerable argument.

On the day after the incident in the kitchen such an argument took place— hardly an argument, for Harmony knew nothing of mental fencing. Anna had taken a heavy cold, and remained at home. Harmony had been practicing, and at

50

the end she played a little winter song by some modern composer. It breathed all the purity of a white winter's day; it was as chaste as ice and as cold; and yet throughout was the thought of green things hiding beneath the snow and the hope of spring.

Harmony, having finished, voiced some such feeling. She was rather ashamed of her thought.

"It seems that way to me," she finished apologetically. "It sounds rather silly. I always think I can tell the sort of person who composes certain things."

"And this gentleman who writes of winter?"

"I think he is very reserved. And that he has never loved any one."

"Indeed!"

"When there is any love in music, any heart, one always feels it, exactly as in books—the difference between a love story and—and—"

"—a dictionary!"

"You always laugh," Harmony complained

"That's better than weeping. When I think of the rotten way things go in this world I want to weep always."

"I don't find it a bad world. Of course there are bad people, but there are good ones."

"Where? Peter and you and I, I suppose."

"There are plenty of good men."

"What do you call a good man?"

Harmony hesitated, then went on bravely:—

"Honorable men."

Anna smiled. "My dear child," she said, "you substitute the code of a gentleman for the Mosaic Law. Of course your good man is a monogamist?"

Harmony nodded, puzzled eyes on Anna.

"Then there are no 'good' people in the polygamous countries, I suppose! When there were twelve women to every man, a man took a dozen wives. To-day in our part of the globe there is one woman—and a fifth over—for every man. Each man gets one woman, and for every five couples there is a derelict like myself, mateless."

Anna's amazing frankness about herself often confused Harmony. Her resentment at her single condition, because it left her childless, brought forth theories that shocked and alarmed the girl. In the atmosphere in which Harmony had been reared single women were always presumed to be thus by choice and to regard with certain tolerance those weaker sisters who had married. Anna, on the contrary, was frankly a derelict, frankly regretted her maiden condition and railed with bitterness against her enforced childlessness. The near approach of Christmas had for years found her morose and resentful. There are, here and there, such women, essentially mothers but not necessarily wives, their sole passion that of maternity.

Anna, argumentative and reckless, talked on. She tore away, in her resentment, every theory of existence the girl had ever known, and offered her instead an

51

incredible liberty in the name of the freedom of the individual. Harmony found all her foundations of living shaken, and though refusing to accept Anna's theories, found her faith in her own weakened. She sat back, pale and silent, listening, while Anna built up out of her discontent a new heaven and a new earth, with liberty written high in its firmament.

When her reckless mood had passed Anna was regretful enough at the girl's stricken face.

"I'm a fool!" she said contritely. "If Peter had been here he'd have throttled me. I deserve it. I'm a theorist, pure and simple, and theorists are the anarchists of society. There's only one comfort about us—we never live up to our convictions. Now forget all this rot I've been talking."

Peter brought up the mail that afternoon, a Christmas card or two for Anna, depressingly early, and a letter from the Big Soprano for Harmony from New York. The Big Soprano was very glad to be back and spent two pages over her chances for concert work.

"... I could have done as well had I stayed at home. If I had had the money they wanted, to go to Geneva and sing 'Brunnhilde,' it would have helped a lot. I could have said I'd sung in opera in Europe and at least have had a hearing at the Met. But I didn't, and I'm back at the church again and glad to get my old salary. If it's at all possible, stay until the master has presented you in a concert. He's quite right, you haven't a chance unless he does. And now I'll quit grumbling.

"Scatchy met her Henry at the dock and looked quite lovely, flushed with excitement and having been up since dawn curling her hair. He was rather a disappointment—small and blond, with light blue eyes, and almost dapper. But oh, my dear, I wouldn't care how pale a man's eyes were if he looked at me the way Henry looked at her.

"They asked me to luncheon with them, but I knew they wanted to be alone together, and so I ate a bite or two, all I could swallow for the lump in my throat, by myself. I was homesick enough in old Wien, but I am just as homesick now that I am here, for we are really homesick only for people, not places. And no one really cared whether I came back or not."

Peter had been miserable all day, not with regret for the day before, but with fear. What if Harmony should decide that the situation was unpleasant and decide to leave? What if a reckless impulse, recklessly carried out, were to break up an arrangement that had made a green oasis of happiness and content for all of them in the desert of their common despair?

If he had only let her go and apologized! But no, he had had to argue, to justify himself, to make an idiot of himself generally. He almost groaned aloud as he opened the gate end crossed the wintry garden.

He need not have feared. Harmony had taken him entirely at his word. "I am not a beast. I'll let you alone," he had said. She had had a bad night, as nights go. She had gone through the painful introspection which, in a thoroughly good girl, always follows such an outburst as Peter's. Had she said or done anything to make him think—Surely she had not! Had she been wrong about Peter after all? Surely not again.

While the Portier's wife, waked, as may happen, by an unaccustomed silence, was standing guard in the hall below, iron candlestick in hand, Harmony, having read the Litany through in the not particularly religious hope of getting to sleep, was dreaming placidly. It was Peter who tossed and turned almost all night. Truly there had been little sleep that night in the old hunting-lodge of Maria Theresa.

Peter, still not quite at ease, that evening kept out of the kitchen while supper was preparing. Anna, radical theories forgotten and wearing a knitted shawl against drafts, was making a salad, and Harmony, all anxiety and flushed with heat, was broiling a steak.

Steak was an extravagance, to be cooked with clear hot coals and prayer.

"Peter," she called, "you may set the table. And try to lay the cloth straight."

Peter, exiled in the salon, came joyously. Obviously the wretched business of yesterday was forgiven. He came to the door, pipe in mouth.

"Suppose I refuse?" he questioned. "You—you haven't been very friendly with me to-day, Harry."

"I?"

"Don't quarrel, you children," cried Anna, beating eggs vigorously. "Harmony is always friendly, too friendly. The Portier loves her."

"I'm sure I said good-evening to you."

"You usually say, 'Good-evening, Peter.'"

"And I did not?"

"You did not."

"Then—Good-evening, Peter."

"Thank you."

His steady eyes met hers. In them there was a renewal of his yesterday's promise, abasement, regret. Harmony met him with forgiveness and restoration.

"Sometimes," said Peter humbly, "when I am in very great favor, you say, 'Good-evening, Peter, dear.'"

"Good-evening, Peter, dear," said Harmony.

CHAPTER XI

The affairs of young Stewart and Marie Jedlicka were not moving smoothly. Having rented their apartment to the Boyers, and through Marie's frugality and the extra month's wages at Christmas, which was Marie's annual perquisite, being temporarily in funds the sky seemed clear enough, and Walter Stewart started on his holiday with a comfortable sense of financial security.

Mrs. Boyer, shown over the flat by Stewart during Marie's temporary exile in the apartment across the hall, was captivated by the comfort of the little suite and by its order. Her housewifely mind, restless with long inactivity in a pension, seized on the bright pans of Marie's kitchen and the promise of the brick-and-sheetiron stove. She disapproved of Stewart, having heard strange stories of him, but there was nothing bacchanal or suspicious about this orderly establishment. Mrs. Boyer was a placid, motherly looking woman, torn from her church and her card club, her grown children, her household gods of thirty years' accumulation, that "Frank" might catch up with his profession.

She had explained it rather tremulously at home.

"Father wants to go," she said. "You children are big enough now to be left. He's always wanted to do it, but we couldn't go while you were little."

"But, mother!" expostulated the oldest girl. "When you are so afraid of the ocean! And a year!"

"What is to be will be," she had replied. "If I'm going to be drowned I'll be drowned, whether it's in the sea or in a bathtub. And I'll not let father go alone."

Fatalism being their mother's last argument and always final, the children gave up. They let her go. More, they prepared for her so elaborate a wardrobe that the poor soul had had no excuse to purchase anything abroad. She had gone through Paris looking straight ahead lest her eyes lead her into the temptation of the shops. In Vienna she wore her home-town outfit with determination, vaguely conscious that the women about her had more style, were different. She priced unsuitable garments wistfully, and went home to her trunks full of best materials that would never wear out. The children, knowing her, had bought the best.

To this couple, then, Stewart had rented his apartment. It is hard to say by what psychology he found their respectability so satisfactory. It was as though his own status gained by it. He had much the same feeling about the order and decency with which Marie managed the apartment, as if irregularity were thus regularized.

Marie had met him once for a walk along the Graben. She had worn an experimental touch of rouge under a veil, and fine lines were drawn under her blue eyes, darkening them. She had looked very pretty, rather frightened. Stewart had sent her home and had sulked for an entire evening.

So curious a thing is the mind masculine, such an order of disorder, so conventional its defiance of convention. Stewart breaking the law and trying to keep the letter!

On the day they left for Semmering Marie was up at dawn. There was much to do. The house must be left clean and shining. There must be no feminine gewgaws to reveal to the Frau Doktor that it was not a purely masculine establishment. At the last moment, so late that it sent her heart into her mouth, she happened on the box of rouge hidden from Stewart's watchful eyes. She gave it to the milk girl.

Finally she folded her meager wardrobe and placed it in the Herr Doktor's American trunk: a marvel, that trunk, so firm, so heavy, bound with iron. And with her own clothing she packed Stewart's, the dress-suit he had worn once to the Embassy, a hat that folded, strange American shoes, and books—always books. The Herr Doktor would study at Semmering. When all was in readiness and Stewart was taking a final survey, Marie ran downstairs and summoned a cab. It did not occur to her to ask him to do it. Marie's small life was one of service, and besides there was an element in their relationship that no one but Marie

54

suspected, and that she hid even from herself. She was very much in love with this indifferent American, this captious temporary god of her domestic altar. Such a contingency had never occurred to Stewart; but Peter, smoking gravely in the little apartment, had more than once caught a look in Marie's eyes as she turned them on the other man, and had surmised it. It made him uncomfortable.

When the train was well under way, however, and he found no disturbing element among the three others in the compartment, Stewart relaxed. Semmering was a favorite resort with the American colony, but not until later in the winter. In December there were rains in the mountains, and low-lying clouds that invested some of the chalets in constant fog. It was not until the middle of January that the little mountain train became crowded with tourists, knickerbockered men with knapsacks, and jaunty feathers in their soft hats, boys carrying ski, women with Alpine cloaks and iron-pointed sticks.

Marie was childishly happy. It was the first real vacation of her life, and more than that she was going to Semmering, in the very shadow of the Raxalpe, the beloved mountain of the Viennese.

Marie had seen the Rax all her life, as it towered thirty miles or so away above the plain. On peaceful Sundays, having climbed the cog railroad, she had seen its white head turn rosy in the setting sun, and once when a German tourist from Munich had handed her his fieldglass she had even made out some of the crosses that showed where travelers had met their deaths. Now she would be very close. If the weather were good, she might even say a prayer in the chapel on its crest for the souls of those who had died. It was of a marvel, truly; so far may one go when one has money and leisure.

The small single-trucked railway carriages bumped and rattled up the mountain sides, always rising, always winding. There were moments when the track held to the cliffs only by gigantic fingers of steel, while far below were peaceful valleys and pink-and-blue houses and churches with gilded spires. There were vistas of snow-peak and avalanche shed, and always there were tunnels. Marie, so wise in some things, was a child in others; she slid close to Stewart in the darkness and touched him for comfort.

"It is so dark," she apologized, "and it frightens me, the mountain heart. In your America, have you so great mountains?"

Stewart patted her hand, a patronizing touch that sent her blood racing.

"Much larger," he said magnificently. "I haven't seen a hill in Europe I'd exchange for the Rockies. And when we cross the mountains there we use railway coaches. These toy railroads are a joke. At home we'd use 'em as street-cars."

"Really! I should like to see America."

"So should I."

The conversation was taking a dangerous trend. Mention of America was apt to put the Herr Doktor in a bad humor or to depress him, which was even worse. Marie, her hand still on his arm and not repulsed, became silent.

At a small way station the three Germans in the compartment left the train. Stewart, lowering a window, bought from a boy on the platform beer and sausages and a bag of pretzels. As the train resumed its clanking progress they ate luncheon, drinking the beer from the bottles and slicing the sausage with a penknife. It was a joyous trip, a red-letter day in the girl's rather sordid if not uneventful life. The Herr Doktor was pleased with her. He liked her hat, and when she flushed with pleasure demanded proof that she was not rouged. Proof was forthcoming. She rubbed her cheeks vigorously with a handkerchief and produced in triumph its unreddened purity.

"Thou suspicious one!" she pouted. "I must take off the skin to assure thee! When the Herr Doktor says no rouge, I use none."

"You're a good child." He stooped over and kissed one scarlet cheek and then being very comfortable and the beer having made him drowsy, he put his head in her lap and slept.

When he awakened they were still higher. The snow-peak towered above and the valleys were dizzying! Semmering was getting near. They were frequently in darkness; and between the tunnels were long lines of granite avalanche sheds. The little passage of the car was full of tourists looking down.

"We are very close, I am sure," an American girl was saying just outside the doorway. "See, isn't that the Kurhaus? There, it is lost again."

The tourists in the passage were Americans and the girl who had spoken was young and attractive. Stewart noticed them for the first time and moved to a more decorous distance from Marie.

Marie Jedlicka took her cue and lapsed into silence, but her thoughts were busy. Perhaps this girl was going to Semmering also and the Herr Doktor would meet her. But that was foolish! There were other resorts besides Semmering, and in the little villa to which they went there would be no Americans. It was childish to worry about a girl whose back and profile only she had seen. Also profiles were deceptive; there was the matter of the ears. Marie's ears were small and set close to her head. If the American Fraulein's ears stuck out or her face were only short and wide! But no. The American Fraulein turned and glanced once swiftly into the compartment. She was quite lovely.

Stewart thought so, too. He got up with a great show of stretching and yawning and lounged into the passage. He did not speak to the girl; Marie noted that with some comfort. But shortly after she saw him conversing easily with a male member of the party. Her heart sank again. Life was moving very fast for Marie Jedlicka that afternoon on the train.

Stewart was duly presented to the party of Americans and offered his own cards, bowing from the waist and clicking his heels together, a German custom he had picked up. The girl was impressed; Marie saw that. When they drew into the station at Semmering Stewart helped the American party off first and then came back for Marie. Less keen eyes than the little Austrian's would have seen his nervous anxiety to escape attention, once they were out of the train and moving toward the gate of the station. He stopped to light a cigarette, he put down the hand-luggage and picked it up again, as though it weighed heavily, whereas it was both small and light. He loitered through the gate and paused to exchange a word with the gateman.

The result was, of course, that the Americans were in a sleigh and well up the mountainside before Stewart and Marie were seated side by side in a straw-lined sledge, their luggage about them, a robe over their knees, and a noisy driver high above them on the driving-seat. Stewart spoke to her then, the first time for half an hour.

Marie found some comfort. The villas at Semmering were scattered wide over the mountain breast, set in dense clumps of evergreens, hidden from the roads and from each other by trees and shrubbery separated by valleys. One might live in one part of Semmering for a month and never suspect the existence of other parts, or wander over steep roads and paths for days and never pass twice over the same one. The Herr Doktor might not see the American girl again—and if he did! Did he not see American girls wherever he went?

The sleigh climbed on. It seemed they would never stop climbing. Below in the valley twilight already reigned, a twilight of blue shadows, of cows with bells wandering home over frosty fields, of houses with dark faces that opened an eye of lamplight as one looked.

Across the valley and far above—Marie pointed without words. Her small heart was very full. Greater than she had ever dreamed it, steeper, more beautiful, more deadly, and crowned with its sunset hue of rose was the Rax. Even Stewart lost his look of irritation as he gazed with her. He reached over and covered both her hands with his large one under the robe.

The sleigh climbed steadily. Marie Jedlicka, in a sort of ecstasy, leaned back and watched the mountain; its crown faded from rose to gold, from gold to purple with a thread of black. There was a shadow on the side that looked like a cross. Marie stopped the sleigh at a wayside shrine, and getting out knelt to say a prayer for the travelers who had died on the Rax. They had taken a room at a small villa where board was cheap, and where the guests were usually Germans of the thriftier sort from Bavaria. Both the season and the modest character of the establishment promised them quiet and seclusion.

To Marie the house seemed the epitome of elegance, even luxury. It clung to a steep hillside. Their room, on the third floor, looked out from the back of the building over the valley, which fell away almost sheer from beneath their windows. A tiny balcony outside, with access to it by a door from the bedroom, looked far down on the tops of tall pines. It made Marie dizzy.

She was cheerful again and busy. The American trunk was to be unpacked and the Herr Doktor's things put away, his shoes in rows, as he liked them, and his shaving materials laid out on the washstand. Then there was a new dress to put on, that she might do him credit at supper.

Stewart's bad humor had returned. He complained of the room and the draft under the balcony door; the light was wrong for shaving. But the truth came out at last and found Marie not unprepared.

"The fact is," he said, "I'm not going to eat with you to-night, dear. I'm going to the hotel."

57

"With the Americans?"

"Yes. I know a chap who went to college with the brother—with the young man you saw."

Marie glanced down at her gala toilet. Then she began slowly to take off the dress, reaching behind her for a hook he had just fastened and fighting back tears as she struggled with it.

"Now, remember, Marie, I will have no sulking."

"I am not sulking."

"Why should you change your clothes?"

"Because the dress was for you. If you are not here I do not wish to wear it."

Stewart went out in a bad humor, which left him before he had walked for five minutes in the clear mountain air. At the hotel he found the party waiting for him, the women in evening gowns. The girl, whose name was Anita, was bewitching in pale green.

That was a memorable night for Walter Stewart, with his own kind once more— a perfect dinner, brisk and clever conversation, enlivened by a bit of sweet champagne, an hour or two on the terrace afterward with the women in furs, and stars making a jeweled crown for the Rax.

He entirely forgot Marie until he returned to the villa and opening the door of the room found her missing.

She had not gone far. At the sound of his steps she moved on the balcony and came in slowly. She was pale and pinched with cold, but she was wise with the wisdom of her kind. She smiled.

"Didst thou have a fine evening?"

"Wonderful!"

"I am sorry if I was unpleasant. I was tired, now I am rested."

"Good, little Marie!"

CHAPTER XII

The card in the American Doctors' Club brought a response finally. It was just in time. Harmony's funds were low, and the Frau Professor Bergmeister had gone to St. Moritz for the winter. She regretted the English lessons, but there were always English at St. Moritz and it cost nothing to talk with them. Before she left she made Harmony a present. "For Christmas," she explained. It was a glass pin-tray, decorated beneath with labels from the Herr Professor's cigars and in the center a picture of the Emperor.

The response came in this wise. Harmony struggling home against an east wind and holding the pin-tray and her violin case, opened the old garden gate by the simple expedient of leaning against it. It flew back violently, almost overthrowing a stout woman in process of egress down the walk. The stout woman was Mrs. Boyer, clad as usual in the best broadcloth and wearing her old sable cape, made over according to her oldest daughter's ideas into a staid stole and muff. The muff lay on the path now and Mrs. Boyer was gasping for breath.

"I'm so sorry!" Harmony exclaimed. "It was stupid of me; but the wind—Is this your muff?"

Mrs. Boyer took the muff coldly. From its depths she proceeded to extract a handkerchief and with the handkerchief she brushed down the broadcloth. Harmony stood apologetically by. It is explanatory of Mrs. Boyer's face, attitude, and costume that the girl addressed her in English.

"I backed in," she explained. "So few people come, and no Americans."

Mrs. Boyer, having finished her brushing and responded to this humble apology in her own tongue, condescended to look at Harmony.

"It really is no matter," she said, still coolly but with indications of thawing. "I am only glad it did not strike my nose. I dare say it would have, but I was looking up to see if it were going to snow." Here she saw the violin case and became almost affable.

"There was a card in the Doctors' Club, and I called—" She hesitated.

"I am Miss Wells. The card is mine."

"One of the women here has a small boy who wishes to take violin lessons and I offered to come. The mother is very busy."

"I see. Will you come in? I can make you a cup of tea and we can talk about it."

Mrs. Boyer was very willing, although she had doubts about the tea. She had had no good tea since she had left England, and was inclined to suspect all of it.

They went in together, Harmony chatting gayly as she ran ahead, explaining this bit of the old staircase, that walled-up door, here an ancient bit of furniture not considered worthy of salvage, there a closed and locked room, home of ghosts and legends. To Harmony this elderly woman, climbing slowly behind her, was a bit of home. There had been many such in her life; women no longer young, friends of her mother's who were friends of hers; women to whom she had been wont to pay the courtesy of a potted hyacinth at Easter or a wreath at Christmas or a bit of custard during an illness. She had missed them all cruelly, as she had missed many things—her mother, her church, her small gayeties. She had thought at first that Frau Professor Bergmeister might allay her longing for these comfortable, middle-aged, placid-eyed friends of hers. But the Frau Professor Bergmeister had proved to be a frivolous and garrulous old woman, who substituted ease for comfort, and who burned a candle on the name-day of her first husband while her second was safely out of the house.

So it was with something of excitement that Harmony led the way up the stairs and into the salon of Maria Theresa.

Peter was there. He was sitting with his back to the door, busily engaged in polishing the horns of the deer. Whatever scruples Harmony had had about the horns, Peter had none whatever, save to get them safely out of the place and to the hospital. So Peter was polishing the horns. Harmony had not expected to find him home, and paused, rather startled.

"Oh, I didn't know you were home."

Peter spoke without turning.

"Try to bear up under it," he said. "I'm home and hungry, sweetheart!"

"Peter, please!"

Peter turned at that and rose instantly. It was rather dark in the salon and he did not immediately recognize Mrs. Boyer. But that keen-eyed lady had known him before he turned, had taken in the domesticity of the scene and Peter's part in it, and had drawn the swift conclusion of the pure of heart.

"I'll come again," she said hurriedly. "I—I must really get home. Dr. Boyer will be there, and wondering—"

"Mrs. Boyer!" Peter knew her.

"Oh, Dr. Byrne, isn't it? How unexpected to find you here!"

"I live here."

"So I surmised."

"Three of us," said Peter. "You know Anna Gates, don't you?"

"I'm afraid not. Really I—"

Peter was determined to explain. His very eagerness was almost damning.

"She and Miss Wells are keeping house here and have kindly taken me in as a boarder. Please sit down."

Harmony found nothing strange in the situation and was frankly puzzled at Peter. The fact that there was anything unusual in two single women and one unmarried man, unrelated and comparative strangers, setting up housekeeping together had never occurred to her. Many a single woman whom she knew at home took a gentleman into the house as a roomer, and thereafter referred to him as "he" and spent hours airing the curtains of smoke and even, as "he" became a member of the family, in sewing on his buttons. There was nothing indecorous about such an arrangement; merely a concession to economic pressure.

She made tea, taking off her jacket and gloves to do it, but bustling about cheerfully, with her hat rather awry and her cheeks flushed with excitement and hope. Just now, when the Frau Professor had gone, the prospect of a music pupil meant everything. An American child, too! Fond as Harmony was of children, the sedate and dignified youngsters who walked the parks daily with a governess, or sat with folded hands and fixed eyes through hours of heavy music at the opera, rather daunted her. They were never alone, those Austrian children—always under surveillance, always restrained, always prepared to kiss the hand of whatever relative might be near and to take themselves of to anywhere so it were somewhere else.

"I am so glad you are going to talk to me about an American child," said Harmony, bringing in the tea.

But Mrs. Boyer was not so sure she was going to talk about the American child. She was not sure of anything, except that the household looked most irregular, and that Peter Byrne was trying to cover a difficult situation with much conversation. He was almost glib, was Peter. The tea was good; that was one thing.

She sat back with her muff on her knee, having refused the concession of putting it on a chair as savoring too much of acceptance if not approval, and sipped her tea out of a spoon as becomes a tea-lover. Peter, who loathed tea, lounged about the room, clearly in the way, but fearful to leave Harmony alone with her. She was quite likely, at the first opportunity, to read her a lesson on the conventions, if nothing worse; to upset the delicate balance of the little household he was guarding. So he stayed, praying for Anna to come and bear out his story, while Harmony toyed with her spoon and waited for some mention of the lessons. None came. Mrs. Boyer, having finished her tea, rose and put down her cup.

"That was very refreshing," she said. "Where shall I find the street-car? I walked out, but it is late."

"I'll take you to the car." Peter picked up his old hat.

"Thank you. I am always lost in this wretched town. I give the conductors double tips to put me down where I want to go; but how can they when it is the wrong car?" She bowed to Harmony without shaking hands. "Thank you for the tea. It was really good. Where do you get it?"

"There is a tea-shop a door or two from the Grand Hotel."

"I must remember that. Thank you again. Good-bye."

Not a word about the lessons or the American child!

"You said something about my card in the Doctors' Club—"

Something wistful in the girl's eyes caught and held Mrs. Boyer.

After all she was the mother of daughters. She held out her hand and her voice was not so hard.

"That will have to wait until another time. I have made a social visit and we'll not spoil it with business."

"But—"

"I really think the boy's mother must attend to that herself. But I shall tell her where to find you, and"—here she glanced at Peter—"all about it."

"Thank you," said Harmony gratefully.

Peter had no finesse. He escorted Mrs. Boyer across the yard and through the gate with hardly a word. With the gate closed behind them he turned and faced her:—

"You are going away with a wrong impression, Mrs. Boyer."

Mrs. Boyer had been thinking hard as she crossed the yard. The result was a resolution to give Peter a piece of her mind. She drew her ample proportions into a dignity that was almost majesty.

"Yes?"

"I—I can understand why you think as you do. It is quite without foundation."

"I am glad of that." There was no conviction in her voice.

"Of course," went on Peter, humbling himself for Harmony's sake, "I suppose it has been rather unconventional, but Dr. Gates is not a young woman by any means, and she takes very good care of Miss Wells. There were reasons why this seemed the best thing to do. Miss Wells was alone and—"

"There is a Dr. Gates?"

"Of course. If you will come back and wait she'll be along very soon."

Mrs. Boyer was convinced and defrauded in one breath; convinced that there might be a Dr. Gates, but equally convinced that the situation was anomalous and certainly suspicious; defrauded in that she had lost the anticipated pleasure of giving Peter a piece of her mind. She walked along beside him without speaking until they reached the street-car line. Then she turned.

"You called her—you spoke to her very affectionately, young man," she accused him.

Peter smiled. The car was close. Some imp of recklessness, some perversion of humor seized him.

"My dear Mrs. Boyer," he said, "that was in jest purely. Besides, I did not know that you were there!"

Mrs. Boyer was a literal person without humor. It was outraged American womanhood incarnate that got into the street-car and settled its broadcloth of the best quality indignantly on the cane seat. It was outraged American womanhood that flung open the door of Marie Jedlicka's flat, and stalking into Marie Jedlicka's sitting room confronted her husband as he read a month-old newspaper from home.

"Did you ever hear of a woman doctor named Gates?" she demanded.

Boyer was not unaccustomed to such verbal attacks. He had learned to meet domestic broadsides with a shield of impenetrable good humor, or at the most with a return fire of mild sarcasm.

"I never hear of a woman doctor if it can be avoided."

"Dr. Gates—Anna Gates?"

"There are a number here. I meet them in the hospital, but I don't know their names."

"Where does Peter Byrne live?"

"In a pension, I believe, my dear. Are we going to have anything to eat or do we sup of Peter Byrne?"

Mrs. Boyer made no immediate reply. She repaired to the bedroom of Marie Jedlicka, and placed her hat, coat and furs on one of the beds with the crocheted coverlets. It is a curious thing about rooms. There was no change in the bedroom apparent to the eye, save that for Marie's tiny slippers at the foot of the wardrobe there were Mrs. Boyer's substantial house shoes. But in some indefinable way the room had changed. About it hung an atmosphere of solid respectability, of impeccable purity that soothed Mrs. Boyer's ruffled virtue into peace. Is it any wonder that there is a theory to the effect that things take on the essential qualities of people who use them, and that we are haunted by things, not people? That when grandfather's wraith is seen in his old armchair it is the chair that produces it, while grandfather himself serenely haunts the shades of some vast wilderness of departed spirits?

Not that Mrs. Boyer troubled herself about such things. She was exceedingly orthodox, even in the matter of a hereafter, where the most orthodox are apt to stretch a point, finding no attraction whatever in the thing they are asked to believe. Mrs. Boyer, who would have regarded it as heterodox to substitute any other instrument for the harp of her expectation, tied on her gingham apron before Marie Jedlicka's mirror, and thought of Harmony and of the girls at home.

She told her husband over the supper-table and found him less shocked than she had expected.

"It's not your affair or mine," he said. "It's Byrne's business."

"Think of the girl!"

"Even if you are right it's rather late, isn't it?"

"You could tell him what you think of him."

Dr. Boyer sighed over a cup of very excellent coffee. Much living with a representative male had never taught his wife the reserves among members of the sex masculine.

"I might, but I don't intend to," he said. "And if you listen to me you'll keep the thing to yourself."

"I'll take precious good care that the girl gets no pupils," snapped Mrs. Boyer. And she did with great thoroughness.

We trace a life by its scars. Destiny, marching on by a thousand painful steps, had left its usual mark, a footprint on a naked soul. The soul was Harmony's; the foot—was it not encased at that moment in Mrs. Boyer's comfortable house shoes?

Anna was very late that night. Peter, having put Mrs. Boyer on her car, went back quickly. He had come out without his overcoat, and with the sunset a bitter wind had risen, but he was too indignant to be cold. He ran up the staircase, hearing on all sides the creaking and banging with which the old house resented a gale, and burst into the salon of Maria Theresa.

Harmony was sitting sidewise in a chair by the tea-table with her face hidden against its worn red velvet. She did not look up when he entered. Peter went over and put a hand on her shoulder. She quivered under it and he took it away.

"Crying?"

"A little," very smothered. "Just dis-disappointment. Don't mind me, Peter."

"You mean about the pupil?"

Harmony sat up and looked at him. She still wore her hat, now more than ever askew, and some of the dye from the velvet had stained her cheek. She looked rather hectic, very lovely.

"Why did she change so when she saw you?"

Peter hesitated. Afterward he thought of a dozen things he might have said, safe things. Not one came to him.

"She—she is an evil-thinking old woman, Harry," he said gravely.

"She did not approve of the way we are living here, is that it?"

"Yes."

"But Anna?"

"She did not believe there was an Anna. Not that it matters," he added hastily. "I'll make Anna go to her and explain. It's her infernal jumping to a conclusion that makes me crazy."

"She will talk, Peter. I am frightened."

"I'll take Anna to-night and we'll go to Boyer's. I'll make that woman get down on her knees to you. I'll—"

"You'll make bad very much worse," said Harmony dejectedly. "When a thing has to be explained it does no good to explain it."

The salon was growing dark. Peter was very close to her again. As in the dusky kitchen only a few days before, he felt the compelling influence of her nearness. He wanted, as he had never wanted anything in his life before, to take her in his arms, to hold her close and bid defiance to evil tongues. He was afraid of himself. To gain a moment he put a chair between them and stood, strong hands gripping its back, looking down at her.

"There is one thing we could do."

"What, Peter?"

"We could marry. If you cared for me even a little it—it might not be so bad for you."

"But I am not in love with you. I care for you, of course, but—not that way, Peter. And I do not wish to marry."

"Not even if I wish it very much?"

"No."

"If you are thinking of my future—"

"I'm thinking for both of us. And although just now you think you care a little for me, you do not care enough, Peter. You are lonely and I am the only person you see much, so you think you want to marry me. You don't really. You want to help me."

Few motives are unmixed. Poor Peter, thus accused, could not deny his altruism.

And in the face of his poverty and the little he could offer, compared with what she must lose, he did not urge what was the compelling motive after all, his need of her.

"It would be a rotten match for you," he agreed. "I only thought, perhaps—You are right, of course; you ought not to marry."

"And what about you?"

"I ought not, of course."

Harmony rose, smiling a little.

"Then that's settled. And for goodness' sake, Peter, stop proposing to me every time things go wrong." Her voice changed, grew grave and older, much older than Peter's. "We must not marry, either of us, Peter. Anna is right. There might be an excuse if we were very much in love: but we are not. And loneliness is not a reason."

"I am very lonely," said Peter wistfully.

CHAPTER XIII

Peter took the polished horns to the hospital the next morning and approached Jimmy with his hands behind him and an atmosphere of mystery that enshrouded him like a cloak. Jimmy, having had a good night and having taken the morning's

64

medicine without argument, had been allowed up in a roller chair. It struck Peter with a pang that the boy looked more frail day by day, more transparent.

"I have brought you," said Peter gravely, "the cod-liver oil."

"I've had it!"

"Then guess."

"Dad's letter?"

"You've just had one. Don't be a piggy."

"Animal, vegetable, or mineral?"

"Vegetable," said Peter shamelessly.

"Soft or hard!"

"Soft."

This was plainly a disappointment. A pair of horns might be vegetable; they could hardly be soft.

"A kitten?"

"A kitten is not vegetable, James."

"I know. A bowl of gelatin from Harry!" For by this time Harmony was his very good friend, admitted to the Jimmy club, which consisted of Nurse Elisabet, the Dozent with the red beard, Anna and Peter, and of course the sentry, who did not know that he belonged.

"Gelatin, to be sure," replied Peter, and produced the horns.

It was a joyous moment in the long low ward, with its triple row of beds, its barred windows, its clean, uneven old floor. As if to add a touch of completeness the sentry outside, peering in, saw the wheeled chair with its occupant, and celebrated this advance along the road to recovery by placing on the window-ledge a wooden replica of himself, bayonet and all, carved from a bit of cigar box.

"Everybody is very nice to me," said Jimmy contentedly. "When my father comes back I shall tell him. He is very fond of people who are kind to me. There was a woman on the ship—What is bulging your pocket, Peter?"

"My handkerchief."

"That is not where you mostly carry your handkerchief."

Peter was injured. He scowled ferociously at being doubted and stood up before the wheeled chair to be searched. The ward watched joyously, while from pocket after pocket of Peter's old gray suit came Jimmy's salvage—two nuts, a packet of figs, a postcard that represented a stout colonel of hussars on his back on a frozen lake, with a private soldier waiting to go through the various salutations due his rank before assisting him. A gala day, indeed, if one could forget the grave in the little mountain town with only a name on the cross at its head, and if one did not notice that the boy was thinner than ever, that his hands soon tired of playing and lay in his lap, that Nurse Elisabet, who was much inured to death and lived her days with tragedy, caught him to her almost fiercely as she lifted him back from the chair into the smooth white bed.

He fell asleep with Peter's arm under his head and the horns of the deer beside him. On the bedside stand stood the wooden sentry, keeping guard. As Peter drew his arm away he became aware of the Nurse Elisabet beckoning to him from a

65

door at the end of the ward Peter left the sentinel on guard and tiptoed down the room. Just outside, round a corner, was the Dozent's laboratory, and beyond the tiny closet where he slept, where on a stand was the photograph of the lady he would marry when he had become a professor and required no one's consent.

The Dozent was waiting for Peter. In the amiable conspiracy which kept the boy happy he was arch-plotter. His familiarity with Austrian intrigue had made him invaluable. He it was who had originated the idea of making Jimmy responsible for the order of the ward, so that a burly Trager quarreling over his daily tobacco with the nurse in charge, or brawling over his soup with another patient, was likely to be hailed in a thin soprano, and to stand, grinning sheepishly, while Jimmy, in mixed English and German, restored the decorum of the ward. They were a quarrelsome lot, the convalescents. Jimmy was so busy some days settling disputes and awarding decisions that he slept almost all night. This was as it should be.

The Dozent waited for Peter. His red beard twitched and his white coat, stained from the laboratory table, looked quite villainous. He held out a letter.

"This has come for the child," he said in quite good English. He was obliged to speak English. Day by day he taught in the clinics Americans who scorned his native tongue, and who brought him the money with which some day he would marry. He liked the English language; he liked Americans because they learned quickly. He held out an envelope with a black border and Peter took it.

"From Paris!" he said. "Who in the world—I suppose I'd better open it."

"So I thought. It appears a letter of—how you say it? Ah, yes, condolence."

Peter opened the letter and read it. Then without a word he gave it open to the Dozent. There was silence in the laboratory while the Dozent read it, silence except for his canary, which was chipping at a lump of sugar. Peter's face was very sober.

"So. A mother! You knew nothing of a mother?"

"Something from the papers I found. She left when the boy was a baby—went on the stage, I think. He has no recollection of her, which is a good thing. She seems to have been a bad lot."

"She comes to take him away. That is impossible."

"Of course it is impossible," said Peter savagely. "She's not going to see the child if I can help it. She left because—she's the boy's mother, but that's the best you can say of her. This letter—Well, you've read it."

"She is as a stranger to him?"

"Absolutely. She will come in mourning—look at that black border—and tell him his father is dead, and kill him. I know the type."

The canary chipped at his sugar; the red beard of the Dozent twitched, as does the beard of one who plots. Peter re-read the gushing letter in his hand and thought fiercely.

"She is on her way here," said the Dozent. "That is bad. Paris to Wien is two days and a night. She may hourly arrive."

"We might send him away—to another hospital."

The Dozent shrugged his shoulders.

66

"Had I a home—" he said, and glanced through the door to the portrait on the stand. "It would be possible to hide the boy, at least for a time. In the interval the mother might be watched, and if she proved a fit person the boy could be given to her. It is, of course, an affair of police."

This gave Peter pause. He had no money for fines, no time for imprisonment, and he shared the common horror of the great jail. He read the letter again, and tried to read into the lines Jimmy's mother, and failed. He glanced into the ward. Still Jimmy slept. A burly convalescent, with a saber cut from temple to ear and the general appearance of an assassin, had stopped beside the bed and was drawing up the blanket round the small shoulders.

"I can give orders that the woman be not admitted to-day," said the Dozent. "That gives us a few hours. She will go to the police, and to-morrow she will be admitted. In the mean time—"

"In the mean time," Peter replied, "I'll try to think of something. If I thought she could be warned and would leave him here—"

"She will not. She will buy him garments and she will travel with him through the Riviera and to Nice. She says Nice. She wishes to be there for carnival, and the boy will die."

Peter took the letter and went home. He rode, that he might read it again in the bus. But no scrap of comfort could he get from it. It spoke of the dead father coldly, and the father had been the boy's idol. No good woman could have been so heartless. It offered the boy a seat in one of the least reputable of the Paris theaters to hear his mother sing. And in the envelope, overlooked before, Peter found a cutting from a French newspaper, a picture of the music-hall type that made him groan. It was indorsed "Mamma."

Harmony had had a busy morning. First she had put her house in order, working deftly, her pretty hair pinned up in a towel—all in order but Peter's room. That was to have a special cleaning later. Next, still with her hair tied up, she had spent two hours with her violin, standing very close to the stove to save fuel and keep her fingers warm. She played well that morning: even her own critical ears were satisfied, and the Portier, repairing a window lock in an empty room below, was entranced. He sat on the window sill in the biting cold and listened. Many music students had lived in the apartment with the great salon; there had been much music of one sort and another, but none like this.

"She tears my heart from my bosom," muttered the Portier, sighing, and almost swallowed a screw that he held in his teeth.

After the practicing Harmony cleaned Peter's room. She felt very tender toward Peter that day. The hurt left by Mrs. Boyer's visit had died away, but there remained a clear vision of Peter standing behind the chair and offering himself humbly in marriage, so that a bad situation might be made better. And as with a man tenderness expresses itself in the giving of gifts, so with a woman it means giving of service. Harmony cleaned Peter's room.

It was really rather tidy. Peter's few belongings did not spread to any extent and years of bachelorhood had taught him the rudiments of order. Harmony took the covers from washstand and dressing table and washed and ironed them. She cleaned Peter's worn brushes and brought a pincushion of her own for his one extra scarfpin. Finally she brought her own steamer rug and folded it across the foot of the bed. There was no stove in the room; it had been Harmony's room once, and she knew to the full how cold it could be.

Having made all comfortable for the outer man she prepared for the inner. She was in the kitchen, still with her hair tied up, when Anna came home.

Anna was preoccupied. Instead of her cheery greeting she came somberly back to the kitchen, a letter in her hand. History was making fast that day.

"Hello, Harry," she said. "I'm going to take a bite and hurry off. Don't bother, I'll attend to myself." She stuffed the letter in her belt and got a plate from a shelf. "How pretty you look with your head tied up! If stupid Peter saw you now he would fall in love with you."

"Then I shall take it off. Peter must be saved!"

Anna sat down at the tiny table and drank her tea. She felt rather better after the tea. Harmony, having taken the towel off, was busy over the brick stove. There was nothing said for a moment. Then:—

"I am out of patience with Peter," said Anna.

"Why?"

"Because he hasn't fallen in love with you. Where are his eyes?"

"Please, Anna!"

"It's better as it is, no doubt, for both of you. But it's superhuman of Peter. I wonder—"

"Yes?"

"I think I'll not tell you what I wonder."

And Harmony, rather afraid of Anna's frank speech, did not insist.

As she drank her tea and made a pretense at eating, Anna's thoughts wandered from Peter to Harmony to the letter in her belt and back again to Peter and Harmony. For some time she had been suspicious of Peter. From her dozen years of advantage in age and experience she looked down on Peter's thirty years of youth, and thought she knew something that Peter himself did not suspect. Peter being unintrospective, Anna did his heart-searching for him. She believed he was madly in love with Harmony and did not himself suspect it. As she watched the girl over her teacup, revealing herself in a thousand unposed gestures of youth and grace, a thousand lovelinesses, something of the responsibility she and Peter had assumed came over her. She sighed and felt for her letter.

"I've had rather bad news," she said at last.

"From home?"

"Yes. My father—did you know I have a father?"

"You hadn't spoken of him."

"I never do. As a father he hasn't amounted to much. But he's very ill, and—I 've a conscience."

Harmony turned a startled face to her.

"You are not going back to America?"

"Oh, no, not now, anyhow. If I become hag ridden with remorse and do go I'll find some one to take my place. Don't worry."

The lunch was a silent meal. Anna was hurrying off as Peter came in, and there was no time to discuss Peter's new complication with her. Harmony and Peter ate together, Harmony rather silent. Anna's unfortunate comment about Peter had made her constrained. After the meal Peter, pipe in mouth, carried the dishes to the kitchen, and there it was that he gave her the letter. What Peter's slower mind had been a perceptible time in grasping Harmony comprehended at once—and not only the situation, but its solution.

"Don't let her have him!" she said, putting down the letter. "Bring him here. Oh, Peter, how good we must be to him!"

And that after all was how the thing was settled. So simple, so obvious was it that these three expatriates, these waifs and estrays, banded together against a common poverty, a common loneliness, should share without question whatever was theirs to divide. Peter and Anna gave cheerfully of their substance, Harmony of her labor, that a small boy should be saved a tragic knowledge until he was well enough to bear it, or until, if God so willed, he might learn it himself without pain.

The friendly sentry on duty again that night proved singularly blind. Thus it happened that, although the night was clear when the twin dials of the Votivkirche showed nine o'clock, he did not notice a cab that halted across the street from the hospital.

Still more strange that, although Peter passed within a dozen feet of him, carrying a wriggling and excited figure wrapped in a blanket and insisting on uncovering its feet, the sentry was able the next day to say that he had observed such a person carrying a bundle, but that it was a short stocky person, quite lame, and that the bundle was undoubtedly clothing going to the laundry.

Perhaps—it is just possible—the sentry had his suspicions. It is undeniable that as Jimmy in the cab on Peter's knee, with Peter's arm close about him, looked back at the hospital, the sentry was going through the manual of arms very solemnly under the stars and facing toward the carriage.

CHAPTER XIV

For two days at Semmering it rained. The Raxalpe and the Schneeberg sulked behind walls of mist. From the little balcony of the Pension Waldheim one looked out over a sea of cloud, pierced here and there by islands that were crags or by the tops of sunken masts that were evergreen trees. The roads were masses of slippery mud, up which the horses steamed and sweated. The gray cloud fog hung over everything; the barking of a dog loomed out of it near at hand where no dog was to be seen. Children cried and wild birds squawked; one saw them not.

During the second night a landslide occurred on the side of the mountain with a rumble like the noise of fifty trains. In the morning, the rain clouds lifting for a moment, Marie saw the narrow yellow line of the slip.

Everything was saturated with moisture. It did no good to close the heavy wooden shutters at night: in the morning the air of the room was sticky and clothing was moist to the touch. Stewart, confined to the house, grew irritable.

Marie watched him anxiously. She knew quite well by what slender tenure she held her man. They had nothing in common, neither speech nor thought. And the little Marie's love for Stewart, grown to be a part of her, was largely maternal. She held him by mothering him, by keeping him comfortable, not by a great reciprocal passion that might in time have brought him to her in chains.

And now he was uncomfortable. He chafed against the confinement; he resented the food, the weather. Even Marie's content at her unusual leisure irked him. He accused her of purring like a cat by the fire, and stamped out more than once, only to be driven in by the curious thunderstorms of early Alpine winter.

On the night of the second day the weather changed. Marie, awakening early, stepped out on to the balcony and closed the door carefully behind her. A new world lay beneath her, a marvel of glittering branches, of white plain far below; the snowy mane of the Raxalpe was become a garment. And from behind the villa came the cheerful sound of sleigh-bells, of horses' feet on crisp snow, of runners sliding easily along frozen roads. Even the barking of the dog in the next yard had ceased rumbling and become sharp staccato.

The balcony extended round the corner of the house. Marie, eagerly discovering her new world, peered about, and seeing no one near ventured so far. The road was in view, and a small girl on ski was struggling to prevent a collision between two plump feet. Even as Marie saw her the inevitable happened and she went headlong into a drift. A governess who had been kneeling before a shrine by the road hastily crossed herself and ran to the rescue.

It was a marvelous morning, a day of days. The governess and the child went on out of vision. Marie stood still, looking at the shrine. A drift had piled about its foot, where the governess had placed a bunch of Alpine flowers. Down on her knees on the balcony went the little Marie, regardless of the snow, and prayed to the shrine of the Virgin below—for what? For forgiveness? For a better life? Not at all. She prayed that the heels of the American girl would keep her in out of the snow.

The prayer of the wicked availeth nothing; even the godly at times must suffer disappointment. And when one prays of heels, who can know of the yearning back of the praying? Marie, rising and dusting her chilled knees, saw the party of Americans on the road, clad in stout boots and swinging along gayly. Marie shrugged her shoulders resignedly. She should have gone to the shrine itself; a balcony was not a holy place. But one thing she determined—the Americans went toward the Sonnwendstein. She would advise against the Sonnwendstein for that day.

Marie's day of days had begun wrong after all. For Stewart rose with the Sonnwendstein in his mind, and no suggestion of Marie's that in another day a path would be broken had any effect on him. He was eager to be off, committed the extravagance of ordering an egg apiece for breakfast, and finally proclaimed that if Marie feared the climb he would go alone.

Marie made many delays: she dressed slowly, and must run back to see if the balcony door was securely closed. At a little shop where they stopped to buy mountain sticks she must purchase postcards and send them at once. Stewart was fairly patient: air and exercise were having their effect.

It was eleven o'clock when, having crossed the valley, they commenced to mount the slope of the Sonnwendstein. The climb was easy; the road wound back and forward on itself so that one ascended with hardly an effort. Stewart gave Marie a hand here and there, and even paused to let her sit on a boulder and rest. The snow was not heavy; he showed her the footprints of a party that had gone ahead, and to amuse her tried to count the number of people. When he found it was five he grew thoughtful. There were five in Anita's party. Thanks to Marie's delays they met the Americans coming down. The meeting was a short one: the party went on down, gayly talking. Marie and Stewart climbed silently. Marie's day was spoiled; Stewart had promised to dine at the hotel.

Even the view at the tourist house did not restore Marie's fallen spirits. What were the Vienna plain and the Styrian Alps to her, with this impatient and frowning man beside her consulting his watch and computing the time until he might see the American again? What was prayer, if this were its answer?

They descended rapidly, Stewart always in the lead and setting a pace that Marie struggled in vain to meet. To her tentative and breathless remarks he made brief answer, and only once in all that time did he volunteer a remark. They had reached the Hotel Erzherzog in the valley. The hotel was still closed, and Marie, panting, sat down on an edge of the terrace.

"We have been very foolish," he said.

"Why?"

"Being seen together like that."

"But why? Could you not walk with any woman?"

"It's not that," said Stewart hastily. "I suppose once does not matter. But we can't be seen together all the time."

Marie turned white. The time had gone by when an incident of the sort could have been met with scorn or with threats; things had changed for Marie Jedlicka since the day Peter had refused to introduce her to Harmony. Then it had been vanity; now it was life itself.

"What you mean," she said with pale lips, "is that we must not be seen together at all. Must I—do you wish me to remain a prisoner while you—" she choked.

"For Heaven's sake," he broke out brutally, "don't make a scene. There are men cutting ice over there. Of course you are not a prisoner. You may go where you like."

Marie rose and picked up her muff.

Marie's sordid little tragedy played itself out in Semmering. Stewart neglected her almost completely; he took fewer and fewer meals at the villa. In two weeks he spent one evening with the girl, and was so irritable that she went to bed crying. The little mountain resort was filling up; there were more and more Americans. Christmas was drawing near and a dozen or so American doctors came up, bringing their families for the holidays. It was difficult to enter a shop without encountering some of them. To add to the difficulty, the party at the hotel, finding it crowded there, decided to go into a pension and suggested moving to the Waldheim.

Stewart himself was wretchedly uncomfortable. Marie's tragedy was his predicament. He disliked himself very cordially, loathing himself and his situation with the new-born humility of the lover. For Stewart was in love for the first time in his life. Marie knew it. She had not lived with him for months without knowing his every thought, every mood. She grew bitter and hard those days, sitting alone by the green stove in the Pension Waldheim, or leaning, elbows on the rail, looking from the balcony over the valley far below. Bitter and hard, that is, during his absences; he had but to enter the room and her rage died, to be replaced with yearning and little, shy, tentative advances that he only tolerated. Wild thoughts came to Marie, especially at night, when the stars made a crown over the Rax, and in the hotel an orchestra played, while people dined and laughed and loved.

She grew obstinate, too. When in his desperation Stewart suggested that they go back to Vienna she openly scoffed.

"Why?" she demanded. "That you may come back here to her, leaving me there?"

"My dear girl," he flung back exasperated, "this affair was not a permanent one. You knew that at the start."

"You have taken me away from my work. I have two months' vacation. It is but one month."

"Go back and let me pay—"

"No!"

In pursuance of the plan to leave the hotel the American party came to see the Waldheim, and catastrophe almost ensued. Luckily Marie was on the balcony when the landlady flung open the door, and announced it as Stewart's apartment. But Stewart had a bad five minutes and took it out, manlike, on the girl.

Stewart had another reason for not wishing to leave Semmering. Anita was beautiful, a bit of a coquette, too; as are most pretty women. And Stewart was not alone in his devotion. A member of the party, a New Yorker named Adam, was much in love with the girl and indifferent who knew it. Stewart detested him.

In his despair Stewart wrote to Peter Byrne. It was characteristic of Peter that, however indifferent people might be in prosperity, they always turned to him in trouble. Stewart's letter concluded:—

"I have made out a poor case for myself; but I'm in a hole, as you can see. I would like to chuck everything here and sail for home with these people who go in January. But, confound it, Byrne, what am I to do with Marie? And that brings me to what I 've been wanting to say all along, and haven't had the courage to. Marie likes you and you rather liked her, didn't you? You could talk her into reason if anybody could. Now that you know how things are, can't you come up over Sunday? It's asking a lot, and I know it; but things are pretty bad."

Peter received the letter on the morning of the day before Christmas. He read it several times and, recalling the look he had seen more than once in Marie Jedlicka's eyes, he knew that things were very bad, indeed.

But Peter was a man of family in those days, and Christmas is a family festival not to be lightly ignored. He wired to Stewart that he would come up as soon as possible after Christmas. Then, because of the look in Marie's eyes and because he feared for her a sad Christmas, full of heartaches and God knows what loneliness, he bought her a most hideous brooch, which he thought admirable in every way and highly ornamental and which he could not afford at all. This he mailed, with a cheery greeting, and feeling happier and much poorer made his way homeward.

CHAPTER XV

Christmas-Eve in the saloon of Maria Theresa! Christmas-Eve, with the great chandelier recklessly ablaze and a pig's head with cranberry eyes for supper! Christmas-Eve, with a two-foot tree gleaming with candles on the stand, and beside the stand, in a huge chair, Jimmy!

It had been a busy day for Harmony. In the morning there had been shopping and marketing, and such a temptation to be reckless, with the shops full of ecstasies and the old flower women fairly overburdened. There had been anxieties, too, such as the pig's head, which must be done a certain way, and Jimmy, who must be left with the Portier's wife as nurse while all of them went to the hospital. The house revolved around Jimmy now, Jimmy, who seemed the better for the moving, and whose mother as yet had failed to materialize.

In the afternoon Harmony played at the hospital. Peter took her as the early twilight was falling in through the gate where the sentry kept guard and so to the great courtyard. In this grim playground men wandered about, smoking their daily allowance of tobacco and moving to keep warm, offscourings of the barracks, derelicts of the slums, with here and there an honest citizen lamenting a Christmas away from home. The hospital was always pathetic to Harmony; on this Christmas-Eve she found it harrowing. Its very size shocked her, that there should be so much suffering, so much that was appalling, frightful, insupportable. Peter felt her quiver under his hand. A hospital in festivity is very affecting. It smiles through its tears. And in every assemblage there are sharply defined lines of difference. There are those who are going home soon, God willing; there are those who will go home some time after long days and longer nights. And there are those who will never go home and who know it. And because of this the ones who are never going home are most festively clad, as if, by way of compensation, the nurses mean to give them all future Christmasses in one. They receive an extra orange, or a pair of gloves, perhaps,—and they are not the less grateful because

73

they understand. And when everything is over they lay away in the bedside stand the gloves they will never wear, and divide the extra orange with a less fortunate one who is almost recovered. Their last Christmas is past.

"How beautiful the tree was!" they say. Or, "Did you hear how the children sang? So little, to sing like that! It made me think—of angels."

Peter led Harmony across the courtyard, through many twisting corridors, and up and down more twisting staircases to the room where she was to play. There were many Christmas trees in the hospital that afternoon; no one hall could have held the thousands of patients, the doctors, the nurses. Sometimes a single ward had its own tree, its own entertainment. Occasionally two or three joined forces, preempted a lecture-room, and wheeled or hobbled or carried in their convalescents. In such case an imposing audience was the result.

Into such a room Peter led Harmony. It was an amphitheater, the seats rising in tiers, half circle above half circle, to the dusk of the roof. In the pit stood the tree, candle-lighted. There was no other illumination in the room. The semi-darkness, the blazing tree, the rows of hopeful, hoping, hopeless, rising above, white faces over white gowns, the soft rustle of expectancy, the silence when the Dozent with the red beard stepped out and began to read an address—all caught Harmony by the throat. Peter, keenly alive to everything she did, felt rather than heard her soft sob.

Peter saw the hospital anew that dark afternoon, saw it through Harmony's eyes. Layer after layer his professional callus fell away, leaving him quick again. He had lived so long close to the heart of humanity that he had reduced its throbbing to beats that might be counted. Now, once more, Peter was back in the early days, when a heart was not a pump, but a thing that ached or thrilled or struggled, that loved or hated or yearned.

The orchestra, insisting on sadly sentimental music, was fast turning festivity into gloom. It played Handel's "Largo"; it threw its whole soul into the assurance that the world, after all, was only a poor place, that Heaven was a better. It preached resignation with every deep vibration of the cello. Harmony fidgeted.

"How terrible!" she whispered. "To turn their Christmas-Eve into mourning! Stop them!"

"Stop a German orchestra?"

"They are crying, some of them. Oh, Peter!"

The music came to an end at last. Tears were dried. Followed recitations, gifts, a speech of thanks from Nurse Elisabet for the patients. Then—Harmony.

Harmony never remembered afterward what she had played. It was joyous, she knew, for the whole atmosphere changed. Laughter came; even the candles burned more cheerfully. When she had finished, a student in a white coat asked her to play a German Volkspiel, and roared it out to her accompaniment with much vigor and humor. The audience joined in, at first timidly, then lustily.

Harmony stood alone by the tree, violin poised, smiling at the applause. Her eyes, running along the dim amphitheater, sought Peter's, and finding them dwelt there a moment. Then she began to play softly and as softly the others sang.

74

"Stille Nacht, heilige Nacht,"—they sang, with upturned eyes.

"Alles schlaeft, einsam wacht..."

Visions came to Peter that afternoon in the darkness, visions in which his poverty was forgotten or mattered not at all. Visions of a Christmas-Eve in a home that he had earned, of a tree, of a girl-woman, of a still and holy night, of a child.

"Nur das traute, hoch heilige Paar Holder Knabe im lockigen Haar Schlaf' in himmlischer Ruh', Schlaf' in himmlischer Ruh'," they sang.

There was real festivity at the old lodge of Maria Theresa that night.

Jimmy had taken his full place in the household. The best room, which had been Anna's, had been given up to him. Here, carefully tended, with a fire all day in the stove, Jimmy reigned from the bed. To him Harmony brought her small puzzles and together they solved them.

"Shall it be a steak to-night?" thus Harmony humbly. "Or chops?"

"With tomato sauce?"

"If Peter allows, yes."

Much thinking on Jimmy's part, and then:—

"Fish," he would decide. "Fish with egg dressing."

They would argue for a time, and compromise on fish.

The boy was better. Peter shook his head over any permanent improvement, but Anna fiercely seized each crumb of hope. Many and bitter were the battles she and Peter fought at night over his treatment, frightful the litter of authorities Harmony put straight every morning.

The extra expense was not much, but it told. Peter's carefully calculated expenditures felt the strain. He gave up a course in X-ray on which he had set his heart and cut off his hour in the coffee-house as a luxury. There was no hardship about the latter renunciation. Life for Peter was spelling itself very much in terms of Harmony and Jimmy those days. He resented anything that took him from them.

There were anxieties of a different sort also. Anna's father was failing. He had written her a feeble, half-senile appeal to let bygones be bygones and come back to see him before he died. Anna was Peter's great prop. What would he do should she decide to go home? He had built his house on the sand, indeed.

So far the threatened danger of a mother to Jimmy had not materialized. Peter was puzzled, but satisfied. He still wrote letters of marvelous adventure; Jimmy still watched for them, listened breathless, treasured them under his pillow. But he spoke less of his father. The open page of his childish mind was being written over with new impressions. "Dad" was already a memory; Peter and Harmony and Anna were realities. Sometimes he called Peter "Dad." At those times Peter caught the boy to him in an agony of tenderness.

And as the little apartment revolved round Jimmy, so was this Christmas-Eve given up to him. All day he had stayed in bed for the privilege of an extra hour propped up among pillows in the salon. All day he had strung little red berries that looked like cranberries for the tree, or fastened threads to the tiny cakes that were for trimming only, and sternly forbidden to eat.

A marvelous day that for Jimmy. Late in the afternoon the Portier, with a collar on, had mounted the stairs and sheepishly presented him with a pair of white mice in a wooden cage. Jimmy was thrilled. The cage was on his knees all evening, and one of the mice was clearly ill of a cake with pink icing. The Portier's gift was a stealthy one, while his wife was having coffee with her cousin, the brushmaker. But the spirit Of Christmas does strange things. That very evening, while the Portier was roistering in a beer hall preparatory to the midnight mass, came the Portier's wife, puffing from the stairs, and brought a puzzle book that only the initiated could open, and when one succeeded at last there was a picture of the Christ-Child within.

Young McLean came to call that evening—came to call and remained to worship. It was the first time since Mrs. Boyer that a visitor had come. McLean, interested with everything and palpably not shocked, was a comforting caller. He seemed to Harmony, who had had bad moments since the day of Mrs. Boyer's visit, to put the hallmark of respectability on the household, to restore it to something it had lost or had never had.

She was quite unconscious of McLean's admiration. She and Anna put Jimmy to bed. The tree candles were burned out; Peter was extinguishing the dying remnants when Harmony came back. McLean was at the piano, thrumming softly. Peter, turning round suddenly, surprised an expression on the younger man's face that startled him.

For that one night Harmony had laid aside her mourning, and wore white, soft white, tucked in at the neck, short-sleeved, trailing. Peter had never seen her in white before.

It was Peter's way to sit back and listen: his steady eyes were always alert, good-humored, but he talked very little. That night he was unusually silent. He sat in the shadow away from the lamp and watched the two at the piano: McLean playing a bit of this or that, the girl bending over a string of her violin. Anna came in and sat down near him.

"The boy is quite fascinated," she whispered. "Watch his eyes!"

"He is a nice boy." This from Peter, as if he argued with himself.

"As men go!" This was a challenge Peter was usually quick to accept. That night he only smiled. "It would be a good thing for her: his people are wealthy."

Money, always money! Peter ground his teeth over his pipestem. Eminently it would be a good thing for Harmony, this nice boy in his well-made evening clothes, who spoke Harmony's own language of music, who was almost speechless over her playing, and who looked up at her with eyes in which admiration was not unmixed with adoration.

Peter was restless. As the music went on he tiptoed out of the room and took to pacing up and down the little corridor. Each time as he passed the door he tried not to glance in; each time he paused involuntarily. Jealousy had her will of him that night, jealousy, when he had never acknowledged even to himself how much the girl was to him.

Jimmy was restless. Usually Harmony's music put him to sleep; but that night he lay awake, even after Peter had closed all the doors. Peter came in and sat with him in the dark, going over now and then to cover him, or to give him a drink, or to pick up the cage of mice which Jimmy insisted on having beside him and which constantly slipped off on to the floor. After a time Peter lighted the night-light, a bit of wick on a cork floating in a saucer of lard oil, and set it on the bedside table. Then round it he arranged Jimmy's treasures, the deer antlers, the cage of mice, the box, the wooden sentry. The boy fell asleep. Peter sat in the room, his dead pipe in his teeth, and thought of many things.

It was very late when young McLean left. The two had played until they stopped for very weariness. Anna had yawned herself off to bed. From Jimmy's room Peter could hear the soft hum of their voices.

"You have been awfully good to me," McLean said as he finally rose to go. "I—I want you to know that I'll never forget this evening, never."

"It has been splendid, hasn't it? Since little Scatchy left there has been no one for the piano. I have been lonely sometimes for some one to talk music to."

Lonely! Poor Peter!

"Then you will let me come back?"

"Will I, indeed! I—I'll be grateful."

"How soon would be proper? I dare say to-morrow you'll be busy—Christmas and all that."

"Do you mean you would like to come to-morrow?"

"If old Peter wouldn't be fussed. He might think—"

"Peter always wants every one to be happy. So if you really care—"

"And I'll not bore you?"

"Rather not!"

"How—about what time?"

"In the afternoon would be pleasant, I think. And then Jimmy can listen. He loves music."

McLean, having found his fur-lined coat, got into it as slowly as possible. Then he missed a glove, and it must be searched for in all the dark corners of the salon until found in his pocket. Even then he hesitated, lingered, loath to break up this little world of two.

"You play wonderfully," he said.

"So do you."

"If only something comes of it! It's curious, isn't it, when you think of it? You and I meeting here in the center of Europe and both of us working our heads off for something that may never pan out."

There was something reminiscent about that to Harmony. It was not until after young McLean had gone that she recalled. It was almost word for word what Peter had said to her in the coffee-house the night they met. She thought it very curious, the coincidence, and pondered it, being ignorant of the fact that it is always a matter for wonder when the man meets the woman, no matter where. Nothing is less curious, more inevitable, more amazing. "You and I," forsooth, said Peter!

"You and I," cried young McLean!

CHAPTER XVI

Quite suddenly Peter's house, built on the sand, collapsed. The shock came on Christmas-Day, after young McLean, now frankly infatuated, had been driven home by Peter.

Peter did it after his own fashion. Harmony, with unflagging enthusiasm, was looking tired. Suggestions to this effect rolled off McLean's back like rain off a roof. Finally Peter gathered up the fur-lined coat, the velours hat, gloves, and stick, and placed them on the piano in front of the younger man.

"I'm sorry you must go," said Peter calmly, "but, as you say, Miss Wells is tired and there is supper to be eaten. Don't let me hurry you."

The Portier was at the door as McLean, laughing and protesting, went out. He brought a cablegram for Anna. Peter took it to her door and waited uneasily while she read it.

It was an urgent summons home; the old father was very low. He was calling for her, and a few days or week' would see the end. There were things that must be looked after. The need of her was imperative. With the death the old man's pension would cease and Anna was the bread-winner.

Anna held the paper out to Peter and sat down. Her nervous strength seemed to have deserted her. All at once she was a stricken, elderly woman, with hope wiped out of her face and something nearer resentment than grief in its place.

"It has come, Peter," she said dully. "I always knew it couldn't last. They've always hung about my neck, and now—"

"Do you think you must go? Isn't there some way? If things are so bad you could hardly get there in time, and—you must think of yourself a little, Anna."

"I am not thinking of anything else. Peter, I'm an uncommonly selfish woman, but I—"

Quite without warning she burst out crying, unlovely, audible weeping that shook her narrow shoulders. Harmony heard the sound and joined them. After a look at Anna she sat down beside her and put a white arm over her shoulders. She did not try to speak. Anna's noisy grief subsided as suddenly as it came. She patted Harmony's hand in mute acknowledgment and dried her eyes.

"I'm not grieving, child," she said; "I'm only realizing what a selfish old maid I am. I'm crying because I'm a disappointment to myself. Harry, I'm going back to America."

And that, after hours of discussion, was where they ended. Anna must go at once. Peter must keep the apartment, having Jimmy to look after and to hide. What was a frightful dilemma to him and to Harmony Anna took rather lightly.

"You'll find some one else to take my place," she said. "If I had a day I could find a dozen."

"And in the interval?" Harmony asked, without looking at Peter.

"The interval! Tut! Peter is your brother, to all intents and purposes. And if you are thinking of scandal-mongers, who will know?"

Having determined to go, no arguments moved Anna, nor could either of the two think of anything to urge beyond a situation she refused to see, or rather a situation she refused to acknowledge. She was not as comfortable as she pretended. During all that long night, while snow sifted down into the ugly yard and made it beautiful, while Jimmy slept and the white mice played, while Harmony tossed and tried to sleep and Peter sat in his cold room and smoked his pipe, Anna packed her untidy belongings and added a name now and then to a list that was meant for Peter, a list of possible substitutes for herself in the little household.

She left early the next morning, a grim little person who bent over the sleeping boy hungrily, and insisted on carrying her own bag down the stairs. Harmony did not go to the station, but stayed at home, pale and silent, hovering around against Jimmy's awakening and struggling against a feeling of panic. Not that she feared Peter or herself. But she was conventional; shielded girls are accustomed to lean for a certain support on the proprieties, as bridgeplayers depend on rules.

Peter came back to breakfast, but ate little. Harmony did not even sit down, but drank her cup of coffee standing, looking down at the snow below. Jimmy still slept.

"Won't you sit down?" said Peter.

"I'm not hungry, thank you."

"You can sit down without eating."

Peter was nervous. To cover his uneasiness he was distinctly gruff. He pulled a chair out for her and she sat down. Now that they were face to face the tension was lessened. Peter laid Anna's list on the table between them and bent over it toward her.

"You are hurting me very much, Harry," he said. "Do you know why?"

"I? I am only sorry about Anna. I miss her. I—I was fond of her."

"So was I. But that isn't it, Harry. It's something else."

"I'm uncomfortable, Peter."

"So am I. I'm sorry you don't trust me. For that's it."

"Not at all. But, Peter, what will people say?"

"A great deal, if they know. Who is to know? How many people know about us? A handful, at the most, McLean and Mrs. Boyer and one or two others. Of course I can go away until we get some one to take Anna's place, but you'd be here alone at night, and if the youngster had an attack—"

"Oh, no, don't leave him!"

"It's holiday time. There are no clinics until next week. If you'll put up with me —"

"Put up with you, when it is your apartment I use, your food I eat!" She almost choked. "Peter, I must talk about money."

"I'm coming to that. Don't you suppose you more than earn everything?

79

Doesn't it humiliate me hourly to see you working here?"

"Peter! Would you rob me of my last vestige of self-respect?"

This being unanswerable, Peter fell back on his major premise.

"If you'll put up with me for a day or so I'll take this list of Anna's and hunt up some body. Just describe the person you desire and I'll find her." He assumed a certainty he was far from feeling, but it reassured the girl. "A woman, of course?"

"Of course. And not young."

"'Not young,'" wrote Peter. "Fat?"

Harmony recalled Mrs. Boyer's ample figure and shook her head.

"Not too stout. And agreeable. That's most important."

"'Agreeable,'" wrote Peter. "Although Anna was hardly agreeable, in the strict sense of the word, was she?"

"She was interesting, and—and human."

"'Human!'" wrote Peter. "Wanted, a woman, not young, not too stout, agreeable and human. Shall I advertise?"

The strain was quite gone by that time. Harmony was smiling. Jimmy, waking, called for food, and the morning of the first day was under way.

Peter was well content that morning, in spite of an undercurrent of uneasiness. Before this Anna had shared his proprietorship with him. Now the little household was his. His vicarious domesticity pleased him. He strutted about, taking a new view of his domain; he tightened a doorknob and fastened a noisy window. He inspected the coal-supply and grumbled over its quality. He filled the copper kettle on the stove, carried in the water for Jimmy's morning bath, cleaned the mouse cage. He even insisted on peeling the little German potatoes, until Harmony cried aloud at his wastefulness and took the knife from him.

And afterward, while Harmony in the sickroom read aloud and Jimmy put the wooden sentry into the cage to keep order, he got out his books and tried to study. But he did little work. His book lay on his knee, his pipe died beside him. The strangeness of the situation came over him, sitting there, and left him rather frightened. He tried to see it from the viewpoint of an outsider, and found himself incredulous and doubting. McLean would resent the situation. Even the Portier was a person to reckon with. The skepticism of the American colony was a thing to fear and avoid.

And over all hung the incessant worry about money; he could just manage alone. He could not, by any method he knew of, stretch his resources to cover a separate arrangement for himself. But he had undertaken to shield a girl-woman and a child, and shield them he would and could.

Brave thoughts were Peter's that snowy morning in the great salon of Maria Theresa, with the cat of the Portier purring before the fire; brave thoughts, cool reason, with Harmony practicing scales very softly while Jimmy slept, and with Anna speeding through a white world, to the accompaniment of bitter meditation.

Peter had meant to go to Semmering that day, but even the urgency of Marie's need faded before his own situation. He wired Stewart that he would come as soon as he could, and immediately after lunch departed for the club, Anna's list in his pocket, Harmony's requirements in mind. He paused at Jimmy's door on his way out.

"What shall it be to-day?" he inquired. "A postcard or a crayon?"

"I wish I could have a dog."

"We'll have a dog when you are better and can take him walking. Wait until spring, son."

"Some more mice?"

"You will have them—but not to-day."

"What holiday comes next?"

"New Year's Day. Suppose I bring you a New Year's card."

"That's right," agreed Jimmy. "One I can send to Dad. Do you think he will come back this year?" wistfully.

Peter dropped on his baggy knees beside the bed and drew the little wasted figure to him.

"I think you'll surely see him this year, old man," he said huskily.

Peter walked to the Doctors' Club. On the way he happened on little Georgiev, the Bulgarian, and they went on together. Peter managed to make out that Georgiev was studying English, and that he desired to know the state of health and the abode of the Fraulein Wells. Peter evaded the latter by the simple expedient of pretending not to understand. The little Bulgarian watched him earnestly, his smouldering eyes not without suspicion. There had been much talk in the Pension Schwarz about the departure together of the three Americans. The Jew from Galicia still raved over Harmony's beauty.

Georgiev rather hoped, by staying by Peter, to be led toward his star. But Peter left him at the Doctors' Club, still amiable, but absolutely obtuse to the question nearest the little spy's heart.

The club was almost deserted. The holidays had taken many of the members out of town. Other men were taking advantage of the vacation to see the city, or to make acquaintance again with families they had hardly seen during the busy weeks before Christmas. The room at the top of the stairs where the wives of the members were apt to meet for chocolate and to exchange the addresses of dressmakers was empty; in the reading room he found McLean. Although not a member, McLean was a sort of honorary habitue, being allowed the privilege of the club in exchange for a dependable willingness to play at entertainments of all sorts.

It was in Peter's mind to enlist McLean's assistance in his difficulties. McLean knew a good many people. He was popular, goodlooking, and in a colony where, unlike London and Paris, the great majority were people of moderate means, he was conspicuously well off. But he was also much younger than Peter and intolerant with the insolence of youth. Peter was thinking hard as he took off his overcoat and ordered beer.

The boy was in love with Harmony already; Peter had seen that, as he saw many things. How far his love might carry him, Peter had no idea. It seemed to him, as he sat across the reading-table and studied him over his magazine, that McLean would resent bitterly the girl's position, and that when he learned it a crisis might be precipitated.

One of three things might happen: He might bend all his energies to second Peter's effort to fill Anna's place, to find the right person; he might suggest taking Anna's place himself, and insist that his presence in the apartment would be as justifiable as Peter's; or he might do at once the thing Peter felt he would do eventually, cut the knot of the difficulty by asking Harmony to marry him. Peter, greeting him pleasantly, decided not to tell him anything, to keep him away if possible until the thing was straightened out, and to wait for an hour at the club in the hope that a solution might stroll in for chocolate and gossip.

In any event explanation to McLean would have required justification. Peter disliked the idea. He could humble himself, if necessary, to a woman; he could admit his asininity in assuming the responsibility of Jimmy, for instance, and any woman worthy of the name, or worthy of living in the house with Harmony, would understand. But McLean was young, intolerant. He was more than that, though Peter, concealing from himself just what Harmony meant to him, would not have admitted a rival for what he had never claimed. But a rival the boy was. Peter, calmly reading a magazine and drinking his Munich beer, was in the grip of the fiercest jealousy. He turned pages automatically, to recall nothing of what he had read.

McLean, sitting across from him, watched him surreptitiously. Big Peter, aggressively masculine, heavy of shoulder, direct of speech and eye, was to him the embodiment of all that a woman should desire in a man. He, too, was jealous, but humbly so. Unlike Peter he knew his situation, was young enough to glory in it. Shameless love is always young; with years comes discretion, perhaps loss of confidence. The Crusaders were youths, pursuing an idea to the ends of the earth and flaunting a lady's guerdon from spear or saddle-bow. The older men among them tucked the handkerchief or bit of a gauntleted glove under jerkin and armor near the heart, and flung to the air the guerdon of some light o' love. McLean would have shouted Harmony's name from the housetops. Peter did not acknowledge even to himself that he was in love with her.

It occurred to McLean after a time that Peter being in the club, and Harmony being in all probability at home, it might be possible to see her alone for a few minutes. He had not intended to go back to the house in the Siebensternstrasse so soon after being peremptorily put out; he had come to the club with the intention of clinching his resolution with a game of cribbage. But fate was playing into his hands. There was no cribbage player round, and Peter himself sat across deeply immersed in a magazine. McLean rose, not stealthily, but without unnecessary noise.

So far so good. Peter turned a page and went on reading. McLean sauntered to a window, hands in pockets. He even whistled a trifle, under his breath, to prove how very casual were his intentions. Still whistling, he moved toward the door. Peter turned another page, which was curiously soon to have read two columns of small type without illustrations.

Once out in the hall McLean's movements gained aim and precision. He got his coat, hat and stick, flung the first over his arm and the second on his head, and—

"Going out?" asked Peter calmly.

"Yes, nothing to do here. I've read all the infernal old magazines until I'm sick of them." Indignant, too, from his tone.

"Walking?"

"Yes."

"Mind if I go with you?"

"Not at all."

Peter, taking down his old overcoat from its hook, turned and caught the boy's eye. It was a swift exchange of glances, but illuminating—Peter's whimsical, but with a sort of grim determination; McLean's sheepish, but equally determined.

"Rotten afternoon," said McLean as they started for the stairs. "Half rain, half snow. Streets are ankle-deep."

"I'm not particularly keen about walking, but—I don't care for this tomb alone."

Nothing was further from McLean's mind than a walk with Peter that afternoon. He hesitated halfway down the upper flight.

"You don't care for cribbage, do you?"

"Don't know anything about it. How about pinochle?"

They had both stopped, equally determined, equally hesitating.

"Pinochle it is," acquiesced McLean. "I was only going because there was nothing to do."

Things went very well for Peter that afternoon—up to a certain point. He beat McLean unmercifully, playing with cold deliberation. McLean wearied, fidgeted, railed at his luck. Peter played on grimly.

The club filled up toward the coffee-hour. Two or three women, wives of members, a young girl to whom McLean had been rather attentive before he met Harmony and who bridled at the abstracted bow he gave her. And, finally, when hope in Peter was dead, one of the women on Anna's list.

Peter, laying down pairs and marking up score, went over Harmony's requirements. Dr. Jennings seemed to fit them all, a woman, not young, not too stout, agreeable and human. She was a large, almost bovinely placid person, not at all reminiscent of Anna. She was neat where Anna had been disorderly, well dressed and breezy against Anna's dowdiness and sharpness. Peter, having totaled the score, rose and looked down at McLean.

"You're a nice lad," he said, smiling. "Sometime I shall teach you the game."

"How about a lesson to-night in Seven-Star Street?"

"To-night? Why, I'm sorry. We have an engagement for to-night."

The "we" was deliberate and cruel. McLean writhed. Also the statement was false, but the boy was spared that knowledge for the moment.

Things went well. Dr. Jennings was badly off for quarters. She would make a change if she could better herself. Peter drew her off to a corner and stated his case. She listened attentively, albeit not without disapproval.

She frankly discredited the altruism of Peter's motives when he told her about Harmony. But as the recital went on she found herself rather touched. The story of Jimmy appealed to her. She scolded and lauded Peter in one breath, and what was more to the point, she promised to visit the house in the Siebensternstrasse the next day.

"So Anna Gates has gone home!" she reflected. "When?"

"This morning."

"Then the girl is there alone?"

"Yes. She is very young and inexperienced, and the boy—it's myocarditis. She's afraid to be left with him."

"Is she quite alone?"

"Absolutely, and without funds, except enough for her lessons. Our arrangement was that she should keep the house going; that was her share."

Dr. Jennings was impressed. It was impossible to talk to Peter and not believe him. Women trusted Peter always.

"You've been very foolish, Dr. Byrne," she said as she rose; "but you've been disinterested enough to offset that and to put some of us to shame. To-morrow at three, if it suits you. You said the Siebensternstrasse?"

Peter went home exultant.

CHAPTER XVII

Christmas-Day had had a softening effect on Mrs. Boyer. It had opened badly. It was the first Christmas she had spent away from her children, and there had been little of the holiday spirit in her attitude as she prepared the Christmas breakfast. After that, however, things happened.

In the first place, under her plate she had found a frivolous chain and pendant which she had admired. And when her eyes filled up, as they did whenever she was emotionally moved, the doctor had come round the table and put both his arms about her.

"Too young for you? Not a bit!" he said heartily. "You're better-looking then you ever were, Jennie; and if you weren't you're the only woman for me, anyhow. Don't you think I realize what this exile means to you and that you're doing it for me?"

"I—I don't mind it."

"Yes, you do. To-night we'll go out and make a night of it, shall we? Supper at the Grand, the theater, and then the Tabarin, eh?"

She loosened herself from his arms.

"What shall I wear? Those horrible things the children bought me—"

"Throw 'em away."

"They're not worn at all."

"Throw them out. Get rid of the things the children got you. Go out to-morrow and buy something you like—not that I don't like you in anything or

84

without—"

"Frank!"

"Be happy, that's the thing. It's the first Christmas without the family, and I miss them too. But we're together, dear. That's the big thing. Merry Christmas."

An auspicious opening, that, to Christmas-Day. And they had carried out the program as outlined. Mrs. Boyer had enjoyed it, albeit a bit horrified at the Christmas gayety at the Tabarin.

The next morning, however, she awakened with a keen reaction. Her head ached. She had a sense of taint over her. She was virtue rampant again, as on the day she had first visited the old lodge in the Siebensternstrasse.

It is hardly astonishing that by association of ideas Harmony came into her mind again, a brand that might even yet be snatched from the burning. She had been a bit hasty before, she admitted to herself. There was a woman doctor named Gates, although her address at the club was given as Pension Schwarz. She determined to do her shopping early and then to visit the house in the Siebensternstrasse. She was not a hard woman, for all her inflexible morality, and more than once she had had an uneasy memory of Harmony's bewildered, almost stricken face the afternoon of her visit. She had been a watchful mother over a not particularly handsome family of daughters. This lovely young girl needed mothering and she had refused it. She would go back, and if she found she had been wrong and the girl was deserving and honest, she would see what could be done.

The day was wretched. The snow had turned to rain. Mrs. Boyer, shopping, dragged wet skirts and damp feet from store to store. She found nothing that she cared for after all. The garments that looked chic in the windows or on manikins in the shops, were absurd on her. Her insistent bosom bulged, straight lines became curves or tortuous zigzags, plackets gaped, collars choked her or shocked her by their absence. In the mirror of Marie Jedlicka, clad in familiar garments that had accommodated themselves to the idiosyncrasies of her figure, Mrs. Boyer was a plump, rather comely matron. Here before the plate glass of the modiste, under the glare of a hundred lights, side by side with a slim Austrian girl who looked like a willow wand, Mrs. Boyer was grotesque, ridiculous, monstrous. She shuddered. She almost wept.

It was bad preparation for a visit to the Siebensternstrasse. Mrs. Boyer, finding her vanity gone, convinced that she was an absurdity physically, fell back for comfort on her soul. She had been a good wife and mother; she was chaste, righteous. God had been cruel to her in the flesh, but He had given her the spirit.

"Madame wishes not the gown? It is beautiful—see the embroidery! And the neck may be filled with chiffon."

"Young woman," she said grimly, "I see the embroidery; and the neck may be filled with chiffon, but not for me! And when you have had five children, you will not buy clothes like that either."

All the kindliness was gone from the visit to the Siebensternstrasse; only the determination remained. Wounded to the heart of her self-esteem, her pride in

85

tatters, she took her way to the old lodge and climbed the stairs.

She found a condition of mild excitement. Jimmy had slept long after his bath. Harmony practiced, cut up a chicken for broth, aired blankets for the chair into which Peter on his return was to lift the boy.

She was called to inspect the mouse-cage, which, according to Jimmy, had strawberries in it.

"Far back," he explained. "There in the cotton, Harry."

But it was not strawberries. Harmony opened the cage and very tenderly took out the cotton nest. Eight tiny pink baby mice, clean washed by the mother, lay curled in a heap.

It was a stupendous moment. The joy of vicarious parentage was Jimmy's. He named them all immediately and demanded food for them. On Harmony's delicate explanation that this was unnecessary, life took on a new meaning for Jimmy. He watched the mother lest she slight one. His responsibility weighed on him. Also his inquiring mind was very busy.

"But how did they get there?" he demanded.

"God sent them, just as he sends babies of all sorts."

"Did he send me?"

"Of course."

"That's a good one on you, Harry. My father found me in a hollow tree."

"But don't you think God had something to do with it?"

Jimmy pondered this.

"I suppose," he reflected, "God sent Daddy to find me so that I would be his little boy. You never happened to see any babies when you were out walking, did you, Harry?"

"Not in stumps—but I probably wasn't looking."

Jimmy eyed her with sympathy.

"You may some day. Would you like to have one?"

"Very much," said Harmony, and flushed delightfully.

Jimmy was disposed to press the matter, to urge immediate maternity on her.

"You could lay it here on the bed," he offered, "and I'd watch it. When they yell you let 'em suck your finger. I knew a woman once that had a baby and she did that. And it could watch Isabella." Isabella was the mother mouse. "And when I'm better I could take it walking."

"That," said Harmony gravely, "is mighty fine of you, Jimmy boy. I—I'll think about it." She never denied Jimmy anything, so now she temporized.

"I'll ask Peter."

Harmony had a half-hysterical moment; then:

"Wouldn't it be better," she asked, "to keep anything of that sort a secret? And to surprise Peter?"

The boy loved a secret. He played with it in lieu of other occupation. His uncertain future was sown thick with secrets that would never flower into reality. Thus Peter had shamelessly promised him a visit to the circus when he was able to go, Harmony not to be told until the tickets were bought. Anna had similarly

86

promised to send him from America a pitcher's glove and a baseball bat. To this list of futurities he now added Harmony's baby.

Harmony brought in her violin and played softly to him, not to disturb the sleeping mice. She sang, too, a verse that the Big Soprano had been fond of and that Jimmy loved. Not much of a voice was Harmony's, but sweet and low and very true, as became her violinist's ear.

"Ah, well! For us all some sweet hope lies
  Deeply buried from human eyes,"
she sang, her clear eyes luminous.
"And in the hereafter, angels may
  Roll the stone from its grave away!"

Mrs. Boyer mounted the stairs. She was in a very bad humor. She had snagged her skirt on a nail in the old gate, and although that very morning she had detested the suit, her round of shopping had again endeared it to her. She told the Portier in English what she thought of him, and climbed ponderously, pausing at each landing to examine the damage.

Harmony, having sung Jimmy to sleep, was in the throes of an experiment. She was trying to smoke.

A very human young person was Harmony, apt to be exceedingly wretched if her hat were of last year's fashion, anxious to be inconspicuous by doing what every one else was doing, conventional as are the very young, fearful of being an exception.

And nearly every one was smoking. Many of the young women whom she met at the master's house had yellowed fingers and smoked in the anteroom; the Big Soprano had smoked; Anna and Scatchy had smoked; in the coffee-houses milliners' apprentices produced little silver mouth-pieces to prevent soiling their pretty lips and smoked endlessly. Even Peter had admitted that it was not a vice, but only a comfortable bad habit. And Anna had left a handful of cigarettes.

Harmony was not smoking; she was experimenting. Peter and Anna had smoked together and it had looked comradely. Perhaps, without reasoning it out, Harmony was experimenting toward the end of establishing her relations with Peter still further on friendly and comradely grounds. Two men might smoke together; a man and a woman might smoke together as friends. According to Harmony's ideas, a girl paring potatoes might inspire sentiment, but smoking a cigarette— never!

She did not like it. She thought, standing before her little mirror, that she looked fast, after all. She tried pursing her lips together, as she had seen Anna do, and blowing out the smoke in a thin line. She smoked very hard, so that she stood in the center of a gray nimbus. She hated it, but she persisted. Perhaps it grew on one; perhaps, also, if she walked about it would choke her less. She practiced holding the thing between her first and second fingers, and found that easier than smoking. Then she went to the salon where there was more air, and tried exhaling through her nose. It made her sneeze.

On the sneeze came Mrs. Boyer's ring. Harmony thought very fast. It might be

87

the bread or the milk, but again—She flung the cigarette into the stove, shut the door, and answered the bell.

Mrs. Boyer's greeting was colder than she had intended. It put Harmony on the defensive at once, made her uncomfortable. Like all the innocent falsely accused she looked guiltier than the guiltiest. Under Mrs. Boyer's searching eyes the enormity of her situation overwhelmed her. And over all, through salon and passage, hung the damning odor of the cigarette. Harmony, leading the way in, was a sheep before her shearer.

"I'm calling on all of you," said Mrs. Boyer, sniping. "I meant to bring Dr. Boyer's cards for every one, including Dr. Byrne."

"I'm sorry. Dr. Byrne is out."

"And Dr. Gates?"

"She—she is away."

Mrs. Boyer raised her eyebrows and ostentatiously changed the subject, requesting a needle and thread to draw the rent together. It had been in Harmony's mind to explain the situation, to show Jimmy to Mrs. Boyer, to throw herself on the older woman's sympathy, to ask advice. But the visitor's attitude made this difficult. To add to her discomfort, through the grating in the stove door was coming a thin thread of smoke.

It was, after all, Mrs. Boyer who broached the subject again. She had had a cup of tea, and Harmony, sitting on a stool, had mended the rent so that it could hardly be seen. Mrs. Boyer, softened by the tea and by the proximity of Harmony's lovely head bent over her task, grew slightly more expansive.

"I ought to tell you something, Miss Wells," she said. "You remember my other visit?"

"Perfectly." Harmony bent still lower.

"I did you an injustice at that time. I've been sorry ever since. I thought that there was no Dr. Gates. I'm sorry, but I'm not going to deny it. People do things in this wicked city that they wouldn't do at home. I confess I misjudged Peter Byrne. You can give him my apologies, since he won't see me."

"But he isn't here or of course he'd see you."

"Then," demanded Mrs. Boyer grimly, "if Peter Byrne is not here, who has been smoking cigarettes in this room? There is one still burning in that stove!"

Harmony's hand was forced. She was white as she cut the brown-silk thread and rose to her feet.

"I think," she said, "that I'd better go back a few weeks, Mrs. Boyer, and tell you a story, if you have time to listen."

"If it is disagreeable—"

"Not at all. It is about Peter Byrne and myself, and—some others. It is really about Peter. Mrs. Boyer, will you come very quietly across the hall?"

Mrs. Boyer, expecting Heaven knows what, rose with celerity. Harmony led the way to Jimmy's door and opened it. He was still asleep, a wasted small figure on the narrow bed. Beside him the mice frolicked in their cage, the sentry kept guard over Peter's shameless letters from the Tyrol, the strawberry babies wriggled in their cotton.

"We are not going to have him very long," said Harmony softly. "Peter is making him happy for a little while."

Back in the salon of Maria Theresa she told the whole story. Mrs. Boyer found it very affecting. Harmony sat beside her on a stool and she kept her hand on the girl's shoulder. When the narrative reached Anna's going away, however, she took it away. From that point on she sat uncompromisingly rigid and listened.

"Then you mean to say," she exploded when Harmony had finished, "that you intend to stay on here, just the two of you?"

"And Jimmy."

"Bah! What has the child to do with it?"

"We will find some one to take Anna's place."

"I doubt it. And until you do?"

"There is nothing wicked in what we are doing. Don't you see, Mrs. Boyer, I can't leave the boy."

"Since Peter is so altruistic, let him hire a nurse."

Bad as things were, Harmony smiled.

"A nurse!" she said. "Why, do you realize that he is keeping three people now on what is starvation for one?"

"Then he's a fool!" Mrs. Boyer rose in majesty. "I'm not going to leave you here."

"I'm sorry. You must see—"

"I see nothing but a girl deliberately putting herself in a compromising portion and worse."

"Mrs. Boyer!"

"Get your things on. I guess Dr. Boyer and I can look after you until we can send you home."

"I am not going home—yet," said poor Harmony, biting her lip to steady it.

Back and forth waged the battle, Mrs. Boyer assailing, Harmony offering little defense but standing firm on her refusal to go as long as Peter would let her remain.

"It means so much to me," she ventured, goaded. "And I earn my lodging and board. I work hard and—I make him comfortable. It costs him very little and I give him something in exchange. All men are not alike. If the sort you have known are—are different—"

This was unfortunate. Mrs. Boyer stiffened. She ceased offensive tactics, and retired grimly into the dignity of her high calling of virtuous wife and mother. She washed her hands of Harmony and Peter. She tied on her veil with shaking hands, and prepared to leave Harmony to her fate.

"Give me your mother's address," she demanded.

"Certainly not."

"You absolutely refuse to save yourself?"

"From what? From Peter? There are many worse people than Peter to save myself from, Mrs. Boyer—uncharitable people, and—and cruel people."

89

Mrs. Boyer shrugged her plump shoulders.

"Meaning me!" she retorted. "My dear child, people are always cruel who try to save us from ourselves."

Unluckily for Harmony, one of Anna's specious arguments must pop into her head at that instant and demand expression.

"People are living their own lives these days, Mrs. Boyer; old standards have gone. It is what one's conscience condemns that is wrong, isn't it? Not merely breaking laws that were made to fit the average, not the exception."

Anna! Anna!

Mrs. Boyer flung up her hands.

"You are impossible!" she snapped. "After all, I believe it is Peter who needs protection! I shall speak to him."

She started down the staircase, but turned for a parting volley.

"And just a word of advice: Perhaps the old standards have gone. But if you really expect to find a respectable woman to chaperon YOU, keep your views to yourself."

Harmony, a bruised and wounded thing, crept into Jimmy's room and sank on her knees beside the bed. One small hand lay on the coverlet; she dared not touch it for fear of waking him—but she laid her cheek close to it for comfort. When Peter came in, much later, he found the boy wide awake and Harmony asleep, a crumpled heap beside the bed.

"I think she's been crying," Jimmy whispered. "She's been sobbing in her sleep. And strike a match, Peter; there may be more mice."

CHAPTER XVIII

Mrs. Boyer, bursting with indignation, went to the Doctors' Club. It was typical of the way things were going with Peter that Dr. Boyer was not there, and that the only woman in the clubrooms should be Dr. Jennings. Young McLean was in the reading room, eating his heart out with jealousy of Peter, vacillating between the desire to see Harmony that night and fear lest Peter forbid him the house permanently if he made the attempt. He had found a picture of the Fraulein Engel, from the opera, in a magazine, and was sitting with it open before him. Very deeply and really in love was McLean that afternoon, and the Fraulein Engel and Harmony were not unlike. The double doors between the reading room and the reception room adjoining were open. McLean, lost in a rosy future in which he and Harmony sat together for indefinite periods, with no Peter to scowl over his books at them, a future in which life was one long piano-violin duo, with the candles in the chandelier going out one by one, leaving them at last alone in scented darkness together—McLean heard nothing until the mention of the Siebensternstrasse roused him.

After that he listened. He heard that Dr. Jennings was contemplating taking Anna's place at the lodge, and he comprehended after a moment that Anna was already gone. Even then the significance of the situation was a little time in dawning on him. When it did, however, he rose with a stifled oath.

Mrs. Boyer was speaking.

"It is exactly as I tell you," she was saying. "If Peter Byrne is trying to protect her reputation he is late doing it. Personally I have been there twice. I never saw Anna Gates. And she is registered here at the club as living in the Pension Schwarz. Whatever the facts may be, one thing remains, she is not there now."

McLean waited to hear no more. He was beside himself with rage. He found a "comfortable" at the curb. The driver was asleep inside the carriage. McLean dragged him out by the shoulder and shouted an address to him. The cab bumped along over the rough streets to an accompaniment of protests from its frantic passenger.

The boy was white-lipped with wrath and fear. Peter's silence that afternoon as to the state of affairs loomed large and significant. He had thought once or twice that Peter was in love with Harmony; he knew it now in the clearer vision of the moment. He recalled things that maddened him: the dozen intimacies of the little menage, the caress in Peter's voice when he spoke to the girl, Peter's steady eyes in the semi-gloom of the salon while Harmony played.

At a corner they must pause for the inevitable regiment. McLean cursed, bending out to see how long the delay would be. Peter had been gone for half an hour, perhaps, but Peter would walk. If he could only see the girl first, talk to her, tell her what she would be doing by remaining—

He was there at last, flinging across the courtyard like a madman. Peter was already there; his footprints were fresh in the slush of the path. The house door was closed but not locked. McLean ran up the stairs. It was barely twilight outside, but the staircase well was dark. At the upper landing he was compelled to fumble for the bell.

Peter admitted him. The corridor was unlighted, but from the salon came a glow of lamplight. McLean, out of breath and furious, faced Peter.

"I want to see Harmony," he said without preface.

Peter eyed him. He knew what had happened, had expected it when the bell rang, had anticipated it when Harmony told him of Mrs. Boyer's visit. In the second between the peal of the bell and his opening the door he had decided what to do.

"Come in."

McLean stepped inside. He was smaller than Peter, not so much shorter as slenderer. Even Peter winced before the look in his eyes.

"Where is she?"

"In the kitchen, I think. Come into the salon."

McLean flung off his coat. Peter closed the door behind him and stood just inside. He had his pipe as usual. "I came to see her, not you, Byrne."

"So I gather. I'll let you see her, of course, but don't you want to see me first?"

"I want to take her away from here."

"Why? Are you better able to care for her than I am?"

91

McLean stood rigid. He had thrust his clenched hands into his pockets.

"You're a scoundrel, Byrne," he said steadily. "Why didn't you tell me this this afternoon?"

"Because I knew if I did you'd do just what you are doing."

"Are you going to keep her here?"

Peter changed color at the thrust, but he kept himself in hand.

"I'm not keeping her here," he said patiently. "I'm doing the best I can under the circumstances."

"Then your best is pretty bad."

"Perhaps. If you would try to remember the circumstances, McLean,—that the girl has no place else to go, practically no money, and that I—"

"I remember one circumstance, that you are living here alone with her and that you're crazy in love with her."

"That has nothing to do with you. As long as I treat her—"

"Bah!"

"Will you be good enough to let me finish what I am trying to say? She's safe with me. When I say that I mean it. She will not go away from here with you or with any one else if I can prevent it. And if you care enough about her to try to keep her happy you'll not let her know you have been here. I've got a woman coming to take Anna's place. That ought to satisfy you."

"Dr. Jennings?"

"Yes."

"She'll not come. Mrs. Boyer has been talking to her. Inside of an hour the whole club will have it—every American in Vienna will know about it in a day or so. I tell you, Byrne, you're doing an awful thing."

Peter drew a long breath. He had had his bad half-hour before McLean came; had had to stand by, wordless, and see Harmony trying to smile, see her dragging about, languid and white, see her tragic attempts to greet him on the old familiar footing. Through it all he had been sustained by the thought that a day or two days would see the old footing reestablished, another woman in the house, life again worth the living and Harmony smiling up frankly into his eyes. Now this hope had departed.

"You can't keep me from seeing her, you know," McLean persisted. "I've got to put this thing to her. She's got to choose."

"What alternative have you to suggest?"

"I'd marry her if she'd have me."

After all Peter had expected that. And, if she cared for the boy wouldn't that be best for her? What had he to offer against that? He couldn't marry. He could only offer her shelter, against everything else. Even then he did not dislike McLean. He was a man, every slender inch of him, this boy musician. Peter's heart sank, but he put down his pipe and turned to the door.

"I'll call her," he said. "But, since this concerns me very vitally, I should like to be here while you put the thing to her. After that if you like—"

He called Harmony. She had given Jimmy his supper and was carrying out a tray that seemed hardly touched.

"He won't eat to-night," she said miserably. "Peter, if he stops eating, what can we do? He is so weak!"

Peter, took the tray from her gently.

"Harry dear," he said, "I want you to come into the salon. Some one wishes to speak to you."

"To me?"

"Yes. Harry, do you remember that evening in the kitchen when—Do you recall what I promised?"

"Yes, Peter."

"You are sure you know what I mean?"

"Yes."

"That's all right, then. McLean wants to see you."

She hesitated, looking up at him.

"McLean? You look so grave, Peter. What is it?"

"He will tell you. Nothing alarming."

Peter gave McLean a minute alone after all, while he carried the tray to the kitchen. He had no desire to play watchdog over the girl, he told himself savagely; only to keep himself straight with her and to save her from McLean's impetuosity. He even waited in the kitchen to fill and light his pipe.

McLean had worked himself into a very fair passion. He was intense, almost theatrical, as he stood with folded arms waiting for Harmony. So entirely did the girl fill his existence that he forgot, or did not care to remember, how short a time he had known her. As Harmony she dominated his life and his thoughts; as Harmony he addressed her when, rather startled, she entered the salon and stood just inside the closed door.

"Peter said you wanted to speak to me."

McLean groaned. "Peter!" he said. "It is always Peter. Look here, Harmony, you cannot stay here."

"It is only for a few hours. To-morrow some one is coming. And, anyhow, Peter is going to Semmering. We know it is unusual, but what can we do?"

"Unusual! It's—it's damnable. It's the appearance of the thing, don't you see that?"

"I think it is rather silly to talk of appearance when there is no one to care. And how can I leave? Jimmy needs me all the time—"

"That's another idiocy of Peter's. What does he mean by putting you in this position?"

"I am one of Peter's idiocies."

Peter entered on that. He took in the situation with a glance, and Harmony turned to him; but if she had expected Peter to support her, she was disappointed. Whatever decision she was to make must be her own, in Peter's troubled mind. He crossed the room and stood at one of the windows, looking out, a passive participant in the scene.

The day had been a trying one for Harmony. What she chose to consider Peter's

93

defection was a fresh stab. She glanced from McLean, flushed and excited, to Peter's impassive back. Then she sat down, rather limp, and threw out her hands helplessly.

"What am I to do?" she demanded. "Every one comes with cruel things to say, but no one tells me what to do."

Peter turned away from the window.

"You can leave here," ventured McLean. "That's the first thing. After that—"

"Yes, and after that, what?"

McLean glanced at Peter. Then he took a step toward the girl.

"You could marry me, Harmony," he said unsteadily. "I hadn't expected to tell you so soon, or before a third person." He faltered before Harmony's eyes, full of bewilderment. "I'd be very happy if you—if you could see it that way. I care a great deal, you see."

It seemed hours to Peter before she made any reply, and that her voice came from miles away.

"Is it really as bad as that?" she asked. "Have I made such a mess of things that some one, either you or Peter, must marry me to straighten things out? I don't want to marry any one. Do I have to?"

"Certainly you don't have to," said Peter. There was relief in his voice, relief and also something of exultation. "McLean, you mean well, but marriage isn't the solution. We were getting along all right until our friends stepped in. Let Mrs. Boyer howl all over the colony; there will be one sensible woman somewhere to come and be comfortable here with us. In the interval we'll manage, unless Harmony is afraid. In that case—"

"Afraid of what?"

The two men exchanged glances, McLean helpless, Peter triumphant.

"I do not care what Mrs. Boyer says, at least not much. And I am not afraid of anything else at all."

McLean picked up his overcoat.

"At least," he appealed to Peter, "you'll come over to my place?"

"No!" said Peter.

McLean made a final appeal to Harmony.

"If this gets out," he said, "you are going to regret it all your life."

"I shall have nothing to regret," she retorted proudly.

Had Peter not been there McLean would have made a better case, would have pleaded with her, would have made less of a situation that roused her resentment and more of his love for her. He was very hard hit, very young. He was almost hysterical with rage and helplessness; he wanted to slap her, to take her in his arms. He writhed under the restraint of Peter's steady eyes.

He got to the door and turned, furious.

"Then it's up to you," he flung at Peter. "You're old enough to know better; she isn't. And don't look so damned superior. You're human, like the rest of us. And if any harm comes to her—"

Here unexpectedly Peter held out his hand, and after a sheepish moment

94

McLean took it.

"Good-night, old man," said Peter. "And—don't be an ass."

As was Peter's way, the words meant little, the tone much. McLean knew what in his heart he had known all along—that the girl was safe enough; that all that was to fear was the gossip of scandal-lovers. He took Peter's hand, and then going to Harmony stood before her very erect.

"I suppose I've said too much; I always do," he said contritely. "But you know the reason. Don't forget the reason, will you?"

"I am only sorry."

He bent over and kissed her hand lingeringly. It was a tragic moment for him, poor lad! He turned and went blindly out the door and down the dark stone staircase. It was rather anticlimax, after all that, to have Peter discover he had gone without his hat and toss it down to him a flight below.

All the frankness had gone out of the relationship between Harmony and Peter. They made painful efforts at ease, talked during the meal of careful abstractions, such as Jimmy, and Peter's proposed trip to Semmering, avoided each other's eyes, ate little or nothing. Once when Harmony passed Peter his coffee-cup their fingers touched, and between them they dropped the cup. Harmony was flushed and pallid by turns, Peter wretched and silent.

Out of the darkness came one ray of light. Stewart had wired from Semmering, urging Peter to come. He would be away for two days. In two days much might happen; Dr. Jennings might come or some one else. In two days some of the restraint would have worn off. Things would never be the same, but they would be forty-eight hours better.

Peter spent the early part of the evening with Jimmy, reading aloud to him. After the child had dropped to sleep he packed a valise for the next day's journey and counted out into an envelope half of the money he had with him. This he labeled "Household Expenses" and set it up on his table, leaning against his collar-box. There was no sign of Harmony about. The salon was dark except for the study lamp turned down.

Peter was restless. He put on his shabby dressing-gown and worn slippers and wandered about. The Portier had brought coal to the landing; Peter carried it in. He inspected the medicine bottles on Jimmy's stand and wrote full directions for every emergency he could imagine. Then, finding it still only nine o'clock, he turned up the lamp in the salon and wrote an exciting letter from Jimmy's father, in which a lost lamb, wandering on the mountain-side, had been picked up by an avalanche and carried down into the fold and the arms of the shepherd. And because he stood so in loco parentis, and because it seemed so inevitable that before long Jimmy would be in the arms of the Shepherd, and, of course, because it had been a trying day all through, Peter's lips were none too steady as he folded up the letter.

The fire was dead in the stove; Peter put out the salon lamp and closed the shutters. In the warm darkness he put out his hand to feel his way through the room. It touched a little sweater coat of Harmony's, hanging over the back of a chair. Peter picked it up in a very passion of tenderness and held it to him.

"Little girl!" he choked. "My little girl! God help me!"

He was rather ashamed, considerably startled. It alarmed him to find that the mere unexpected touch of a familiar garment could rouse such a storm in him. It made him pause. He put down the coat and pulled himself up sharply. McLean was right; he was only human stuff, very poor human stuff. He put the little coat down hastily, only to lift it again gently to his lips.

"Good-night, dear," he whispered. "Goodnight, Harmony."

Frau Schwarz had had two visitors between the hours of coffee and supper that day. The reason of their call proved to be neither rooms nor pension. They came to make inquiries.

The Frau Schwarz made this out at last, and sat down on the edge of the bed in the room that had once been Peter's and that still lacked an occupant.

Mrs. Boyer had no German; Dr. Jennings very little and that chiefly medical. There is, however, a sort of code that answers instead of language frequently, when two or three women of later middle life are gathered together, a code born of mutual understanding, mutual disillusion, mutual distrust, a language of outspread hands, raised eyebrows, portentous shakings of the head. Frau Schwarz, on the edge of Peter's tub-shaped bed, needed no English to convey the fact that Peter was a bad lot. Not that she resorted only to the sign language.

"The women were also wicked," she said. "Of a man what does one expect? But of a woman! And the younger one looked—Herr Gott! She had the eyes of a saint! The little Georgiev was mad for her. When the three of them left, disgraced, as one may say, he came to me, he threatened me. The Herr Schwarz, God rest his soul, was a violent man, but never spoke he so to me!"

"She says," interpreted Dr. Jennings, "that they were a bad lot—that the younger one made eyes at the Herr Schwarz!"

Mrs. Boyer drew her ancient sables about her and put a tremulous hand on the other woman's arm.

"What an escape for you!" she said. "If you had gone there to live and then found the establishment—queer!"

From the kitchen of the pension, Olga was listening, an ear to the door. Behind her, also listening, but less advantageously, was Katrina.

"American ladies!" said Olga. "Two, old and fat."

"More hot water!" growled Katrina. "Why do not the Americans stay in their own country, where the water, I have learned, comes hot from the earth."

Olga, bending forward, opened the door a crack wider.

"Sh! They do not come for rooms. They inquire for the Herr Doktor Byrne and the others!"

"No!"

"Of a certainty."

"Then let me to the door!"

"A moment. She tells them everything and more. She says—how she is wicked, Katrina! She says the Fraulein Harmony was not good, that she sent them all away. Here, take the door!"

Thus it happened that Dr. Jennings and Mrs. Boyer, having shaken off the dust of a pension that had once harbored three malefactors, and having retired Peter and Anna and Harmony into the limbo of things best forgotten or ignored, found themselves, at the corner, confronted by a slovenly girl in heelless slippers and wearing a knitted shawl over her head. "The Frau Schwarz is wrong," cried Olga passionately in Vienna dialect. "They were good, all of them!"

"What in the world—"

"And, please, tell me where lives the Fraulein Harmony. The Herr Georgiev eats not nor sleeps that he cannot find her."

Dr. Jennings was puzzled.

"She wishes to know where the girl lives," she interpreted to Mrs. Boyer. "A man wishes to know."

"Naturally!" said Mrs. Boyer. "Well, don't tell her."

Olga gathered from the tone rather than the words that she was not to be told. She burst into a despairing appeal in which the Herr Georgiev, Peter, a necktie Peter had forgotten, open windows, and hot water were inextricably confused. Dr. Jennings listened, then waved her back with a gesture.

"She says," she interpreted as they walked on, "that Dr. Peter—by which I suppose she means Dr. Byrne—has left a necktie, and that she'll be in hot water if she does not return it."

Mrs. Boyer sniffed.

"In love with him, probably, like the others!" she said.

CHAPTER XIX

Peter went to Semmering the next morning, tiptoeing out very early and without breakfast. He went in to cover Jimmy, lying diagonally across his small bed amid a riot of tossed blankets. The communicating door into Harmony's room was open. Peter kept his eyes carefully from it, but his ears were less under control. He could hear her soft breathing. There were days coming when Peter would stand where he stood then and listen, and find only silence.

He tore himself away at last, closing the outer door carefully behind him and lighting a match to find his way down the staircase. The Portier was not awake. Peter had to rouse him, and to stand by while he donned the trousers which he deemed necessary to the dignity of his position before he opened the street door.

Reluctant as he had been to go, the change was good for Peter. The dawn grew rosy, promised sunshine, fulfilled its promise. The hurrying crowds at the depot interested him: he enjoyed his coffee, taken from a bare table in the station. The horizontal morning sunlight, shining in through marvelously clean windows, warmed the marble of the floor, made black shadows beside the heaps of hand luggage everywhere, turned into gold the hair of a toddling baby venturing on a tour of discovery. The same morning light, alas! revealed to Peter a break across

97

the toe of one of his shoes. Peter sighed, then smiled. The baby was catching at the bits of dust that floated in the sunshine.

Suddenly a great wave of happiness overwhelmed Peter. It was a passing thing, born of nothing, but for the instant that it lasted Peter was a king. Everything was well. The world was his oyster. Life was his, to make it what he would—youth and hope and joy. Under the beatific influence he expanded, grew, almost shone. Youth and hope and joy—that cometh in the morning.

The ecstasy passed away, but without reaction. Peter no longer shone; he still glowed. He picked up the golden-haired baby and hugged it. He hunted out a beggar he had passed and gave him five Hellers. He helped a suspicious old lady with an oilcloth-covered bundle; he called the guard on the train "son" and forced a grin out of that dignitary.

Peter traveled third-class, which was quite comfortable, and no bother about "Nicht Rauchen" signs. His unreasonable cheerfulness persisted as far as Gloggnitz. There, with the increasing ruggedness of the scenery and his first view of the Raxalpe, came recollection of the urgency of Stewart's last message, of Marie Jedlicka, of the sordid little tragedy that awaited him at the end of his journey.

Peter sobered. Life was rather a mess, after all, he reflected. Love was a blessing, but it was also a curse. After that he sat back in his corner and let the mountain scenery take care of itself, while he recalled the look he had surprised once or twice in Marie's eyes when she looked at Stewart. It was sad, pitiful. Marie was a clever little thing. If only she'd had a chance!—Why wasn't he rich enough to help the ones who needed help. Marie could start again in America, with no one the wiser, and make her way.

"Smart as the devil, these Austrian girls!" Peter reflected. "Poor little guttersnipe!"

The weather was beautiful. The sleet of the previous day in Vienna had been a deep snowfall on the mountains. The Schwarza was frozen, the castle of Liechtenstein was gray against a white world. A little pilgrimage church far below seemed snowed in against the faithful. The third-class compartment filled with noisy skiing parties. The old woman opened her oilcloth bundle, and taking a cat out of a box inside fed it a sausage.

Up and up, past the Weinzettelwand and the Station Breitenstein, across the highest viaduct, the Kalte Rinne, and so at last to Semmering.

The glow had died at last for Peter. He did not like his errand, was very vague, indeed, as to just what that errand might be. He was stiff and rather cold. Also he thought the cat might stifle in the oilcloth, but the old woman too clearly distrusted him to make it possible to interfere. Anyhow, he did not know the German for either cat or oilcloth.

He had wired Stewart; but the latter was not at the station. This made him vaguely uneasy, he hardly knew why. He did not know Stewart well enough to know whether he was punctilious in such matters or not: as a matter of fact he hardly knew him at all. It was because he had appealed to him that Peter was there, it being only necessary to Peter to be needed, and he was anywhere.

The Pension Waldheim was well up the mountains. He shouldered his valise and started up—first long flights of steps through the pines, then a steep road. Peter climbed easily. Here and there he met groups coming down, men that he thought probably American, pretty women in "tams" and sweaters. He watched for Marie, but there was no sign of her.

He was half an hour, perhaps, in reaching the Waldheim. As he turned in at the gate he noticed a sledge, with a dozen people following it, coming toward him. It was a singularly silent party. Peter, with his hand on the door-knocker, watched its approach with some curiosity.

It stopped, and the men who had been following closed up round it. Even then Peter did not understand. He did not understand until he saw Stewart, limp and unconscious, lifted out of the straw and carried toward him.

Suicide may be moral cowardice; but it requires physical bravery. And Marie was not brave. The balcony had attracted her: it opened possibilities of escape, of unceasing regret and repentance for Stewart, of publicity that would mean an end to the situation. But every inch of her soul was craven at the thought. She crept out often and looked down, and as often drew back, shuddering. To fall down, down on to the tree tops, to be dropped from branch to branch, a broken thing, and perhaps even not yet dead—that was the unthinkable thing, to live for a time and suffer!

Stewart was not ignorant of all that went on in her mind. She had threatened him with the balcony, just as, earlier in the winter, it had been a window-ledge with which she had frightened him. But there was this difference, whereas before he had drawn her back from the window and clapped her into sanity, now he let her alone. At the end of one of their quarrels she had flung out on to the balcony, and then had watched him through the opening in the shutter. He had lighted a cigarette!

Stewart spent every daylight hour at the hotel, or walking over the mountain roads, seldom alone with Anita, but always near her. He left Marie sulking or sewing, as the case might be. He returned in the evening to find her still sulking, still sewing.

But Marie did not sulk all day, or sew. She too was out, never far from Stewart, always watching. Many times she escaped discovery only by a miracle, as when she stooped behind an oxcart, pretending to tie her shoe, or once when they all met face to face, and although she lowered her veil Stewart must have known her instantly had he not been so intent on helping Anita over a slippery gutter.

She planned a dozen forms of revenge and found them impossible of execution. Stewart himself was frightfully unhappy. For the first time in his life he was really in love, with all the humility of the condition. There were days when he would not touch Anita's hand, when he hardly spoke, when the girl herself would have been outraged at his conduct had she not now and then caught him watching her, seen the wretchedness in his eyes.

The form of Marie's revenge was unpremeditated, after all. The light mountain snow was augmented by a storm; roads were ploughed through early in the morning, leaving great banks on either side. Sleigh-bells were everywhere. Coasting parties made the steep roads a menace to the pedestrian; every up-climbing sleigh carried behind it a string of sleds, going back to the starting-point.

Below the hotel was the Serpentine Coast, a long and dangerous course, full of high-banked curves, of sudden descents, of long straightaway dashes through the woodland. Two miles, perhaps three, it wound its tortuous way down the mountain. Up by the highroad to the crest again, only a mile or less. Thus it happened that the track was always clear, except for speeding sleds. No coasters, dragging sleds back up the slide, interfered.

The track was crowded. Every minute a sled set out, sped down the straightaway, dipped, turned, disappeared. A dozen would be lined up, waiting for the interval and the signal. And here, watching from the porch of the church, in the very shadow of the saints, Marie found her revenge.

Stewart had given her a little wrist watch. Stewart and Anita were twelfth in line. By the watch, then, twelve minutes down the mountain-side, straight down through the trees to a curve that Marie knew well, a bad curve, only to be taken by running well up on the snowbank. Beyond the snowbank there was a drop, fifteen feet, perhaps more, into the yard of a Russian villa. Stewart and Anita were twelfth; a man in a green stocking-cap was eleventh. The hillside was steep. Marie negotiated it by running from tree to tree, catching herself, steadying for a second, then down again. Once she fell and rolled a little distance. There was no time to think; perhaps had she thought she would have weakened. She had no real courage, only desperation.

As she reached the track the man in the green stocking-cap was in sight. A minute and a half she had then, not more. She looked about her hastily. A stone might serve her purpose, almost anything that would throw the sled out of its course. She saw a tree branch just above the track and dragged at it frantically. Some one was shouting at her from an upper window of the Russian villa. She did not hear. Stewart and Anita had made the curve above and were coming down at frantic speed. Marie stood, her back to the oncoming rush of the sled, swaying slightly. When she could hear the singing of the runners she stooped and slid the tree branch out against the track.

She had acted almost by instinct, but with devilish skill. The sled swung to one side up the snowbank, and launched itself into the air. Marie heard the thud and the silence that followed it. Then she turned and scuttled like a hunted thing up the mountain side.

Peter put in a bad day. Marie was not about, could not be located. Stewart, suffering from concussion, lay insensible all day and all of the night. Peter could find no fracture, but felt it wise to get another opinion. In the afternoon he sent for a doctor from the Kurhaus and learned for the first time that Anita had also been hurt—a broken arm. "Not serious," said the Kurhaus man. "She is brave, very brave, the young woman. I believe they are engaged?" Peter said he did not know and thought very hard. Where was Marie? Not gone surely. Here about him lay all her belongings, even her purse.

Toward evening Stewart showed some improvement. He was not conscious, but he swallowed better and began to toss about. Peter, who had had a long day and very little sleep the night before, began to look jaded. He would have sent for a nurse from the Kurhaus, but he doubted Stewart's ability to stand any extra financial strain, and Peter could not help any.

The time for supper passed, and no Marie.

The landlady sent up a tray to Peter, stewed meat and potatoes, a salad, coffee. Peter sat in a corner with his back to Stewart and ate ravenously. He had had nothing since the morning's coffee. After that he sat down again by the bed to watch. There was little to do but watch.

The meal had made him drowsy. He thought of his pipe. Perhaps if he got some fresh air and a smoke! He remembered the balcony.

It was there on the balcony that he found Marie, a cowering thing that pushed his hands away when he would have caught her and broke into passionate crying.

"I cannot! I cannot!"

"Cannot what?" demanded Peter gently, watching her. So near was the balcony rail!

"Throw myself over. I've tried, Peter. I cannot!"

"I should think not!" said Peter sternly. "Just now when we need you, too! Come in and don't be a foolish child."

But Marie would not go in. She held back, clinging tight to Peter's big hand, moaning out in the dialect of the people that always confused him her story of the day, of what she had done, of watching Stewart brought back, of stealing into the house and through an adjacent room to the balcony, of her desperation and her cowardice.

She was numb with cold, exhaustion, and hunger, quite childish, helpless. Peter stood out on the balcony with his arm round her, while the night wind beat about them, and pondered what was best to do. He thought she might come in and care for Stewart, at least, until he was conscious. He could get her some supper.

"How can I?" she asked. "I was seen. They are searching for me now. Oh, Peter! Peter!"

"Who is searching for you? Who saw you?"

"The people in the Russian villa."

"Did they see your face?"

"I wore a veil. I think not."

"Then come in and change your clothes. There is a train down at midnight. You can take it."

"I have no money."

This raised a delicate question. Marie absolutely refused to take Stewart's money. She had almost none of her own. And there were other complications—where was she to go? The family of the injured girl did not suspect her since they did not know of her existence. She might get away without trouble. But after that, what?

101

Peter pondered this on the balcony, while Marie in the bedroom was changing her clothing, soaked with a day in the snow. He came to the inevitable decision, the decision he knew at the beginning that he was going to make.

"If I could only put it up to Harmony first!" he reflected. "But she will understand when I tell her. She always understands."

Standing there on the little balcony, with tragedy the thickness of a pine board beyond him, Peter experienced a bit of the glow of the morning, as of one who stumbling along in a dark place puts a hand on a friend.

He went into the room. Stewart was lying very still and breathing easily. On her knees beside the bed knelt Marie. At Peter's step she rose and faced him.

"I am leaving him, Peter, for always."

"Good!" said Peter heartily. "Better for you and better for him."

Marie drew a long breath. "The night train," she said listlessly, "is an express. I had forgotten. It is double fare."

"What of that, little sister?" said Peter. "What is a double fare when it means life, liberty and the pursuit of happiness? And there will be happiness, little sister."

He put his hand in his pocket.

CHAPTER XX

The Portier was almost happy that morning. For one thing, he had won honorable mention at the Schubert Society the night before; for another, that night the Engel was to sing Mignon, and the Portier had spent his Christmas tips for a ticket. All day long he had been poring over the score.

"'Kennst du das Land wo die Citronen bluhen?'" he sang with feeling while he polished the floors. He polished them with his feet, wearing felt boots for the purpose, and executing in the doing a sort of ungainly dance—a sprinkle of wax, right foot forward and back, left foot forward and back, both feet forward and back in a sort of double shuffle; more wax, more vigorous polishing, more singing, with longer pauses for breath. "'Knowest thou the land where the lemon trees bloom?'" he bellowed—sprinkle of wax, right foot, left foot, any foot at all. Now and then he took the score from his pocket and pored over it, humming the air, raising his eyebrows over the high notes, dropping his chin to the low ones. It was a wonderful morning. Between greetings to neighbors he sang—a bit of talk, a bit of song.

"'Kennst du das Land'—Good-morning, sir—the old Rax wears a crown. It will snow soon. 'Kennst du das Land wo die Citronen'—Ah, madam the milk Frau, and are the cows frozen up to-day like the pump? No? Marvelous! Dost thou know that to-night is Mignon at the Opera, and that the Engel sings? 'Kennst du das Land'—"

At eleven came Rosa with her husband, the soldier from Salzburg with one lung. He was having a holiday from his sentry duty at the hospital, and the one lung seemed to be a libel, for while the women had coffee together and a bit of mackerel he sang a very fair bass to the Portier's tenor. Together they pored over the score, and even on their way to the beer hall hummed together such bits as they recalled.

On one point they differed. The score was old and soiled with much thumbing. At one point, destroyed long since, the sentry sang A sharp: the Portier insisted on A natural. They argued together over three Steins of beer; the waiter, referred to, decided for A flat. It was a serious matter to have one's teeth set, as one may say, for a natural and then to be shocked with an unexpected half-tone up or down! It destroyed the illusion; it disappointed; it hurt.

The sentry stuck to the sharp—it was sung so at the Salzburg opera. The Portier snapped his thumb at the Salzburg opera. Things were looking serious; they walked back to the locale in silence. The sentry coughed. Possibly there was something, after all, in the one-lung rumor.

It was then that the Portier remembered Harmony. She would know; perhaps she had the score.

Harmony was having a bad morning. She had slept little until dawn, and Peter's stealthy closing of the outer door had wakened her by its very caution. After that there had been no more sleep. She had sat up in bed with her chin in her hands and thought.

In the pitiless dawn, with no Peter to restore her to cheerfulness, things looked black, indeed. To what had she fallen, that first one man and then another must propose marriage to her to save her. To save her from what? From what people thought, or—each from the other?

Were men so evil that they never trusted each other? McLean had frankly distrusted Peter, had said so. Or could it be that there was something about her, something light and frivolous? She had been frivolous. She always laughed at Peter's foolishnesses. Perhaps that was it. That was it. They were afraid for her. She had thrown herself on Peter's hands—almost into his arms. She had made this situation.

She must get away, of course. If only she had some one to care for Jimmy until Peter returned! But there was no one. The Portier's wife was fond of Jimmy, but not skillful. And suppose he were to wake in the night and call for her and she would not come. She cried a little over this. After a time she pattered across the room in her bare feet and got from a bureau drawer the money she had left. There was not half enough to take her home. She could write; the little mother might get some for her, but at infinite cost, infinite humiliation. That would have to be a final, desperate resort.

She felt a little more cheerful when she had had a cup of coffee. Jimmy wakened about that time, and she went through the details of his morning toilet with all the brightness she could assume—bath blankets, warm bath, toenails, finger-nails, fresh nightgown, fresh sheets, and—final touch of all—a real barber's part straight from crown to brow. After that ten minutes under extra comforters while the room aired.

She hung over the boy that morning in an agony of tenderness—he was so

103

little, so frail, and she must leave him. Only one thing sustained her. The boy loved her, but it was Peter he idolized. When he had Peter he needed nothing else. In some curious process of his childish mind Peter and Daddy mingled in inextricable confusion. More than once he had recalled events in the roving life he and his father had led.

"You remember that, don't you?" he would say.

"Certainly I remember," Peter would reply heartily.

"That evening on the steamer when I ate so many raisins."

"Of course. And were ill."

"Not ill—not that time. But you said I'd make a good pudding! You remember that, don't you?"

And Peter would recall it all.

Peter would be left. That was the girl's comfort.

She made a beginning at gathering her things together that morning, while the boy dozed and the white mice scurried about the little cage. She could not take her trunk, or Peter would trace it. She would have to carry her belongings, a few at a time, to wherever she found a room. Then when Peter came back she could slip away and he would never find her.

At noon came the Portier and the sentry, now no longer friends, and rang the doorbell. Harmony was rather startled. McLean and Mrs. Boyer had been her only callers, and she did not wish to see either of them. But after a second ring she gathered her courage in her hands and opened the door.

She turned pale when she saw the sentry in his belted blue-gray tunic and high cap. She thought, of course, that Jimmy had been traced and that now he would be taken away. If the sentry knew her, however, he kept his face impassive and merely touched his cap. The Portier stated their errand. Harmony's face cleared. She even smiled as the Portier extended to her the thumbed score with its missing corner. What, after all, does it matter which was right—whether it was A sharp or A natural? What really matters is that Harmony, having settled the dispute and clinched the decision by running over the score for a page or two, turned to find the Portier, ecstatic eyes upturned, hands folded on paunch, enjoying a delirium of pleasure, and the sentry nowhere in sight.

He was discovered a moment later in the doorway of Jimmy's room, where, taciturn as ever, severe, martial, he stood at attention, shoulders back, arms at his sides, thumbs in. In this position he was making, with amazing rapidity, a series of hideous grimaces for the benefit of the little boy in the bed: marvelous faces they were, in which nose, mouth, and eyes seemed interchangeable, where features played leapfrog with one another. When all was over—perhaps when his repertoire was exhausted—the sentry returned his nose to the center of his face, replaced eyes and mouth, and wiped the ensemble with a blue cotton handkerchief. Then, still in silence, he saluted and withdrew, leaving the youngster enraptured, staring at the doorway.

Harmony had decided the approximate location of her room. In the higher part of the city, in the sixteenth district, there were many unpretentious buildings. She had hunted board there and she knew. It was far from the Stadt, far from the fashionable part of town, a neighborhood of small shops, of frank indigence. There surely she could find a room, and perhaps in one of the small stores what she failed to secure in the larger, a position.

Rosa having taken her soldier away, Harmony secured the Portier's wife to sit with Jimmy and spent two hours that afternoon looking about for a room. She succeeded finally in finding one, a small and wretchedly furnished bedroom, part of the suite of a cheap dressmaker. The approach was forbidding enough. One entered a cavelike, cobble-paved court under the building, filled with wagons, feeding horses, quarrelsome and swearing teamsters. From the side a stone staircase took off and led, twisting from one landing cave to another, to the upper floor.

Here lived the dressmaker, amid the constant whirring of sewing-machines, the Babel of workpeople. Harmony, seeking not a home but a hiding-place, took the room at once. She was asked for no reference. In a sort of agony lest this haven fail her she paid for a week in advance. The wooden bed, the cracked mirror over the table, even the pigeons outside on the windowsill were hers for a week.

The dressmaker was friendly, almost garrulous.

"I will have it cleaned," she explained. "I have been so busy: the masquerade season is on. The Fraulein is American, is she not?"

"Yes."

"One knows the Americans. They are chic, not like the English. I have some American customers."

Harmony started. The dressmaker was shrewd. Many people hid in the sixteenth district. She hastened to reassure the girl.

"They will not disturb you. And just now I have but one, a dancer. I shall have the room cleaned. Good-bye, Fraulein."

So far, good. She had a refuge now, one spot that the venom of scandal could not poison, where she could study and work—work hard, although there could be no more lessons—one spot where Peter would not have to protect her, where Peter, indeed, would never find her. This thought, which should have brought comfort, brought only new misery. Peace seemed dearly bought all at once; shabby, wholesome, hearty Peter, with his rough hair and quiet voice, his bulging pockets and steady eyes—she was leaving Peter forever, exchanging his companionship for that of a row of pigeons on a window-sill. He would find some one, of course; but who would know that he liked toast made hard and plenty of butter, or to leave his bed-clothing loose at the foot, Peter being very long and apt to lop over? The lopping over brought a tear or two. A very teary and tragic young heroine, this Harmony, prone to go about for the last day or two with a damp little handkerchief tucked in her sleeve.

She felt her way down the staircase and into the cave below. Fate hangs by a very slender thread sometimes. If a wagon had not lumbered by as she reached the lowest step, so that she must wait and thus had time to lower her veil, she would have been recognized at once by the little Georgiev, waiting to ascend. But

105

the wagon was there, Harmony lowered her veil, the little Georgiev, passing a veiled young woman in the gloom, went up the staircase with even pulses and calm and judicial bearing, up to the tiny room a floor or two below Harmony's, where he wrote reports to the Minister of War and mixed them with sonnets—to Harmony.

Harmony went back to the Siebensternstrasse, having accomplished what she had set out to do and being very wretched in consequence. Because she was leaving the boy so soon she strove to atone for her coming defection by making it a gala evening. The child was very happy. She tucked him up in the salon, lighted all the candles, served him the daintiest of suppers there. She brought in the mice and tied tiny bows on their necks; she played checkers with him while the supper dishes waited, and went down to defeat in three hilarious games; and last of all she played to him, joyous music at first, then slower, drowsier airs, until his heavy head dropped on his shoulder and she gathered him up in tender arms and carried him to bed.

It was dawn when Marie arrived. Harmony was sleeping soundly when the bell rang. Her first thought was that Peter had come back—but Peter carried a key. The bell rang again, and she slipped on the old kimono and went to the door.

"Is it Peter?" she called, hand on knob.

"I come from Peter. I have a letter," in German.

"Who is it?"

"You do not know me—Marie Jedlicka. Please let me come in."

Bewildered, Harmony opened the door, and like a gray ghost Marie slipped by her and into the hall.

There was a gaslight burning very low; Harmony turned it up and faced her visitor. She recognized her at once—the girl Dr. Stewart had been with in the coffee-house.

"Something has happened to Peter!"

"No. He is well. He sent this to the Fraulein Wells."

"I am the Fraulein Wells."

Marie held out the letter and staggered. Harmony put her in a chair; she was bewildered, almost frightened. Crisis of some sort was written on Marie's face. Harmony felt very young, very incapable. The other girl refused coffee, would not even go into the salon until Peter's letter had been read. She was a fugitive, a criminal; the Austrian law is severe to those that harbor criminals. Let Harmony read:—

"DEAR HARRY,—Will you forgive me for this and spread the wings of your splendid charity over this poor child? Perhaps I am doing wrong in sending her to you, but just now it is all I can think of. If she wants to talk let her talk. It will probably help her. Also feed her, will you? And if she cannot sleep, give her one of the blue powders I fixed for Jimmy. I'll be back later to-day if I can make it.

"PETER"

Harmony glanced up from the letter. Marie sat drooping in her chair. Her eyes were sunken in her head. She had recognized her at once, but any surprise she may have felt at finding Harmony in Peter's apartment was sunk in a general apathy, a compound of nervous reaction and fatigue. During the long hours in the express she had worn herself out with fright and remorse: there was nothing left now but exhaustion.

Harmony was bewildered, but obedient. She went back to the cold kitchen and lighted a fire. She made Marie as comfortable as she could in the salon, and then went into her room to dress. There she read the letter again, and wondered if Peter had gone through life like this, picking up waifs and strays and shouldering their burdens for them. Decidedly, life with Peter was full of surprises.

She remembered, as she hurried into her clothes; the boys' club back in America and the spelling-matches. Decidedly, also, Peter was an occupation, a state of mind, a career. No musician, hoping for a career of her own, could possibly marry Peter.

That was a curious morning in the old lodge of Maria Theresa, while Stewart in the Pension Waldheim struggled back to consciousness, while Peter sat beside him and figured on an old envelope the problem of dividing among four enough money to support one, while McLean ate his heart out in wretchedness in his hotel.

Marie told her story over the early breakfast, sitting with her thin elbows on the table, her pointed chin in her palms.

"And now I am sorry," she finished. "It has done no good. If it had only killed her but she was not much hurt. I saw her rise and bend over him."

Harmony was silent. She had no stock of aphorisms for the situation, no worldly knowledge, only pity.

"Did Peter say he would recover?"

"Yes. They will both recover and go to America. And he will marry her."

Perhaps Harmony would have been less comfortable, Marie less frank, had Marie realized that this establishment of Peter's was not on the same basis as Stewart's had been, or had Harmony divined her thought.

The presence of the boy was discovered by his waking. Marie was taken in and presented. She looked stupefied. Certainly the Americans were a marvelous people—to have taken into their house and their hearts this strange child—if he were strange. Marie's suspicious little slum mind was not certain.

In the safety and comfort of the little apartment the Viennese expanded, cheered. She devoted herself to the boy, telling him strange folk tales, singing snatches of songs for him. The youngster took a liking to her at once. It seemed to Harmony, going about her morning routine, that Marie was her solution and Peter's.

During the afternoon she took a package to the branch post-office and mailed it by parcel-post to the Wollbadgasse. On the way she met Mrs. Boyer face to face. That lady looked severely ahead, and Harmony passed her with her chin well up and the eyes of a wounded animal.

McLean sent a great box of flowers that day. She put them, for lack of a vase, in a pitcher beside Jimmy's bed.

107

At dusk a telegram came to say that Stewart was better and that Peter was on his way down to Vienna. He would arrive at eight. Time was very short now—seconds flashed by, minutes galloped. Harmony stewed a chicken for supper, and creamed the breast for Jimmy. She fixed the table, flowers in the center, the best cloth, Peter's favorite cheese. Six o'clock, six-thirty, seven; Marie was telling Jimmy a fairy tale and making the fairies out of rosebuds. The studylamp was lighted, the stove glowing, Peter's slippers were out, his old smoking-coat, his pipe.

A quarter past seven. Peter would be near Vienna now and hungry. If he could only eat his supper before he learned—but that was impossible. He would come in, as he always did, and slam the outer door, and open it again to close it gently, as he always did, and then he would look for her, going from room to room until he found her—only to-night he would not find her.

She did not say good-bye to Jimmy. She stood in the doorway and said a little prayer for him. Marie had made the flower fairies on needles, and they stood about his head on the pillow—pink and yellow and white elves with fluffy skirts. Then, very silently, she put on her hat and jacket and closed the outer door behind her. In the courtyard she turned and looked up. The great chandelier in the salon was not lighted, but from the casement windows shone out the comfortable glow of Peter's lamp.

CHAPTER XXI

Peter had had many things to think over during the ride down the mountains. He had the third-class compartment to himself, and sat in a corner, soft hat over his eyes. Life had never been particularly simple to Peter—his own life, yes; a matter of three meals a day—he had had fewer—a roof, clothing. But other lives had always touched him closely, and at the contact points Peter glowed, fused, amalgamated. Thus he had been many people—good, indifferent, bad, but all needy. Thus, also, Peter had committed vicarious crimes, suffered vicarious illnesses, starved, died, loved—vicariously.

And now, after years of living for others, Peter was living at last for himself—and suffering.

Not that he understood exactly what ailed him. He thought he was tired, which was true enough, having had little sleep for two or three nights. Also he explained to himself that he was smoking too much, and resolutely—lighted another cigarette.

Two things had revealed Peter's condition to himself: McLean had said: "You are crazy in love with her." McLean's statement, lacking subtlety, had had a certain quality of directness. Even then Peter, utterly miserable, had refused to capitulate, when to capitulate would have meant the surrender of the house in the Siebensternstrasse. And the absence from Harmony had shown him just where he stood.

He was in love, crazy in love. Every fiber of his long body glowed with it, ached

108

with it. And every atom of his reason told him what mad folly it was, this love. Even if Harmony cared—and at the mere thought his heart pounded—what madness for her, what idiocy for him! To ask her to accept the half of—nothing, to give up a career to share his struggle for one, to ask her to bury her splendid talent and her beauty under a bushel that he might wave aloft his feeble light!

And there was no way out, no royal road to fortune by the route he had chosen; nothing but grinding work, with a result problematical and years ahead. There were even no legacies to expect, he thought whimsically. Peter had known a chap once, struggling along in gynecology, who had had a fortune left him by a G. P., which being interpreted is Grateful Patient. Peter's patients had a way of living, and when they did drop out, as happened now and then, had also a way of leaving Peter an unpaid bill in token of appreciation; Peter had even occasionally helped to bury them, by way, he defended himself, of covering up his mistakes.

Peter, sitting back in his corner, allowed the wonderful scenery to slip by unnoticed. He put Harmony the Desirable out of his mind, and took to calculating on a scrap of paper what could be done for Harmony the Musician. He could hold out for three months, he calculated, and still have enough to send Harmony home and to get home himself on a slow boat. The Canadian lines were cheap. If Jimmy lived perhaps he could take him along: if not—

He would have to put six months' work in the next three. That was not so hard. He had got along before with less sleep, and thrived on it. Also there must be no more idle evenings, with Jimmy in the salon propped in a chair and Harmony playing, the room dark save for the glow from the stove and for the one candle at Harmony's elbow.

All roads lead to Rome. Peter's thoughts, having traveled in a circle, were back again to Harmony the Desirable—Harmony playing in the firelight, Harmony Hushed over the brick stove, Harmony paring potatoes that night in the kitchen when he—Harmony! Harmony!

Stewart knew all about the accident and its cause. Peter had surmised as much when the injured man failed to ask for Marie.

He tested him finally by bringing Marie's name into the conversation. Stewart ignored it, accepted her absence, refused to be drawn.

That was at first. During the day, however, as he gained strength, he grew restless and uneasy. As the time approached for Peter to leave, he was clearly struggling with himself. The landlady had agreed to care for him and was bustling about the room. During one of her absences he turned to Peter.

"I suppose Marie hasn't been round?"

"She came back last night."

"Did she tell you?"

"Yes, poor child."

"She's a devil!" Stewart said, and lay silent. Then: "I saw her shoot that thing out in front of us, but there was no time—Where is she now?"

"Marie? I sent her to Vienna."

Stewart fell back, relieved, not even curious.

109

"Thank Heaven for that!" he said. "I don't want to see her again. I'd do something I'd be sorry for. The kindest thing to say for her is that she was not sane."

"No," said Peter gravely, "she was hardly sane."

Stewart caught his steady gaze and glanced away. For him Marie's little tragedy had been written and erased. He would forget it magnanimously. He had divided what he had with her, and she had repaid him by attempting his life. And not only his life, but Anita's. Peter followed his line of reasoning easily.

"It's quite a frequent complication, Stewart," he said, "but every man to whom it happens regards himself more or less as a victim. She fell in love with you, that's all. Her conduct is contrary to the ethics of the game, but she's been playing poor cards all along."

"Where is she?"

"That doesn't matter, does it?"

Stewart had lain back and closed his eyes. No, it didn't matter. A sense of great relief overwhelmed him. Marie was gone, frightened into hiding. It was as if a band that had been about him was suddenly loosed: he breathed deep, he threw out his arms and laughed from sheer reaction. Then, catching Peter's not particularly approving eyes, he colored.

"Good Lord, Peter!" he said, "you don't know what I've gone through with that little devil. And now she's gone!" He glanced round the disordered room, where bandages and medicines crowded toilet articles on the dressing-table, where one of Marie's small slippers still lay where it had fallen under the foot of the bed, where her rosary still hung over the corner of the table. "Ring for the maid, Peter, will you! I've got to get this junk out of here. Some of Anita's people may come."

During that afternoon ride, while the train clump-clumped down the mountains, Peter thought of all this. Some of Marie's "junk" was in his bag; her rosary lay in his breastpocket, along with the pin he had sent her at Christmas. Peter happened on it, still in its box, which looked as if it had been cried over. He had brought it with him. He admired it very much, and it had cost money he could ill afford to spend.

It was late when the train drew into the station. Peter, encumbered with Marie's luggage and his own, lowered his window and added his voice to the chorus of plaintive calls: "Portier! Portier!" they shouted. "Portier!" bawled Peter.

He was obliged to resort to the extravagance of a taxicab. Possibly a fiacre would have done as well, but it cost almost as much and was slower. Moments counted now: a second was an hour, an hour a decade. For he was on his way to Harmony. Extravagance became recklessness. As soon die for a sheep as a lamb! He stopped the taxicab and bought a bunch of violets, stopped again and bought lilies of the valley to combine with the violets, went out of his way to the American grocery and bought a jar of preserved fruit.

By that time he was laden. The jar of preserves hung in one shabby pocket, Marie's rosary dangled from another; the violets were buttoned under his overcoat against the cold.

110

At the very last he held the taxi an extra moment and darted into the delicatessen shop across the Siebensternstrasse. From there, standing inside the doorway, he could see the lights in the salon across the way, the glow of his lamp, the flicker that was the fire. Peter whistled, stamped his cold feet, quite neglected —in spite of repeated warnings from Harmony—to watch the Herr Schenkenkaufer weigh the cheese, accepted without a glance a ten-Kronen piece with a hole in it.

"And how is the child to-day?" asked the Herr Schenkenkaufer, covering the defective gold piece with conversation.

"I do not know; I have been away," said Peter. He almost sang it.

"All is well or I would have heard. Wilhelm the Portier was but just now here."

"All well, of course," sang Peter, eyes on the comfortable Floor of his lamp, the flicker that was the fire. "Auf wiedersehen, Herr Schenkenkaufer."

"Auf wiedersehen, Herr Doktor."

Violets, lilies-of-the-valley, cheese, rosary, luggage—thus Peter climbed the stairs. The Portier wished to assist him, but Peter declined. The Portier was noisy. There was to be a moment when Peter, having admitted himself with extreme caution, would present himself without so much as a creak to betray him, would stand in a doorway until some one, Harmony perhaps—ah, Peter!—would turn and see him. She had a way of putting one slender hand over her heart when she was startled.

Peter put down the jar of preserved peaches outside. It was to be a second surprise. Also he put down the flowers; they were to be brought in last of all. One surprise after another is a cumulative happiness. Peter did not wish to swallow all his cake in one bite.

For once he did not slam the outer door, although he very nearly did, and only caught it at the cost of a bruised finger. Inside he listened. There was no clatter of dishes, no scurrying back and forth from table to stove in the final excitement of dishing up. There was, however, a highly agreeable odor of stewing chicken, a crisp smell of baking biscuit.

In the darkened hall Peter had to pause to steady himself. For he had a sudden mad impulse to shout Harmony's name, to hold out his arms, to call her to him there in the warm darkness, and when she had come, to catch her to him, to tell his love in one long embrace, his arms about her, his rough cheek against her soft one. No wonder he grew somewhat dizzy and had to pull himself together.

The silence rather surprised him, until he recalled that Harmony was probably sewing in the salon, as she did sometimes when dinner was ready to serve. The boy was asleep, no doubt. He stole along on tiptoe, hardly breathing, to the first doorway, which was Jimmy's.

Jimmy was asleep. Round him were the pink and yellow and white flower fairies with violet heads. Peter saw them and smiled. Then, his eyes growing accustomed to the light, he saw Marie, face down on the floor, her head on her arms. Still as she was, Peter knew she was not sleeping, only fighting her battle over again and losing.

111

Some of the joyousness of his return fled from Peter, never to come back. The two silent figures were too close to tragedy. Peter, with a long breath, stole past the door and on to the salon. No Harmony there, but the great room was warm and cheery. The table was drawn near the stove and laid for Abendessen. The white porcelain coffee-pot had boiled and extinguished itself, according to its method, and now gently steamed.

On to the kitchen. Much odor of food here, two candles lighted but burning low, a small platter with money on it, quite a little money—almost all he had left Harmony when he went away.

Peter was dazed at first. Even when Marie, hastily summoned, had discovered that Harmony's clothing was gone, when a search of the rooms revealed the absence of her violin and her music, when at last the fact stared them, incontestable, in the face, Peter refused to accept it. He sat for a half-hour or even more by the fire in the salon, obstinately refusing to believe she was gone, keeping the supper warm against her return. He did not think or reason, he sat and waited, saying nothing, hardly moving, save when a gust of wind slammed the garden gate. Then he was all alive, sat erect, ears straining for her hand on the knob of the outer door.

The numbness of the shock passed at last, to be succeeded by alarm. During all the time that followed, that condition persisted, fright, almost terror. Harmony alone in the city, helpless, dependent, poverty-stricken. Harmony seeking employment under conditions Peter knew too well. But with his alarm came rage.

Marie had never seen Peter angry. She shrank from this gaunt and gray-faced man who raved up and down the salon, questioning the frightened Portier, swearing fierce oaths, bringing accusation after accusation against some unnamed woman to whom he applied epithets that Marie's English luckily did not comprehend. Not a particularly heroic figure was Peter that night: a frantic, disheveled individual, before whom the Portier cowered, who struggled back to sanity through a berserk haze and was liable to swift relapses into fury again.

To this succeeded at last the mental condition that was to be Peter's for many days, hopelessness and alarm and a grim determination to keep on searching.

There were no clues. The Portier made inquiries of all the cabstands in the neighborhood. Harmony had not taken a cab. The delicatessen seller had seen her go out that afternoon with a bundle and return without it. She had been gone only an hour or so. That gave Peter a ray of hope that she might have found a haven in the neighborhood—until he recalled the parcel-post.

One possibility he clung to: Mrs. Boyer had made the mischief, but she had also offered the girl a home. She might be at the Boyers'. Peter, flinging on a hat and without his overcoat, went to the Boyers'. Time was valuable, and he had wasted an hour, two hours, in useless rage. So he took a taxicab, and being by this time utterly reckless of cost let it stand while he interviewed the Boyers.

Boyer himself, partially undressed, opened the door to his ring. Peter was past explanation or ceremonial.

"Is Harmony here?" he demanded.

112

"Harmony?"

"Harmony Wells. She's disappeared, missing."

"Come in," said Boyer, alive to the strain in Peter's voice. "I don't know, I haven't heard anything. I'll ask Mrs. Boyer."

During the interval it took for a whispered colloquy in the bedroom, and for Mrs. Boyer to don her flannel wrapper, Peter suffered the tortures of the damned. Whatever Mrs. Boyer had meant to say by way of protest at the intrusion on the sacred privacy of eleven o'clock and bedtime died in her throat. Her plump and terraced chin shook with agitation, perhaps with guilt. Peter, however, had got himself in hand. He told a quiet story; Boyer listened; Mrs. Boyer, clutching her wrapper about her unstayed figure, listened.

"I thought," finished Peter, "that since you had offered her a refuge—from me —she might have come here."

"I offered her a refuge—before I had been to the Pension Schwarz."

"Ah!" said Peter slowly. "And what about the Pension Schwarz?"

"Need you ask? I learned that you were all put out there. I am obliged to say, Dr. Byrne, that under the circumstances had the girl come here I could hardly— Frank, I will speak!—I could hardly have taken her in."

Peter went white and ducked as from a physical blow, stumbling out into the hall again. There he thought of something to say in reply, repudiation, thought better of it, started down the stairs.

Boyer followed him helplessly. At the street door, however, he put his hand on Peter's shoulder. "You know, old man, I don't believe that. These women—"

"I know," said Peter simply. "Thank you. Good-night."

CHAPTER XXII

Harmony's only thought had been flight, from Peter, from McLean, from Mrs. Boyer. She had devoted all her energies to losing herself, to cutting the threads that bound her to the life in the Siebensternstrasse. She had drawn all her money, as Peter discovered later. The discovery caused him even more acute anxiety. The city was full of thieves; poverty and its companion, crime, lurked on every shadowy staircase of the barracklike houses, or peered, red-eyed, from every alleyway.

And into this city of contrasts—of gray women of the night hugging gratings for warmth and accosting passers-by with loathsome gestures, of smug civilians hiding sensuous mouths under great mustaches, of dapper soldiers to whom the young girl unattended was potential prey, into this night city of terror, this day city of frightful contrasts, ermine rubbing elbows with frost-nipped flesh, destitution sauntering along the fashionable Prater for lack of shelter, gilt wheels of royalty and yellow wheels of courtesans—Harmony had ventured alone for the second time.

And this time there was no Peter Byrne to accost her cheerily in the twilight and

113

win her by sheer friendliness. She was alone. Her funds were lower, much lower. And something else had gone—her faith. Mrs. Boyer had seen to that. In the autumn Harmony had faced the city clear-eyed and unafraid; now she feared it, met it with averted eyes, alas! understood it.

It was not the Harmony who had bade a brave farewell to Scatchy and the Big Soprano in the station who fled to her refuge on the upper floor of the house in the Wollbadgasse. This was a hunted creature, alternately flushed and pale, who locked her door behind her before she took off her hat, and who, having taken off her hat and surveyed her hiding-place with tragic eyes, fell suddenly to trembling, alone there in the gaslight.

She had had no plans beyond flight. She had meant, once alone, to think the thing out. But the room was cold, she had had nothing to eat, and the single slovenly maid was a Hungarian and spoke no German. The dressmaker had gone to the Ronacher. Harmony did not know where to find a restaurant, was afraid to trust herself to the streets alone. She went to bed supperless, with a tiny picture of Peter and Jimmy and the wooden sentry under her cheek.

The pigeons, cooing on the window-sill, wakened her early. She was confused at first, got up to see if Jimmy had thrown off his blankets, and wakened to full consciousness with the sickening realization that Jimmy was not there.

The dressmaker, whose name was Monia Reiff, slept late after her evening out. Harmony, collapsing with hunger and faintness, waited as long as she could. Then she put on her things desperately and ventured out. Surely at this hour Peter would not be searching, and even if he were he would never think of the sixteenth district. He would make inquiries, of course—the Pension Schwarz, Boyers', the master's.

The breakfast brought back her strength and the morning air gave her confidence. The district, too, was less formidable than the neighborhood of the Karntnerstrasse and the Graben. The shops were smaller. The windows exhibited cheaper goods. There was a sort of family atmosphere about many of them; the head of the establishment in the doorway, the wife at the cashier's desk, daughters, cousins, nieces behind the wooden counters. The shopkeepers were approachable, instead of familiar. Harmony met no rebuffs, was respectfully greeted and cheerfully listened to. In many cases the application ended in a general consultation, shopkeeper, wife, daughters, nieces, slim clerks with tiny mustaches. She got addresses, followed them up, more consultations, more addresses, but no work. The reason dawned on her after a day of tramping, during which she kept carefully away from that part of the city where Peter might be searching for her.

The fact was, of course, that her knowledge of English was her sole asset as a clerk. And there were few English and no tourists in the sixteenth district. She was marketing a commodity for which there was no demand.

She lunched at a Konditorei, more to rest her tired body than because she needed food. The afternoon was as the morning. At six o'clock, long after the midwinter darkness had fallen, she stumbled back to the Wollbadgasse and up the whitewashed staircase.

She had a shock at the second landing. A man had stepped into the angle to let her pass. A gasjet dared over his head, and she recognized the short heavy figure and ardent eyes of Georgiev. She had her veil down luckily, and he gave no sign of recognition. She passed on, and she heard him a second later descending. But there had been something reminiscent after all in her figure and carriage. The little Georgiev paused, halfway down, and thought a moment. It was impossible, of course. All women reminded him of the American. Had he not, only the day before, followed for two city blocks a woman old enough to be his mother, merely because she carried a violin case? But there was something about the girl he had just passed—Bah!

A bad week for Harmony followed, a week of weary days and restless nights when she slept only to dream of Peter—of his hurt and incredulous eyes when he found she had gone; of Jimmy—that he needed her, was worse, was dying. More than once she heard him sobbing and wakened to the cooing of the pigeons on the window-sill. She grew thin and sunken-eyed; took to dividing her small hoard, half of it with her, half under the carpet, so that in case of accident all would not be gone.

This, as it happened, was serious. One day, the sixth, she came back wet to the skin from an all-day rain, to find that the carpet bank had been looted. There was no clue. The stolid Hungarian, startled out of her lethargy, protested innocence; the little dressmaker, who seemed honest and friendly, wept in sheer sympathy. The fact remained—half the small hoard was gone.

Two days more, a Sunday and a Monday. On Sunday Harmony played, and Georgiev in the room below, translating into cipher a recent conference between the Austrian Minister of War and the German Ambassador, put aside his work and listened. She played, as once before she had played when life seemed sad and tragic, the "Humoresque." Georgiev, hands behind his head and eyes upturned, was back in the Pension Schwarz that night months ago when Harmony played the "Humoresque" and Peter stooped outside her door. The little Bulgarian sighed and dreamed.

Harmony, a little sadder, a little more forlorn each day, pursued her hopeless quest. She ventured into the heart of the Stadt and paid a part of her remaining money to an employment bureau, to teach English or violin, whichever offered, or even both. After she had paid they told her it would be difficult, almost impossible without references. She had another narrow escape as she was leaving. She almost collided with Olga, the chambermaid, who, having clashed for the last time with Katrina, was seeking new employment. On another occasion she saw Marie in the crowd and was obsessed with a longing to call to her, to ask for Peter, for Jimmy. That meeting took the heart out of the girl. Marie was white and weary —perhaps the boy was worse. Perhaps Peter—Her heart contracted. But that was absurd, of course, Peter was always well and strong.

Two things occurred that week, one unexpected, the other inevitable. The unexpected occurrence was that Monia Reiff, finding Harmony being pressed for work, offered the girl a situation. The wage was small, but she could live on it.

The inevitable was that she met Georgiev on the stairs without her veil.

It was the first day in the workroom. The apprentices were carrying home boxes for a ball that night. Thread was needed, and quickly. Harmony, who did odds and ends of sewing, was most easily spared. She slipped on her jacket and hat and ran down to the shop near by.

It was on the return that she met Georgiev coming down. The afternoon was dark and the staircase unlighted. In the gloom one face was as another. Georgiev, listening intently, hearing footsteps, drew back into the embrasure of a window and waited. His swarthy face was tense, expectant. As the steps drew near, were light feminine instead of stealthy, the little spy relaxed somewhat. But still he waited, crouched.

It was a second before he recognized Harmony, another instant before he realized his good fortune. She had almost passed. He put out an unsteady hand.

"Fraulein!"

"Herr Georgiev!"

The little Bulgarian was profoundly stirred. His fervid eyes gleamed. He struggled against the barrier of language, broke out in passionate Bulgar, switched to German punctuated with an English word here and there. Made intelligible, it was that he had found her at last. Harmony held her spools of thread and waited for the storm of languages to subside. Then:—

"But you are not to say you have seen me, Herr Georgiev."

"No?"

Harmony colored.

"I am—am hiding," she explained. "Something very uncomfortable happened and I came here. Please don't say you have seen me."

Georgiev was puzzled at first. She had to explain very slowly, with his ardent eyes on her. But he understood at last and agreed of course. His incredulity was turning to certainty. Harmony had actually been in the same building with him while he sought her everywhere else.

"Then," he said at last, "it was you who played Sunday."

"I surely."

She made a move to pass him, but he held out an imploring hand.

"Fraulein, I may see you sometimes?"

"We shall meet again, of course."

"Fraulein,—with all respect,—sometime perhaps you will walk out with me?"

"I am very busy all day."

"At night, then? For the exercise? I, with all respect, Fraulein!"

Harmony was touched.

"Sometime," she consented. And then impulsively: "I am very lonely, Herr Georgiev."

She held out her hand, and the little Bulgarian bent over it and kissed it reverently. The Herr Georgiev's father was a nobleman in his own country, and all the little spy's training had been to make of a girl in Harmony's situation lawful prey. But in the spy's glowing heart there was nothing for Harmony to fear. She knew it. He stood, hat in hand, while she went up the staircase. Then:—

"Fraulein!" anxiously.

"Yes?"

"Was there below at the entrance a tall man in a green velours hat?"

"I saw no one there."

"I thank you, Fraulein."

He watched her slender figure ascend, lose itself in the shadows, listened until she reached the upper floors. Then with a sigh he clapped his hat on his head and made his cautious way down to the street. There was no man in a green velours hat below, but the little spy had an uneasy feeling that eyes watched him, nevertheless. Life was growing complicated for the Herr Georgiev.

Life was pressing very close to Harmony also in those days, a life she had never touched before. She discovered, after a day or two in the work-room, that Monia Reiff's business lay almost altogether among the demi-monde. The sewing-girls, of Marie's type many of them, found in the customers endless topics of conversation. Some things Harmony was spared, much of the talk being in dialect. But a great deal of it she understood, and she learned much that was not spoken. They talked freely of the women, their clothes, and they talked a great deal about a newcomer, an American dancer, for whom Monia was making an elaborate outfit. The American's name was Lillian Le Grande. She was dancing at one of the variety theaters.

Harmony was working on a costume for the Le Grande woman—a gold brocade slashed to the knee at one side and with a fragment of bodice made of gilt tissue. On the day after her encounter with Georgiev she met her.

There was a dispute over the gown, something about the draping. Monia, flushed with irritation, came to the workroom door and glanced over the girls. She singled out Harmony finally and called her.

"Come and put on the American's gown," she ordered. "She wishes—Heaven knows what she wishes!"

Harmony went unwillingly. Nothing she had heard of the Fraulein Le Grande had prepossessed her. Her uneasiness was increased when she found herself obliged to shed her gown and to stand for one terrible moment before the little dressmaker's amused eyes.

"Thou art very lovely, very chic," said Monia. The dress added to rather than relieved Harmony's discomfiture. She donned it in one of the fitting-rooms, made by the simple expedient of curtaining off a corner of the large reception room. The slashed skirt embarrassed her; the low cut made her shrink. Monia was frankly entranced. Above the gold tissue of the bodice rose Harmony's exquisite shoulders. Her hair was gold; even her eyes looked golden. The dressmaker, who worshiped beauty, gave a pull here, a pat there. If only all women were so beautiful in the things she made!

She had an eye for the theatrical also. She posed Harmony behind the curtain, arranged lights, drew down the chiffon so that a bit more of the girl's rounded bosom was revealed. Then she drew the curtain aside and stood smiling.

Le Grande paid the picture the tribute of a second's silence. Then:—

"Exquisite!" she said in English. Then in halting German: "Do not change a line. It is perfect."

Harmony must walk in the gown, turn, sit. Once she caught a glimpse of herself and was startled. She had been wearing black for so long, and now this radiant golden creature was herself. She was enchanted and abashed. The slash in the skirt troubled her: her slender leg had a way of revealing itself.

The ordeal was over at last. The dancer was pleased. She ordered another gown. Harmony, behind the curtain, slipped out of the dress and into her own shabby frock. On the other side of the curtain the dancer was talking. Her voice was loud, but rather agreeable. She smoked a cigarette. Scraps of chatter came to Harmony, and once a laugh.

"That is too pink—something more delicate."

"Here is a shade; hold it to your cheek."

"I am a bad color. I did not sleep last night."

"Still no news, Fraulein?"

"None. He has disappeared utterly. That isn't so bad, is it? I could use more rouge."

"It is being much worn. It is strange, is it not, that a child could be stolen from the hospital and leave no sign!"

The dancer laughed a mirthless laugh. Her voice changed, became nasal, full of venom.

"Oh, they know well enough," she snapped. "Those nurses know, and there's a pig of a red-bearded doctor—I'd like to poison him. Separating mother and child! I'm going to find him, if only to show them they are not so smart after all."

In her anger she had lapsed into English. Harmony, behind her curtain, had clutched at her heart. Jimmy's mother!

CHAPTER XXIII

Jimmy was not so well, although Harmony's flight had had nothing to do with the relapse. He had found Marie a slavishly devoted substitute, and besides Peter had indicated that Harmony's absence was purely temporary. But the breaking-up was inevitable. All day long the child lay in the white bed, apathetic but sleepless. In vain Marie made flower fairies for his pillow, in vain the little mice, now quite tame, played hide-and-seek over the bed, in vain Peter paused long enough in his frantic search for Harmony to buy colored postcards and bring them to him.

He was contented enough; he did not suffer at all; and he had no apprehension of what was coming. He asked for nothing, tried obediently to eat, liked to have Marie in the room. But he did not beg to be taken into the salon, as he once had done. There was a sort of mental confusion also. He liked Marie to read his father's letters; but as he grew weaker the occasional confusing of Peter with his

118

dead father became a fixed idea. Peter was Daddy.

Peter took care of him at night. He had moved into Harmony's adjacent room and dressed there. But he had never slept in the bed. At night he put on his shabby dressing-gown and worn slippers and lay on a haircloth sofa at the foot of Jimmy's bed—lay but hardly slept, so afraid was he that the slender thread of life might snap when it was drawn out to its slenderest during the darkest hours before the dawn. More than once in every night Peter rose and stood, hardly breathing, with the tiny lamp in his hand, watching for the rise and fall of the boy's thin little chest. Peter grew old these days. He turned gray over the ears and developed lines about his mouth that never left him again. He felt gray and old, and sometimes bitter and hard also. The boy's condition could not be helped: it was inevitable, hopeless. But the thing that was eating his heart out had been unnecessary and cruel.

Where was Harmony? When it stormed, as it did almost steadily, he wondered how she was sheltered; when the occasional sun shone he hoped it was bringing her a bit of cheer. Now and then, in the night, when the lamp burned low and gusts of wind shook the old house, fearful thoughts came to him—the canal, with its filthy depths. Daylight brought reason, however. Harmony had been too rational, too sane for such an end.

McLean was Peter's great support in those terrible days. He was young and hopeful. Also he had money. Peter could not afford to grease the machinery of the police service; McLean could and did. In Berlin Harmony could not have remained hidden for two days. In Vienna, however, it was different. Returns were made to the department, but irregularly. An American music student was missing. There were thousands of American music students in the city: one fell over them in the coffee-houses. McLean offered a reward and followed up innumerable music students.

The alternating hope and despair was most trying. Peter became old and haggard; the boy grew thin and white. But there was this difference, that with Peter the strain was cumulative, hour on hour, day on day. With McLean each night found him worn and exhausted, but each following morning he went to work with renewed strength and energy. Perhaps, after all, the iron had not struck so deep into his soul. With Peter it was a life-and-death matter.

Clinics and lectures had begun again, but he had no heart for work. The little household went on methodically. Marie remained; there had seemed nothing else to do. She cooked Peter's food—what little he would eat; she nursed Jimmy while Peter was out on the long search; and she kept the apartment neat. She was never intrusive, never talkative. Indeed, she seemed to have lapsed into definite silence. She deferred absolutely to Peter, adored him, indeed, from afar. She never ate with him, in spite of his protests.

The little apartment was very quiet. Where formerly had been music and Harmony's soft laughter, where Anna Gates had been wont to argue with Peter in loud, incisive tones, where even the prisms of the chandelier had once vibrated in response to Harmony's violin, almost absolute silence now reigned. Even the gate, having been repaired, no longer creaked, and the loud altercations between the Portier and his wife had been silenced out of deference to the sick child.

On the day that Harmony, in the gold dress, had discovered Jimmy's mother in the American dancer Peter had had an unusually bad day. McLean had sent him a note by messenger early in the morning, to the effect that a young girl answering Harmony's description had been seen in the park at Schonbrunn and traced to an apartment near by.

Harmony had liked Schonbrunn, and it seemed possible. They had gone out together, McLean optimistic, Peter afraid to hope. And it had been as he feared—a pretty little violin student, indeed, who had been washing her hair, and only opened the door an inch or two.

McLean made a lame apology, Peter too sick with disappointment to speak. Then back to the city again.

He had taken to making a daily round, to the master's, to the Frau Professor Bergmeister's, along the Graben and the Karntnerstrasse, ending up at the Doctors' Club in the faint hope of a letter. Wrath still smouldered deep in Peter; he would not enter a room at the club if Mrs. Boyer sat within. He had had a long hour with Dr. Jennings, and left that cheerful person writhing in abasement. And he had held a stormy interview with the Frau Schwarz, which left her humble for a week, and exceedingly nervous, being of the impression from Peter's manner that in the event of Harmony not turning up an American gunboat would sail up the right arm of the Danube and bombard the Pension Schwarz.

Schonbrunn having failed them, McLean and, Peter went back to the city in the street-car, neither one saying much. Even McLean's elasticity was deserting him. His eyes, from much peering into crowds, had taken on a strained, concentrated look.

Peter was shabbier than ever beside the other man's ultrafashionable dress. He sat, bent forward, his long arms dangling between his knees, his head down. Their common trouble had drawn the two together, or had drawn McLean close to Peter, as if he recognized that there were degrees in grief and that Peter had received almost a death-wound. His old rage at Peter had died. Harmony's flight had proved the situation as no amount of protestation would have done. The thing now was to find the girl; then he and Peter would start even, and the battle to the best man.

They had the car almost to themselves. Peter had not spoken since he sat down. McLean was busy over a notebook, in which he jotted down from day to day such details of their search as might be worth keeping. Now and then he glanced at Peter as if he wished to say something, hesitated, fell to work again over the notebook. Finally he ventured.

"How's the boy?"

"Not so well to-day. I'm having a couple of men in to see him to-night. He doesn't sleep."

"Do you sleep?"

"Not much. He's on my mind, of course."

120

That and other things, Peter.

"Don't you think—wouldn't it be better to have a nurse. You can't go like this all day and be up all night, you know. And Marie has him most of the day." McLean, of course, had known Marie before. "The boy ought to have a nurse, I think."

"He doesn't move without my hearing him."

"That's an argument for me. Do you want to get sick?"

Peter turned a white face toward McLean, a face in which exasperation struggled with fatigue.

"Good Lord, boy," he rasped, "don't you suppose I'd have a nurse if I could afford it?"

"Would you let me help? I'd like to do something. I'm a useless cub in a sick-room, but I could do that. Who's the woman he liked in the hospital?"

"Nurse Elisabet. I don't know, Mac. There's no reason why I shouldn't let you help, I suppose. It hurts, of course, but—if he would be happier—"

"That's settled, then," said McLean. "Nurse Elisabet, if she can come. And— look here, old man. I 've been trying to say this for a week and haven't had the nerve. Let me help you out for a while. You can send it back when you get it, any time, a year or ten years. I'll not miss it."

But Peter refused. He tempered the refusal in his kindly way.

"I can't take anything now," he said. "But I'll remember it, and if things get very bad I'll come to you. It isn't costing much to live. Marie is a good manager, almost as good as—Harmony was." This with difficulty. He found it always hard to speak of Harmony. His throat seemed to close on the name.

That was the best McLean could do, but he made a mental reservation to see Marie that night and slip her a little money. Peter need never know, would never notice.

At a cross-street the car stopped, and the little Bulgarian, Georgiev, got on. He inspected the car carefully before he came in from the platform, and sat down unobtrusively in a corner. Things were not going well with him either. His small black eyes darted from face to face suspiciously, until they came to a rest on Peter.

It was Georgiev's business to read men. Quickly he put together the bits he had gathered from Harmony on the staircase, added to them Peter's despondent attitude, his strained face, the abstraction which required a touch on the arm from his companion when they reached their destination, recalled Peter outside the door of Harmony's room in the Pension Schwarz—and built him a little story that was not far from the truth.

Peter left the car without seeing him. It was the hour of the promenade, when the Ring and the larger business streets were full of people, when Demel's was thronged with pretty women eating American ices, with military men drinking tea and nibbling Austrian pastry, the hour when the flower women along the Stephansplatz did a rousing business in roses, when sterile women burned candles before the Madonna in the Cathedral, when the lottery did the record business of the day.

It was Peter's forlorn hope that somewhere among the crowd he might happen on Harmony. For some reason he thought of her always as in a crowd, with people close, touching her, men staring at her, following her. He had spent a frightful night in the Opera, scanning seat after seat, not so much because he hoped to find her as because inaction was intolerable.

And so, on that afternoon, he made his slow progress along the Karntnerstrasse, halting now and then to scrutinize the crowd. He even peered through the doors of shops here and there, hoping while he feared that the girl might be seeking employment within, as she had before in the early days of the winter.

Because of his stature and powerful physique, and perhaps, too, because of the wretchedness in his eyes, people noticed him. There was one place where Peter lingered, where a new building was being erected, and where because of the narrowness of the passage the dense crowd was thinned as it passed. He stood by choice outside a hairdresser's window, where a brilliant light shone on each face that passed.

Inside the clerks had noticed him. Two of them standing together by the desk spoke of him: "He is there again, the gray man!"

"Ah, so! But, yes, there is his back!"

"Poor one, it is the Fraulein Engel he waits to see, perhaps."

"More likely Le Grande, the American. He is American."

"He is Russian. Look at his size."

"But his shoes!" triumphantly. "They are American, little one."

The third girl had not spoken; she was wrapping in tissue a great golden rose made for the hair. She placed it in a box carefully.

"I think he is of the police," she said, "or a spy. There is much talk of war."

"Foolishness! Does a police officer sigh always? Or a spy have such sadness in his face? And he grows thin and white."

"The rose, Fraulein."

The clerk who had wrapped up the flower held it out to the customer. The customer, however, was not looking. She was gazing with strange intentness at the back of a worn gray overcoat. Then with a curious clutch at her heart she went white. Harmony, of course, Harmony come to fetch the golden rose that was to complete Le Grande's costume.

She recovered almost at once and made an excuse to leave by another exit.

She took a final look at the gray sleeve that was all she could see of Peter, who had shifted a bit, and stumbled out into the crowd, walking along with her lip trembling under her veil, and with the slow and steady ache at her heart that she had thought she had stilled for good.

It had never occurred to Harmony that Peter loved her. He had proposed to her twice, but that had been in each case to solve a difficulty for her. And once he had taken her in his arms, but that was different. Even then he had not said he loved her—had not even known it, to be exact. Nor had Harmony realized what Peter meant to her until she had put him out of her life.

The sight of the familiar gray coat, the scrap of conversation, so enlightening as to poor Peter's quest, that Peter was growing thin and white, made her almost reel. She had been too occupied with her own position to realize Peter's. With the glimpse of him came a great longing for the house on the Siebensternstrasse, for Jimmy's arms about her neck, for the salon with the lamp lighted and the sleet beating harmlessly against the casement windows, for the little kitchen with the brick stove, for Peter.

Doubts of the wisdom of her course assailed her. But to go back meant, at the best, adding to Peter's burden of Jimmy and Marie, meant the old situation again, too, for Marie most certainly did not add to the respectability of the establishment. And other doubts assailed her. What if Jimmy were not so well, should die, as was possible, and she had not let his mother see him!

Monia Reiff was very busy that day. Harmony did not leave the workroom until eight o'clock. During all that time, while her slim fingers worked over fragile laces and soft chiffons, she was seeing Jimmy as she had seen him last, with the flower fairies on his pillow, and Peter, keeping watch over the crowd in the Karntnerstrasse, looking with his steady eyes for her.

No part of the city was safe for a young girl after night, she knew; the sixteenth district was no better than the rest, rather worse in places. But the longing to see the house on the Siebensternstrasse grew on her, became from an ache a sharp and insistent pain. She must go, must see once again the comfortable glow of Peter's lamp, the flicker that was the fire.

She ate no supper. She was too tired to eat, and there was the pain. She put on her wraps and crept down the whitewashed staircase.

The paved courtyard below was to be crossed and it was poorly lighted. She achieved the street, however, without molestation. To the street-car was only a block, but during that block she was accosted twice. She was white and frightened when she reached the car.

The Siebensternstrasse at last. The street was always dark; the delicatessen shop was closed, but in the wild-game store next a light was burning low, and a flame flickered before the little shrine over the money drawer. The gameseller was a religious man.

The old stucco house dominated the neighborhood. From the time she left the car Harmony saw it, its long flat roof black against the dark sky, its rows of unlighted windows, its long wall broken in the center by the gate. Now from across the street its whole facade lay before her. Peter's lamp was not lighted, but there was a glow of soft firelight from the salon windows. The light was not regular—it disappeared at regular intervals, was blotted out. Harmony knew what that meant. Some one beyond range of where she stood was pacing the floor, back and forward, back and forward. When he was worried or anxious Peter always paced the door.

She did not know how long she stood there. One of the soft rains was falling, or more accurately, condensing. The saturated air was hardly cold. She stood on the pavement unmolested, while the glow died lower and lower, until at last it was impossible to trace the pacing figure. No one came to any of the windows. The

123

little lamp before the shrine in the wild-game shop burned itself out; the Portier across the way came to the door, glanced up at the sky and went in. Harmony heard the rattle of the chain as it was stretched across the door inside.

Not all the windows of the suite opened on the street. Jimmy's windows—and Peter's—opened toward the back of the house, where in a brick-paved courtyard the wife of the Portier hung her washing, and where the Portier himself kept a hutch of rabbits. A wild and reckless desire to see at least the light from the child's room possessed Harmony. Even the light would be something; to go like this, to carry with her only the memory of a dark looming house without cheer was unthinkable. The gate was never locked. If she but went into the garden and round by the spruce tree to the back of the house, it would be something.

She knew the garden quite well. Even the darkness had no horror for her. Little Scatchy had had a habit of leaving various articles on her window-sill and of instigating searches for them at untimely hours of night. Once they had found her hairbrush in the rabbit hutch! So Harmony, ashamed but unalarmed, made her way by the big spruce to the corner of the old lodge and thus to the courtyard.

Ah, this was better! Lights all along the apartment floor and moving shadows; on Jimmy's window-sill a jar of milk. And voices—some one was singing.

Peter was singing, droning softly, as one who puts a drowsy child to sleep. Slower and slower, softer and softer, over and over, the little song Harmony had been wont to sing:—

"Ah well! For us all some sweet hope lies Deeply buried from human eyes. And in the—hereafter—angels may

    Roll—the—stone—from—its—grave—away."

Slower and slower, softer and softer, until it died away altogether. Peter, in his old dressing-gown, came to the window and turned down the gaslight beside it to a blue point. Harmony did not breathe. For a minute, two minutes, he stood there looking out. Far off the twin clocks of the Votivkirche struck the hour. All about lay the lights of the old city, so very old, so wise, so cunning, so cold.

Peter stood looking out, as he had each night since Harmony went away. Each night he sang the boy to sleep, turned down the light and stood by the window. And each night he whispered to the city that sheltered Harmony somewhere, what he had whispered to the little sweater coat the night before he went away:—

"Good-night, dear. Good-night, Harmony."

The rabbits stirred uneasily in the hutch; a passing gust shook the great tree overhead and sent down a sharp shower on to the bricks below. Peter struck a match and lit his pipe; the flickering light illuminated his face, his rough hair, his steady eyes.

"Good-night, Peter," whispered Harmony. "Good-night, dear."

CHAPTER XXIV

Walter Stewart had made an uncomplicated recovery, helped along by relief at the turn events had taken. In a few days he was going about again, weak naturally, rather handsomer than before because a little less florid. But the week's confinement had given him an opportunity to think over many things. Peter had set him thinking, on the day when he had packed up the last of Marie's small belongings and sent them down to Vienna.

Stewart, lying in bed, had watched him. "Just how much talk do you suppose this has made, Byrne?" he asked.

"Haven't an idea. Some probably. The people in the Russian villa saw it, you know."

Stewart's brows contracted.

"Damnation! Then the hotel has it, of course!"

"Probably."

Stewart groaned. Peter closed Marie's American trunk of which she had been so proud, and coming over looked down at the injured man.

"Don't you think you'd better tell the girl all about it?"

"No," doggedly.

"I know, of course, it wouldn't be easy, but—you can't get away with it, Stewart. That's one way of looking at it. There's another."

"What's that?"

"Starting with a clean slate. If she's the sort you want to marry, and not a prude, she'll understand, not at first, but after she gets used to it."

"She wouldn't understand in a thousand years."

"Then you'd better not marry her. You know, Stewart, I have an idea that women imagine a good many pretty rotten things about us, anyhow. A sensible girl would rather know the truth and be done with it. What a man has done with his life before a girl—the right girl—comes into it isn't a personal injury to her, since she wasn't a part of his life then. You know what I mean. But she has a right to know it before she chooses."

"How many would choose under those circumstances?" he jibed.

Peter smiled. "Quite a few," he said cheerfully. "It's a wrong system, of course; but we can get a little truth out of it."

"You can't get away with it" stuck in Stewart's mind for several days. It was the one thing Peter said that did stick. And before Stewart had recovered enough to be up and about he had made up his mind to tell Anita. In his mind he made quite a case for himself; he argued the affair against his conscience and came out victorious.

Anita's party had broken up. The winter sports did not compare, they complained, with St. Moritz. They disliked German cooking. Into the bargain the weather was not good; the night's snows turned soft by midday; and the crowds that began to throng the hotels were solid citizens, not the fashionables of the Riviera. Anita's arm forbade her traveling. In the reassembling of the party she went to the Kurhaus in the valley below the pension with one of the women who wished to take the baths.

It was to the Kurhaus, then, that Stewart made his first excursion after the accident. He went to dinner. Part of the chaperon's treatment called for an early retiring hour, which was highly as he had wished it and rather unnerving after all. A man may decide that a dose of poison is the remedy for all his troubles, but he does not approach his hour with any hilarity. Stewart was a stupid dinner guest, ate very little, and looked haggard beyond belief when the hour came for the older woman to leave.

He did not lack courage however. It was his great asset, physical and mental rather than moral, but courage nevertheless. The evening was quiet, and they elected to sit on the balcony outside Anita's sitting room, the girl swathed in white furs and leaning back in her steamer chair.

Below lay the terrace of the Kurhaus, edged with evergreen trees. Beyond and far below that was the mountain village, a few scattered houses along a frozen stream. The townspeople retired early; light after light was extinguished, until only one in the priest's house remained. A train crept out of one tunnel and into another, like a glowing worm crawling from burrow to burrow.

The girl felt a change in Stewart. During the weeks he had known her there had been a curious restraint in his manner to her. There were times when an avowal seemed to tremble on his lips, when his eyes looked into hers with the look no women ever mistakes; the next moment he would glance away, his face would harden. They were miles apart. And perhaps the situation had piqued the girl. Certainly it had lost nothing for her by its unusualness.

To-night there was a difference in the man. His eyes met hers squarely, without evasion, but with a new quality, a searching, perhaps, for something in her to give him courage. The girl had character, more than ordinary decision. It was what Stewart admired in her most, and the thing, of course, that the little Marie had lacked. Moreover, Anita, barely twenty, was a woman, not a young girl. Her knowledge of the world, not so deep as Marie's, was more comprehensive. Where Marie would have been merciful, Anita would be just, unless she cared for him. In that case she might be less than just, or more.

Anita in daylight was a pretty young woman, rather incisive of speech, very intelligent, having a wit without malice, charming to look at, keenly alive. Anita in the dusk of the balcony, waiting to hear she knew not what, was a judicial white goddess, formidably still, frightfully potential. Stewart, who had embraced many women, did not dare a finger on her arm.

He had decided on a way to tell the girl the story—a preamble about his upbringing, which had been indifferent, his struggle to get to Vienna, his loneliness there, all leading with inevitable steps to Marie. From that, if she did not utterly shrink from him, to his love for her.

It was his big hour, that hour on the balcony. He was reaching, through love, heights of honesty he had never scaled before. But as a matter of fact he reversed utterly his order of procedure. The situation got him, this first evening absolutely

126

alone with her. That and her nearness, and the pathos of her bandaged, useless arm. Still he had not touched her.

The thing he was trying to do was more difficult for that. General credulity to the contrary, men do not often make spoken love first. How many men propose marriage to their women across the drawing-room or from chair to chair? Absurd! The eyes speak first, then the arms, the lips last. The woman is in his arms before he tells his love. It is by her response that he gauges his chances and speaks of marriage. Actually the thing is already settled; tardy speech only follows on swift instinct. Stewart, wooing as men woo, would have taken the girl's hand, gained an encouragement from it, ventured to kiss it, perhaps, and finding no rebuff would then and there have crushed her to him; What need of words? They would follow in due time, not to make a situation but to clarify it.

But he could not woo as men woo. The barrier of his own weakness stood between them and must be painfully taken down.

"I'm afraid this is stupid for you," said Anita out of the silence. "Would you like to go to the music-room?"

"God forbid. I was thinking."

"Of what?" Encouragement this, surely.

"I was thinking how you had come into my life, and stirred it up."

"Really? I?"

"You know that."

"How did I stir it up?"

"That's hardly the way I meant to put it. You've changed everything for me. I care for you—a very great deal."

He was still carefully in hand, his voice steady. And still he did not touch her. Other men had made love to her, but never in this fashion, or was he making love?

"I'm very glad you like me."

"Like you!" Almost out of hand that time. The thrill in his voice was unmistakable. "It's much more than that, Anita, so much more that I'm going to try to do a hideously hard thing. Will you help a little?"

"Yes, if I can." She was stirred, too, and rather frightened.

Stewart drew his chair nearer to her and sat forward, his face set and dogged.

"Have you any idea how you were hurt? Or why?"

"No. There's a certain proportion of accidents that occur at all these places, isn't there?"

"This was not an accident."

"No?"

"The branch of a tree was thrown out in front of the sled to send us over the bank. It was murder, if intention is crime."

After a brief silence—

"Somebody who wished to kill you, or me?"

"Both of us, I believe. It was done by a woman—a girl, Anita. A girl I had been living with."

A brutal way to tell her, no doubt, but admirably courageous. For he was quivering with dread when he said it—the courage of the man who faces a cannon. And here, where a less-poised woman would have broken into speech, Anita took the refuge of her kind and was silent. Stewart watched her as best he could in the darkness, trying to gather further courage to go on. He could not see her face, but her fingers, touching the edge of the chair, quivered.

"May I tell you the rest?"

"I don't think I want to hear it."

"Are you going to condemn me unheard?"

"There isn't anything you can say against the fact?"

But there was much to say, and sitting there in the darkness he made his plea. He made no attempt to put his case. He told what had happened simply; he told of his loneliness and discomfort. And he emphasized the lack of sentiment that prompted the arrangement.

Anita spoke then for the first time: "And when you tried to terminate it she attempted to kill you!"

"I was acting the beast. I brought her up here, and then neglected her for you."

"Then it was hardly only a business arrangement for her."

"It was at first. I never dreamed of any thing else. I swear that, Anita. But lately, in the last month or two, she—I suppose I should have seen that she—"

"That she had fallen in love with you. How old is she?"

"Nineteen."

A sudden memory came to Anita, of a slim young girl, who had watched her with wide, almost childish eyes.

"Then it was she who was in the compartment with you on the train coming up?"

"Yes."

"Where is she now?"

"In Vienna. I have not heard from her. Byrne, the chap who came up to see me after the—after the accident, sent her away. I think he's looking after her. I haven't heard from him."

"Why did you tell me all this?"

"Because I love you, Anita. I want you to marry me."

"What! After that?"

"That, or something similar, is in many men's lives. They don't tell it, that's the difference. I 'm not taking any credit for telling you this. I'm ashamed to the bottom of my soul, and when I look at your bandaged arm I'm suicidal. Peter Byrne urged me to tell you. He said I couldn't get away with it; some time or other it would come out. Then he said something else. He said you'd probably understand, and that if you married me it was better to start with a clean slate."

No love, no passion in the interview now. A clear statement of fact, an offer—his past against hers, his future with hers. Her hand was steady now. The light in the priest's house had been extinguished. The chill of the mountain night penetrated Anita's white furs; and set her—or was it the chill?—to shivering.

128

"If I had not told you, would you have married me?"

"I think so. I'll be honest, too. Yes."

"I am the same man you would have married. Only—more honest."

"I cannot argue about it. I am tired and cold."

Stewart glanced across the valley to where the cluster of villas hugged the mountain-side There was a light in his room; outside was the little balcony where Marie had leaned against the railing and looked down, down. Some of the arrogance of his new virtue left the man. He was suddenly humbled. For the first time he realized a part of what Marie had endured in that small room where the light burned.

"Poor little Marie!" he said softly.

The involuntary exclamation did more for him than any plea he could have made. Anita rose and held out her hand.

"Go and see her," she said quietly. "You owe her that. We'll be leaving here in a day or so and I'll not see you again. But you've been honest, and I will be honest, too. I—I cared a great deal, too."

"And this has killed it?"

"I hardly comprehend it yet. I shall have to have time to think."

"But if you are going away—I'm afraid to leave you. You'll think this thing over, alone, and all the rules of life you've been taught will come—"

"Please, I must think. I will write you, I promise."

He caught her hand and crushed it between both of his.

"I suppose you would rather I did not kiss you?" humbly.

"I do not want you to kiss me."

He released her hand and stood looking down at her in the darkness. If he could only have crushed her to him, made her feel the security of his love, of his sheltering arms! But the barrier of his own building was between them. His voice was husky.

"I want you to try to remember, past what I have told you, to the thing that concerns us both—I love you. I never loved the other woman. I never pretended I loved her. And there will be nothing more like that."

"I shall try to remember."

Anita left Semmering the next day, against the protests of the doctor and the pleadings of the chaperon. She did not see Stewart again. But before she left, with the luggage gone and the fiacre at the door, she went out on the terrace, and looked across to the Villa Waldheim, rising from among its clustering trees. Although it was too far to be certain, she thought she saw the figure of a man on the little balcony standing with folded arms, gazing across the valley to the Kurhaus.

Having promised to see Marie, Stewart proceeded to carry out his promise in his direct fashion. He left Semmering the evening of the following day, for Vienna. The strain of the confession was over, but he was a victim of sickening dread. To one thing only he dared to pin his hopes. Anita had said she cared, cared a great deal. And, after all, what else mattered? The story had been a jolt, he told himself. Girls were full of queer ideas of right and wrong, bless them! But she cared. She cared!

He arrived in Vienna at nine o'clock that night. The imminence of his interview with Marie hung over him like a cloud. He ate a hurried supper, and calling up the Doctors' Club by telephone found Peter's address in the Siebensternstrasse. He had no idea, of course, that Marie was there. He wanted to see Peter to learn where Marie had taken refuge, and incidentally to get from Peter a fresh supply of moral courage for the interview. For he needed courage. In vain on the journey down had he clothed himself in armor of wrath against the girl; the very compartment in the train provoked softened memories of her. Here they had bought a luncheon, there Marie had first seen the Rax. Again at this station she had curled up and put her head on his shoulder for a nap. Ah, but again, at this part of the journey he had first seen Anita!

He took a car to the Siebensternstrasse. His idea of Peter's manner of living those days was exceedingly vague. He had respected Peter's reticence, after the manner of men with each other. Peter had once mentioned a boy he was looking after, in excuse for leaving so soon after the accident. That was all.

The house on the Siebensternstrasse loomed large and unlighted. The street was dark, and it was only after a search that Stewart found the gate. Even then he lost the path, and found himself among a group of trees, to touch the lowest branches of any of which resulted in a shower of raindrops. To add to his discomfort some one was walking in the garden, coming toward him with light, almost stealthy steps.

Stewart by his tree stood still, waiting. The steps approached, were very close, were beside him. So intense was the darkness that even then all he saw was a blacker shadow, and that was visible only because it moved. Then a hand touched his arm, stopped as if paralyzed, drew back slowly, fearfully.

"Good Heavens!" said poor Harmony faintly.

"Please don't be alarmed. I have lost the path." Stewart's voice was almost equally nervous. "Is it to the right or the left?"

It was a moment before Harmony had breath to speak. Then:—

"To the right a dozen paces or so."

"Thank you. Perhaps I can help you to find it."

"I know it quite well. Please don't bother."

The whole situation was so unexpected that only then did it dawn on Stewart that this blacker shadow was a countrywoman speaking God's own language. Together, Harmony a foot or so in advance, they made the path.

"The house is there. Ring hard, the bell is out of order."

"Are you not coming in?"

"No. I—I do not live here."

She must have gone just after that. Stewart, glancing at the dark facade of the house, turned round to find her gone, and a moment later heard the closing of the gate. He was bewildered. What sort of curious place was this, a great looming house that concealed in its garden a fugitive American girl who came and went like a shadow, leaving only the memory of a sweet voice strained with fright?

Stewart was full of his encounter as he took the candle the Portier gave him and followed the gentleman's gruff directions up the staircase. Peter admitted him, looking a trifle uneasy, as well he might with Marie in the salon.

Stewart was too preoccupied to notice Peter's expression. He shook the rain off his hat, smiling.

"How are you?" asked Peter dutifully.

"Pretty good, except for a headache when I'm tired. What sort of a place have you got here anyhow, Byrne?"

"Old hunting-lodge of Maria Theresa," replied Peter, still preoccupied with Marie and what was coming. "Rather interesting old place."

"Rather," commented Stewart, "with goddesses in the garden and all the usual stunts."

"Goddesses?"

"Ran into one just now among the trees. 'A woman I forswore, but thou being a goddess I forswore not thee.' English-speaking goddess, by George!"

Peter was staring at him incredulously; now he bent forward and grasped his arm in fingers of steel.

"For Heaven's sake, Stewart, tell me what you mean! Who was in the garden?"

Stewart was amused and interested. It was not for him to belittle a situation of his own making, an incident of his own telling.

"I lost my way in your garden, wandered among the trees, broke through a hedgerow or two, struck a match and consulted the compass—"

Peter's fingers closed.

"Quick," he said.

Stewart's manner lost its jauntiness.

"There was a girl there," he said shortly. "Couldn't see her. She spoke English. Said she didn't live here, and broke for the gate the minute I got to the path."

"You didn't see her?"

"No. Nice voice, though. Young."

The next moment he was alone. Peter in his dressing-gown was running down the staircase to the lower floor, was shouting to the Portier to unlock the door, was a madman in everything but purpose. The Portier let him out and returned to the bedroom.

"The boy above is worse," he said briefly. "A strange doctor has just come, and but now the Herr Doktor Byrne runs to the drug store."

The Portier's wife shrugged her shoulders even while tears filled her eyes.

"What can one expect?" she demanded. "The good Herr Gott has forbidden theft and Rosa says the boy was stolen. Also the druggist has gone to visit his wife's mother."

"Perhaps I may be of service; I shall go up."

"And see for a moment that hussy of the streets! Remain here. I shall go."

Slowly and ponderously she climbed the stairs.

Stewart, left alone, wandered along the dim corridor. He found Peter's

131

excitement rather amusing. So this was where Peter lived, an old house, isolated in a garden where rambled young women with soft voices. Hello, a youngster asleep! The boy, no doubt.

He wandered on toward the lighted door of the salon and Marie. The place was warm and comfortable, but over it all hung the indescribable odor of drugs that meant illness. He remembered that the boy was frail.

Marie turned as he stopped in the salon doorway, and then rose, white-faced. Across the wide spaces of the room they eyed each other. Marie's crisis had come. Like all crises it was bigger than speech. It was after a distinct pause that she spoke.

"Hast thou brought the police?"

Curiously human, curiously masculine at least was Stewart's mental condition at that moment. He had never loved the girl; it was with tremendous relief he had put her out of his life. And yet—

"So it's old Peter now, is it?"

"No, no, not that, Walter. He has given me shelter, that is all. I swear it. I look after the boy."

"Who else is here?"

"No one else; but—"

"Tell that rot to some one who does not know you."

"It is true. He never even looks at me. I am wicked, but I do not lie." There was a catch of hope in her voice. Marie knew men somewhat, but she still cherished the feminine belief that jealousy is love, whereas it is only injured pride. She took a step toward him. "Walter, I am sorry. Do you hate me?" She had dropped the familiar "thou."

Stewart crossed the room until only Peter's table and lamp stood between them.

"I didn't mean to be brutal," he said, rather largely, entirely conscious of his own magnanimity. "It was pretty bad up there and I know it. I don't hate you, of course. That's hardly possible after—everything."

"You—would take me back?"

"No. It's over, Marie. I wanted to know where you were, that's all; to see that you were comfortable and not frightened. You're a silly child to think of the police."

Marie put a hand to her throat.

"It is the American, of course."

"Yes."

She staggered a trifle, recovered, threw up her head. "Then I wish I had killed her!"

No man ever violently resents the passionate hate of one woman for her rival in his affections. Stewart, finding the situation in hand and Marie only feebly formidable, was rather amused and flattered by the honest fury in her voice. The mouse was under his paw; he would play a bit. "You'll get over feeling that way, kid. You don't really love me."

"You were my God, that is all."

132

"Will you let me help you—money, I mean?"

"Keep it for her."

"Peter will be here in a minute." He bent over the table and eyed her with his old, half-bullying, half-playful manner. "Come round here and kiss me for old times."

"No!"

"Come."

She stood stubbornly still, and Stewart, still smiling, took a step or two toward her. Then he stopped, ceased smiling, drew himself up.

"You are quite right and I'm a rotter." Marie's English did not comprehend "rotter," but she knew the tone. "Listen, Marie, I've told the other girl, and there's a chance for me, anyhow. Some day she may marry me. She asked me to see you."

"I do not wish her pity."

"You are wasting your life here. You cannot marry, you say, without a dot. There is a chance in America for a clever girl. You are clever, little Marie. The first money I can spare I'll send you—if you'll take it. It's all I can do."

This was a new Stewart, a man she had never known. Marie recoiled from him, eyed him nervously, sought in her childish mind for an explanation. When at last she understood that he was sincere, she broke down. Stewart, playing a new part and raw in it, found the situation irritating. But Marie's tears were not entirely bitter. Back of them her busy young mind was weaving a new warp of life, with all of America for its loom. Hope that had died lived again. Before her already lay that great country where women might labor and live by the fruit of their labor, where her tawdry past would be buried in the center of distant Europe. New life beckoned to the little Marie that night in the old salon of Maria Theresa, beckoned to her as it called to Stewart, opportunity to one, love and work to the other. To America!

"I will go," she said at last simply. "And I will not trouble you there."

"Good!" Stewart held out his hand and Marie took it. With a quick gesture she held it to her cheek, dropped it.

Peter came back half an hour later, downcast but not hopeless. He had not found Harmony, but life was not all gray. She was well, still in Vienna, and—she had come back! She had cared then enough to come back. To-morrow he would commence again, would comb the city fine, and when he had found her he would bring her back, the wanderer, to a marvelous welcome.

He found Stewart gone, and Marie feverishly overhauling her few belongings by the salon lamp. She turned to him a face still stained with tears but radiant with hope.

"Peter," she said gravely, "I must prepare my outfit. I go to America."

"With Stewart?"

"Alone, Peter, to work, to be very good, to be something. I am very happy, although—Peter, may I kiss you?"

"Certainly," said Peter, and took her caress gravely, patting her thin shoulder. His thoughts were in the garden with Harmony, who had cared enough to come back.

133

"Life," said Peter soberly, "life is just one damned thing after another, isn't it?"

But Marie was anxiously examining the hem of a skirt.

The letter from Anita reached Stewart the following morning. She said:—

"I have been thinking things over, Walter, and I am going to hurt you very much —but not, believe me, without hurting myself. Perhaps my uppermost thought just now is that I am disappointing you, that I am not so big as you thought I would be. For now, in this final letter, I can tell you how much I cared. Oh, my dear, I did care!

"But I will not marry you. And when this reaches you I shall have gone very quietly out of your life. I find that such philosophy as I have does not support me to-night, that all my little rules of life are inadequate. Individual liberty was one— but there is no liberty of the individual. Life—other lives—press too closely. You, living your life as seemed best and easiest, and carrying down with you into shipwreck the little Marie and—myself!

"For, face to face with the fact, I cannot accept it, Walter. It is not only a question of my past against yours. It is of steady revolt and loathing of the whole thing; not the flash of protest before one succumbs to the inevitable, but a deep-seated hatred that is a part of me and that would never forget.

"You say that you are the same man I would have married, only more honest for concealing nothing. But—and forgive me this, it insists on coming up in my mind —were you honest, really? You told me, and it took courage, but wasn't it partly fear? What motive is unmixed? Honesty—and fear, Walter. You were preparing against a contingency, although you may not admit this to yourself.

"I am not passing judgment on you. God forbid that I should! I am only trying to show you what is in my mind, and that this break is final. The revolt is in myself, against something sordid and horrible which I will not take into my life. And for that reason time will make no difference.

"I am not a child, and I am not unreasonable. But I ask a great deal of this life of mine that stretches ahead, Walter—home and children, the love of a good man, the fulfillment of my ideals. And you ask me to start with a handicap. I cannot do it. I know you are resentful, but—I know that you understand.

"ANITA."

CHAPTER XXV

The little Georgiev was in trouble those days. The Balkan engine was threatening to explode, but continued to gather steam, with Bulgaria sitting on the safety-valve. Austria was mobilizing troops, and there were long conferences in the Burg between the Emperor and various bearded gentlemen, while the military prayed in the churches for war.

The little Georgiev hardly ate or slept. Much hammering went on all day in the small room below Harmony's on the Wollbadgasse. At night, when the man in the green velours hat took a little sleep, mysterious packages were carried down the

134

whitewashed staircase and loaded into wagons waiting below. Once on her window-sill Harmony found among the pigeons a carrier pigeon with a brass tube fastened to its leg.

On the morning after Harmony's flight from the garden in the Street of Seven Stars, she received a visit from Georgiev. She had put in a sleepless night, full of heart-searching. She charged herself with cowardice in running away from Peter and Jimmy when they needed her, and in going back like a thief the night before. The conviction that the boy was not so well brought with it additional introspection—her sacrifice seemed useless, almost childish. She had fled because two men thought it necessary, in order to save her reputation, to marry her; and she did not wish to marry. Marriage was fatal to the career she had promised herself, had been promised. But this career, for which she had given up everything else—would she find it in the workroom of a dressmaker?

Ah, but there was more to it than that. Suppose—how her cheeks burned when she thought of it!—suppose she had taken Peter at his word and married him? What about Peter's career? Was there any way by which Peter's poverty for one would be comfort for two? Was there any reason why Peter, with his splendid ability, should settle down to the hack-work of general practice, the very slough out of which he had so painfully climbed?

Either of two things—go back to Peter, but not to marry him, or stay where she was. How she longed to go back only Harmony knew. There in the little room, with only the pigeons to see, she held out her arms longingly. "Peter!" she said. "Peter, dear!"

She decided, of course, to stay where she was, a burden to no one. The instinct of the young girl to preserve her good name at any cost outweighed the vision of Peter at the window, haggard and tired, looking out. It was Harmony's chance, perhaps, to do a big thing; to prove herself bigger than her fears, stronger than convention. But she was young, bewildered, afraid. And there was this element, stronger than any of the others—Peter had never told her he loved her. To go back, throwing herself again on his mercy, was unthinkable. On his love—that was different. But what if he did not love her? He had been good to her; but then Peter was good to every one.

There was something else. If the boy was worse what about his mother? Whatever she was or had been, she was his mother. Suppose he were to die and his mother not see him? Harmony's sense of fairness rebelled. In the small community at home mother was sacred, her claims insistent.

It was very early, hardly more than dawn. The pigeons cooed on the sill; over the ridge of the church roof, across, a luminous strip foretold the sun. An oxcart, laden with vegetables for the market, lumbered along the streets. Puzzled and unhappy, Harmony rose and lighted her fire, drew on her slippers and the faded silk kimono with the pink butterflies.

In the next room the dressmaker still slept, dreaming early morning dreams of lazy apprentices, overdue bills, complaining customers.

Harmony moved lightly not to disturb her. She set her room in order, fed the

135

pigeons,—it was then she saw the carrier with its message,—made her morning coffee by setting the tiny pot inside the stove. And all the time, moving quietly through her morning routine, she was there in that upper room in body only.

In soul she was again in the courtyard back of the old lodge, in the Street of Seven Stars, with the rabbits stirring in the hutch, and Peter, with rapt eyes, gazing out over the city. Bed, toilet-table, coffee-pot, Peter; pigeons, rolls, Peter; sunrise over the church roof, and Peter again. Always Peter!

Monia Reiff was stirring in the next room. Harmony could hear her, muttering and putting coal on the stove and calling to the Hungarian maid for breakfast. Harmony dressed hastily. It was one of her new duties to prepare the workroom for the day. The luminous streak above the church was rose now, time for the day to begin.

She was not certain at once that some one had knocked at the door, so faint was the sound.

She hesitated, listened. The knob turned slightly. Harmony, expecting Monia, called "Come in."

It was the little Georgiev, very apologetic, rather gray of face. He stood in the doorway with his finger on his lips, one ear toward the stairway. It was very silent. Monia was drinking her coffee in bed, whither she had retired for warmth.

"Pardon!" said the Bulgarian in a whisper. "I listened until I heard you moving about. Ah, Fraulein, that I must disturb you!"

"Something has happened!" exclaimed Harmony, thinking of Peter, of course.

"Not yet. I fear it is about to happen. Fraulein, do me the honor to open your window. My pigeon comes now to you to be fed, and I fear—on the sill, Fraulein."

Harmony opened the window. The wild pigeons scattered at once, but the carrier, flying out a foot or two, came back promptly and set about its breakfast.

"Will he let me catch him?"

"Pardon, Fraulein, If I may enter—"

"Come in, of course."

Evidently the defection of the carrier had been serious. A handful of grain on a wrong window-sill, and kingdoms overthrown! Georgiev caught the pigeon and drew the message from the tube. Even Harmony grasped the seriousness of the situation. The little Bulgarian's face, from gray became livid; tiny beads of cold sweat came out on his forehead.

"What have I done?" cried Harmony. "Oh, what have I done? If I had known about the pigeon—"

Georgiev recovered himself.

"The Fraulein can do nothing wrong," he said. "It is a matter of an hour's delay, that is all. It may not be too late."

Monia Reiff, from the next room, called loudly for more coffee. The sulky Hungarian brought it without a glance in their direction.

"Too late for what?"

"Fraulein, if I may trouble you—but glance from the window to the street

136

below. It is of an urgency, or I—Please, Fraulein!"

Harmony glanced down into the half-light of the street. Georgiev, behind her, watched her, breathless, expectant. Harmony drew in her head.

"Only a man in a green hat," she said. "And down the street a group of soldiers."

"Ah!"

The situation dawned on the girl then, at least partially.

"They are coming for you?"

"It is possible. But there are many soldiers in Vienna."

"And I with the pigeon—Oh, it's too horrible! Herr Georgiev, stay here in this room. Lock the door. Monia will say that it is mine—"

"Ah no, Fraulein! It is quite hopeless. Nor is it a matter of the pigeon. It is war, Fraulein. Do not distress yourself. It is but a matter of—imprisonment."

"There must be something I can do," desperately. "I hear them below. Is there no way to the roof, no escape?"

"None, Fraulein. It was an oversight. War is not my game; I am a man of peace. You have been very kind to me, Fraulein. I thank you."

"You are not going down!"

"Pardon, but it is better so. Soldiers they are of the provinces mostly, and not for a lady to confront."

"They are coming up!"

He listened. The clank of scabbards against the stone stairs was unmistakable. The little Georgiev straightened, threw out his chest, turned to descend, faltered, came back a step or two.

His small black eyes were fixed on Harmony's face.

"Fraulein," he said huskily, "you are very lovely. I carry always in my heart your image. Always so long as I live. Adieu."

He drew his heels together, gave a stiff little bow and was gone down the staircase. Harmony was frightened, stricken. She collapsed in a heap on the floor of her room, her fingers in her ears. But she need not have feared. The little Georgiev made no protest, submitted to the inevitable like a gentleman and a soldier, went out of her life, indeed, as unobtrusively as he had entered it.

The carrier pigeon preened itself comfortably on the edge of the washstand. Harmony ceased her hysterical crying at last and pondered what was best to do. Monia was still breakfasting so incredibly brief are great moments. After a little thought Harmony wrote a tiny message, English, German, and French, and inclosed it in the brass tube.

"The Herr Georgiev has been arrested," she wrote. An hour later the carrier rose lazily from the window-sill, flapped its way over the church roof and disappeared, like Georgiev, out of her life. Grim-visaged war had touched her and passed on.

The incident was not entirely closed, however. A search of the building followed the capture of the little spy. Protesting tenants were turned out, beds were dismantled, closets searched, walls sounded for hidden hollows. In one room

137

on Harmony's floor was found stored a quantity of ammunition.

It was when the three men who had conducted the search had finished, when the boxes of ammunition had been gathered in the hall, and the chattering sewing-girls had gone back to work, that Harmony, on her way to her dismantled room, passed through the upper passage.

She glanced down the staircase where little Georgiev had so manfully descended.

"I carry always in my heart your image. Always so long as I live."

The clatter of soldiers on their way down to the street came to her ears; the soft cooing of the pigeons, the whirr of sewing-machines from the workroom. The incident was closed, except for the heap of ammunition boxes on the landing, guarded by an impassive soldier.

Harmony glanced at him. He was eying her steadily, thumbs in, heels in, toes out, chest out. Harmony put her hand to her heart.

"You!" she said.

The conversation of a sentry, save on a holiday is, "Yea, yea," and "Nay, nay."

"Yes, Fraulein."

Harmony put her hands together, a little gesture of appeal, infinitely touching.

"You will not say that you have found, have seen me?"

"No, Fraulein."

It was in Harmony's mind to ask all her hungry heart craved to learn—of Peter, of Jimmy, of the Portier, of anything that belonged to the old life in the Siebensternstrasse. But there was no time. The sentry's impassive face became rigid; he looked through her, not at her. Harmony turned.

The man in the green hat was coming up the staircase. There was no further chance to question. The sentry was set to carrying the boxes down the staircase.

Full morning now, with the winter sun shining on the beggars in the market, on the crowds in the parks, on the flower sellers in the Stephansplatz; shining on Harmony's golden head as she bent over a bit of chiffon, on the old milkwoman carrying up the whitewashed staircase her heavy cans of milk; on the carrier pigeon winging its way to the south; beating in through bars to the exalted face of Herr Georgiev; resting on Peter's drooping shoulders, on the neglected mice and the wooden soldier, on the closed eyes of a sick child—the worshiped sun, peering forth—the golden window of the East.

CHAPTER XXVI

Jimmy was dying. Peter, fighting hard, was beaten at last. All through the night he had felt it; during the hours before the dawn there had been times when the small pulse wavered, flickered, almost ceased. With the daylight there had been a trifle of recovery, enough for a bit of hope, enough to make harder Peter's acceptance of the inevitable.

The boy was very happy, quite content and comfortable. When he opened his eyes he smiled at Peter, and Peter, gray of face, smiled back. Peter died many deaths that night.

At daylight Jimmy fell into a sleep that was really stupor. Marie, creeping to the door in the faint dawn, found the boy apparently asleep and Peter on his knees beside the bed. He raised his head at her footstep and the girl was startled at the suffering in his face. He motioned her back.

"But you must have a little sleep, Peter."

"No. I'll stay until—Go back to bed. It is very early."

Peter had not been able after all to secure the Nurse Elisabet, and now it was useless. At eight o'clock he let Marie take his place, then he bathed and dressed and prepared to face another day, perhaps another night. For the child's release came slowly. He tried to eat breakfast, but managed only a cup of coffee.

Many things had come to Peter in the long night, and one was insistent—the boy's mother was in Vienna and he was dying without her. Peter might know in his heart that he had done the best thing for the child, but like Harmony his early training was rising now to accuse him. He had separated mother and child. Who was he to have decided the mother's unfitness, to have played destiny? How lightly he had taken the lives of others in his hand, and to what end? Harmony, God knows where; the boy dying without his mother. Whatever that mother might be, her place that day was with her boy. What a wreck he had made of things! He was humbled as well as stricken, poor Peter!

In the morning he sent a note to McLean, asking him to try to trace the mother and inclosing the music-hall clipping and the letter. The letter, signed only "Mamma," was not helpful. The clipping might prove valuable.

"And for Heaven's sake be quick," wrote Peter. "This is a matter of hours. I meant well, but I've done a terrible thing. Bring her, Mac, no matter what she is or where you find her." The Portier carried the note. When he came up to get it he brought in his pocket a small rabbit and a lettuce leaf. Never before had the combination failed to arouse and amuse the boy. He carried the rabbit down again sorrowfully. "He saw it not," he reported sadly to his wife. "Be off to the church while I deliver this letter. And this rabbit we will not cook, but keep in remembrance."

At eleven o'clock Marie called Peter, who was asleep on the horsehair sofa.

"He asks for you."

Peter was instantly awake and on his feet. The boy's eyes were open and fixed on him.

"Is it another day?" he asked.

"Yes, boy; another morning."

"I am cold, Peter."

They blanketed him, although the room was warm. From where he lay he could see the mice. He watched them for a moment. Poor Peter, very humble, found himself wondering in how many ways he had been remiss. To see this small soul launched into eternity without a foreword, without a bit of light for the journey! Peter's religion had been one of life and living, not of creed.

139

Marie, bringing jugs of hot water, bent over Peter.

"He knows, poor little one!" she whispered.

And so, indeed, it would seem. The boy, revived by a spoonful or two of broth, asked to have the two tame mice on the bed. Peter, opening the cage, found one dead, very stiff and stark. The catastrophe he kept from the boy.

"One is sick, Jimmy boy," he said, and placed the mate, forlorn and shivering, on the pillow. After a minute:—

"If the sick one dies will it go to heaven?"

"Yes, honey, I think so."

The boy was silent for a time. Thinking was easier than speech. His mind too worked slowly. It was after a pause, while he lay there with closed eyes, that Peter saw two tears slip from under his long lashes. Peter bent over and wiped them away, a great ache in his heart.

"What is it, dear?"

"I'm afraid—it's going to die!"

"Would that be so terrible, Jimmy boy?" asked Peter gently. "To go to heaven, where there is no more death or dying, where it is always summer and the sun always shines?"

No reply for a moment. The little mouse sat up on the pillow and rubbed its nose with a pinkish paw. The baby mice in the cage nuzzled their dead mother.

"Is there grass?"

"Yes—soft green grass."

"Do—boys in heaven—go in their bare feet?" Ah, small mind and heart, so terrified and yet so curious!

"Indeed, yes." And there on his knees beside the white bed Peter painted such a heaven as no theologue has ever had the humanity to paint—a heaven of babbling brooks and laughing, playing children, a heaven of dear departed puppies and resurrected birds, of friendly deer, of trees in fruit, of speckled fish in bright rivers. Painted his heaven with smiling eyes and death in his heart, a child's heaven of games and friendly Indians, of sunlight and rain, sweet sleep and brisk awakening.

The boy listened. He was silent when Peter had finished. Speech was increasingly an effort.

"I should—like—to go there," he whispered at last.

He did not speak again during all the long afternoon, but just at dusk he roused again.

"I would like—to see—the sentry," he said with difficulty.

And so again, and for the last time, Rosa's soldier from Salzburg with one lung.

Through all that long day, then, Harmony sat over her work, unaccustomed muscles aching, the whirring machines in her ears. Monia, upset over the morning's excitement, was irritable and unreasonable. The gold-tissue costume had come back from Le Grande with a complaint. Below in the courtyard all day curious groups stood gaping up the staircase, where the morning had seen such occurrences.

140

At the noon hour, while the girls heated soup and carried in pails of salad from the corner restaurant, Harmony had fallen into the way of playing for them. To the music-loving Viennese girls this was the hour of the day. To sit back, soup bowl on knee, the machines silent, Monia quarreling in the kitchen with the Hungarian servant, and while the pigeons ate crusts on the window-sills, to hear this American girl play such music as was played at the opera, her slim figure swaying, her whole beautiful face and body glowing with the melody she made, the girls found the situation piquant, altogether delightful. Although she did not suspect it, many rumors were rife about Harmony in the workroom. She was not of the people, they said—the daughter of a great American, of course, run away to escape a loveless marriage. This was borne out by the report of one of them who had glimpsed the silk petticoat. It was rumored also that she wore no chemise, but instead an infinitely coquettish series of lace and nainsook garments —of a fineness!

Harmony played for them that day, played, perhaps, as she had not played since the day she had moved the master to tears, played to Peter as she had seen him at the window, to Jimmy, to the little Georgiev as he went down the staircase. And finally with a choke in her throat to the little mother back home, so hopeful, so ignorant.

In the evening, as was her custom, she took the one real meal of the day at the corner restaurant, going early to avoid the crowd and coming back quickly through the winter night. The staircase was always a peril, to be encountered and conquered night after night and even in the daytime not to be lightly regarded. On her way up this night she heard steps ahead, heavy, measured steps that climbed steadily without pauses. For an instant Harmony thought it sounded like Peter's step and she went dizzy.

But it was not Peter. Standing in the upper hall, much as he had stood that morning over the ammunition boxes, thumbs in, heels in, toes out, chest out, was the sentry.

Harmony's first thought was of Georgiev and more searching of the building. Then she saw that the sentry's impassive face wore lines of trouble. He saluted. "Please, Fraulein."

"Yes?"

"I have not told the Herr Doktor."

"I thank you."

"But the child dies."

"Jimmy?"

"He dies all of last night and to-day. To-night, it is, perhaps, but of moments."

Harmony clutched at the iron stair-rail for support. "You are sure? You are not telling me so that I will go back?"

"He dies, Fraulein. The Herr Doktor has not slept for many hours. My wife, Rosa, sits on the stair to see that none disturb, and her cousin, the wife of the Portier, weeps over the stove. Please, Fraulein, come with me."

"When did you leave the Siebensternstrasse?"

141

"But now."

"And he still lives?"

"Ja, Fraulein, and asks for you."

Now suddenly fell away from the girl all pride, all fear, all that was personal and small and frightened, before the reality of death. She rose, as women by divine gift do rise, to the crisis; ceased trembling, got her hat and coat and her shabby gloves and joined the sentry again. Another moment's delay—to secure the Le Grande's address from Monia. Then out into the night, Harmony to the Siebensternstrasse, the tall soldier to find the dancer at her hotel, or failing that, at the Ronacher Music-Hall.

Harmony took a taxicab—nothing must be spared now—bribed the chauffeur to greater speed, arrived at the house and ran across the garden, still tearless, up the stairs, past Rosa on the upper flight, and rang the bell.

Marie admitted her with only a little gasp of surprise. There was nothing to warn Peter. One moment he sat by the bed, watch in hand, alone, drear, tragic-eyed. The next he had glanced up, saw Harmony and went white, holding to the back of his chair. Their eyes met, agony and hope in them, love and death, rapture and bitterness. In Harmony's, pleading, promise, something of doubt; in Peter's, only yearning, as of empty arms. Then Harmony dared to look at the bed and fell on her knees in a storm of grief beside it. Peter bent over and gently stroked her hair.

Le Grande was singing; the boxes were full. In the body of the immense theater waiters scurried back and forward among the tables. Everywhere was the clatter of silver and steel on porcelain, the clink of glasses. Smoke was everywhere—pipes, cigars, cigarettes. Women smoked between bites at the tables, using small paper or silver mouthpieces, even a gold one shone here and there. Men walked up and down among the diners, spraying the air with chemicals to clear it. At a table just below the stage sat the red-bearded Dozent with the lady of the photograph. They were drinking cheap native wines and were very happy.

From the height of his worldly wisdom he was explaining the people to her.

"In the box—don't stare, Liebchen, he looks—is the princeling I have told you of. Roses, of course. Last night it was orchids."

"Last night! Were you here?" He coughed.

"I have been told, Liebchen. Each night he sits there, and when she finishes her song he rises in the box, kisses the flowers and tosses them to her."

"Shameless! Is she so beautiful?"

"No. But you shall see. She comes."

Le Grande was very popular. She occupied the best place on the program; and because she sang in American, which is not exactly English and more difficult to understand, her songs were considered exceedingly risque. As a matter of fact they were merely ragtime melodies, with a lilt to them that caught the Viennese fancy, accustomed to German sentimental ditties and the artificial forms of grand opera. And there was another reason for her success. She carried with her a chorus of a dozen pickaninnies.

142

In Austria darkies were as rare as cats, and there were no cats! So the little chorus had made good.

Each day she walked in the Prater, ermine from head to foot, and behind her two by two trailed twelve little Southern darkies in red-velvet coats and caps, grinning sociably. When she drove a pair sat on the boot.

Her voice was strong, not sweet, spoiled by years of singing against dishes and bottles in smoky music halls; spoiled by cigarettes and absinthe and foreign cocktails that resembled their American prototypes as the night resembles the day.

She wore the gold dress, decolletee, slashed to the knee over rhinestone-spangled stockings. And back of her trailed the twelve little darkies.

She sang "Dixie," of course, and the "Old Folks at Home"; then a ragtime medley, with the chorus showing rows of white teeth and clogging with all their short legs. Le Grande danced to that, a whirling, nimble dance. The little rhinestones on her stockings flashed; her opulent bosom quivered. The Dozent, eyes on the dancer, squeezed his companion's hand.

"I love thee!" he whispered, rather flushed.

And then she sang "Doan ye cry, mah honey." Her voice, rather coarse but melodious, lent itself to the negro rhythm, the swing and lilt of the lullaby. The little darkies, eyes rolling, preternaturally solemn, linked arms and swayed rhythmically, right, left, right, left. The glasses ceased clinking; sturdy citizens forgot their steak and beer for a moment and listened, knife and fork poised. Under the table the Dozent's hand pressed its captive affectionately, his eyes no longer on Le Grande, but on the woman across, his sweetheart, she who would be mother of his children. The words meant little to the audience; the rich, rolling Southern lullaby held them rapt:—

"Doan ye Cry, mah honey—
Doan ye weep no mo',
Mammy's gwine to hold her baby,
All de udder black trash sleepin' on the flo',"

The little darkies swayed; the singer swayed, empty arms cradled.

She picked the tiniest darky up and held him, woolly head against her breast, and crooned to him, rocking on her jeweled heels. The crowd applauded; the man in the box kissed his flowers and flung them. Glasses and dishes clinked again.

The Dozent bent across the table.

"Some day—" he said.

The girl blushed.

Le Grande made her way into the wings, surrounded by her little troupe. A motherly colored woman took them, shooed them off, rounded them up like a flock of chickens.

And there in the wings, grimly impassive, stood a private soldier of the old Franz Josef, blocking the door to her dressing room. For a moment gold dress and dark blue-gray uniform confronted each other. Then the sentry touched his cap.

"Madam," he said, "the child is in the Riebensternstrasse and to-night he dies."

143

"What child?" Her arms were full of flowers.

"The child from the hospital. Please to make haste."

Jimmy died an hour after midnight, quite peacefully, died with one hand in Harmony's and one between Peter's two big ones.

Toward the last he called Peter "Daddy" and asked for a drink. His eyes, moving slowly round the room, passed without notice the grayfaced woman in a gold dress who stood staring down at him, rested a moment on the cage of mice, came to a stop in the doorway, where stood the sentry, white and weary, but refusing rest.

It was Harmony who divined the child's unspoken wish.

"The manual?" she whispered.

The boy nodded. And so just inside the door of the bedroom across from the old salon of Maria Theresa the sentry, with sad eyes but no lack of vigor, went again through the Austrian manual of arms, and because he had no carbine he used Peter's old walking-stick.

When it was finished the boy smiled faintly, tried to salute, lay still.

CHAPTER XXVII

Peter was going back to America and still he had not told Harmony he loved her. It was necessary that he go back. His money had about given out, and there was no way to get more save by earning it. The drain of Jimmy's illness, the inevitable expense of the small grave and the tiny stone Peter had insisted on buying, had made retreat his only course. True, Le Grande had wished to defray all expenses, but Peter was inexorable. No money earned as the dancer earned hers should purchase peaceful rest for the loved little body. And after seeing Peter's eyes the dancer had not insisted.

A week had seen many changes. Marie was gone. After a conference between Stewart and Peter that had been decided on. Stewart raised the money somehow, and Peter saw her off, palpitant and eager, with the pin he had sent her to Semmering at her throat. She kissed Peter on the cheek in the station, rather to his embarrassment. From the lowered window, as the train pulled out, she waved a moist handkerchief.

"I shall be very good," she promised him. The last words he heard above the grinding of the train were her cheery: "To America!"

Peter was living alone in the Street of Seven Stars, getting food where he might happen to be, buying a little now and then from the delicatessen shop across the street. For Harmony had gone back to the house in the Wollbadgasse. She had stayed until all was over and until Marie's small preparations for departure were over. Then, while Peter was at the station, she slipped away again. But this time she left her address. She wrote:—

"You will come to visit me, dear Peter, because I was so lonely before and that is unnecessary now. But you must know that I cannot stay in the Siebensternstrasse.

We have each our own fight to make, and you have been trying to fight for us all, for Marie, for dear little Jimmy, for me. You must get back to work now; you have lost so much time. And I am managing well. The Frau Professor is back and will take an evening lesson, and soon I shall have more money from Fraulein Reiff. You can see how things are looking up for me. In a few months I shall be able to renew my music lessons. And then, Peter,—the career!

"HARMONY."

Her address was beneath.

Peter had suffered much. He was thinner, grayer, and as he stood with the letter in his hand he felt that Harmony was right. He could offer her nothing but his shabby self, his problematic future. Perhaps, surely, everything would have been settled, without reason, had he only once taken the girl in his arms, told her she was the breath of life itself to him. But adversity, while it had roused his fighting spirit in everything else, had sapped his confidence.

He had found the letter on his dressing-table, and he found himself confronting his image over it, a tall, stooping figure, a tired, lined face, a coat that bore the impress of many days with a sick child's head against its breast.

So it was over. She had come back and gone again, and this time he must let her go. Who was he to detain her? She would carry herself on to success, he felt; she had youth, hope, beauty and ability. And she had proved the thing he had not dared to believe, that she could take care of herself in the old city. Only—to go away and leave her there!

McLean would remain. No doubt he already had Harmony's address in the Wollbadgasse. Peter was not subtle, no psychologist, but he had seen during the last few days how the boy watched Harmony's every word, every gesture. And, perhaps, when loneliness and hard work began to tell on her, McLean's devotion would win its reward. McLean's devotion, with all that it meant, the lessons again, community of taste, their common youth! Peter felt old, very tired.

Nevertheless he went that night to the Wollbadgasse. He sent his gray suit to the Portier's wife to be pressed, and getting out his surgical case, as he had once before in the Pension Schwarz, he sewed a button on his overcoat, using the curved needle and the catgut and working with surgeon's precision. Then, still working very carefully, he trimmed the edges of graying hair over his ears, trimmed his cuffs, trimmed his best silk tie, now almost hopeless. He blacked his shoes, and the suit not coming, he donned his dressing-gown and went into Jimmy's room to feed the mice. Peter stood a moment beside the smooth white bed with his face working. The wooden sentry still stood on the bedside table.

It was in Peter's mind to take the mice to Harmony, confess his defeat and approaching retreat, and ask her to care for them. Then he decided against this palpable appeal for sympathy, elected to go empty-handed and discover merely how comfortable she was or was not. When the time came he would slip out of her life, sending her a letter and leaving McLean on guard.

Harmony was at home. Peter climbed the dark staircase—where Harmony had met the little Georgiev, and where he had gone down to his death—climbed

145

steadily, but without his usual elasticity. The place appalled him—its gloom, its dinginess, its somber quiet. In the daylight, with the pigeons on the sills and the morning sunlight printing the cross of the church steeple on the whitewashed wall, it was peaceful, cloisterlike, with landings that were crypts. But at night it was almost terrifying, that staircase.

Harmony was playing. Peter heard her when he reached the upper landing, playing a sad little strain that gripped his heart. He waited outside before ringing, heard her begin something determinedly cheerful, falter, cease altogether. Peter rang.

Harmony herself admitted him. Perhaps—oh, certainly she had expected him! It would be Peter, of course, to come and see how she was getting on, how she was housed. She held out her hand and Peter took it. Still no words, only a half smile from her and no smile at all from Peter, but his heart in his eyes.

"I hoped you would come, Peter. We may have the reception room."

"You knew I would come," said Peter. "The reception room?"

"Where customers wait." She still carried her violin, and slipped back to her room to put it away. Peter had a glimpse of its poverty and its meagerness. He drew a long breath.

Monia was at the opera, and the Hungarian sat in the kitchen knitting a stocking. The reception room was warm from the day's fire, and in order. All the pins and scraps of the day had been swept up, and the portieres that made fitting-rooms of the corners were pushed back. Peter saw only a big room with empty corners, and that at a glance. His eyes were Harmony's.

He sat down awkwardly on a stiff chair, Harmony on a velvet settee. They were suddenly two strangers meeting for the first time. In the squalor of the Pension Schwarz, in the comfortable intimacies of the Street of Seven Stars, they had been easy, unconstrained. Now suddenly Peter was tongue-tied. Only one thing in him clamored for utterance, and that he sternly silenced.

"I—I could not stay there, Peter. You understood?"

"No. Of course, I understood."

"You were not angry?"

"Why should I be angry? You came, like an angel of light, when I needed you. Only, of course,—"

"Yes?"

"I'll not say that, I think."

"Please say it, Peter!"

Peter writhed; looked everywhere but at her.

"Please, Peter. You said I always came when you needed me, only—"

"Only—I always need you!" Peter, Peter!

"Not always, I think. Of course, when one is in trouble one needs a woman; but —"

"Well, of course—but—I'm generally in trouble, Harry dear."

Frightfully ashamed of himself by that time was Peter, ashamed of his weakness. He sought to give a casual air to the speech by stooping for a neglected

146

pin on the carpet. By the time he had stuck it in his lapel he had saved his mental forces from the rout of Harmony's eyes.

His next speech he made to the center table, and missed a most delectable look in the aforesaid eyes.

"I didn't come to be silly," he said to the table. "I hate people who whine, and I've got into a damnable habit of being sorry for myself! It's to laugh, isn't it, a great, hulking carcass like me, to be—"

"Peter," said Harmony softly, "aren't you going to look at me?"

"I'm afraid."

"That's cowardice. And I've fixed my hair a new way. Do you like it?"

"Splendid," said Peter to the center table.

"You didn't look!"

The rout of Harmony's eyes was supplemented by the rout of Harmony's hair. Peter, goaded, got up and walked about. Harmony was half exasperated; she would have boxed Peter's ears with a tender hand had she dared.

His hands thrust savagely in his pockets, Peter turned and faced her at last.

"First of all," he said, "I am going back to America, Harmony. I've got all I can get here, all I came for—" He stopped, seeing her face. "Well, of course, that's not true, I haven't. But I'm going back, anyhow. You needn't look so stricken: I haven't lost my chance. I'll come back sometime again and finish, when I've earned enough to do it."

"You will never come back, Peter. You have spent all your money on others, and now you are going back just where you were, and—you are leaving me here alone!"

"You are alone, anyhow," said Peter, "making your own way and getting along. And McLean will be here."

"Are you turning me over to him?"

No reply. Peter was pacing the floor.

"Peter!"

"Yes, dear?"

"Do you remember the night in Anna's room at the Schwartz when you proposed to me?"

No reply. Peter found another pin.

"And that night in the old lodge when you proposed to me again?"

Peter turned and looked at her, at her slender, swaying young figure, her luminous eyes, her parted, childish lips.

"Peter, I want you to—to ask me again."

"No!"

"Why?"

"Now, listen to me, Harmony. You're sorry for me, that's all; I don't want to be pitied. You stay here and work. You'll do big things. I had a talk with the master while I was searching for you, and he says you can do anything. But he looked at me—and a sight I was with worry and fright—and he warned me off, Harmony. He says you must not marry."

147

"Old pig!" said Harmony. "I will marry if I please."

Nevertheless Peter's refusal and the master's speech had told somewhat. She was colder, less vibrant. Peter came to her, stood close, looking down at her.

"I've said a lot I didn't mean to," he said. "There's only one thing I haven't said, I oughtn't to say it, dear. I'm not going to marry you—I won't have such a thing on my conscience. But it doesn't hurt a woman to know that a man loves her. I love you, dear. You're my heaven and my earth—even my God, I'm afraid. But I will not marry you."

"Not even if I ask you to?"

"Not even then, dear. To share my struggle—"

"I see," slowly. "It is to be a struggle?"

"A hard fight, Harmony. I'm a pauper practically."

"And what am I?"

"Two poverties don't make a wealth, even of happiness," said Peter steadily. "In the time to come, when you would think of what you might have been, it would be a thousand deaths to me, dear."

"People have married, women have married and carried on their work, too, Peter."

"Not your sort of women or your sort of work. And not my sort of man, Harry. I'm jealous—jealous of every one about you. It would have to be the music or me."

"And you make the choice!" said Harmony proudly. "Very well, Peter, I shall do as you say. But I think it is a very curious sort of love."

"I wonder," Peter cried, "if you realize what love it is that loves you enough to give you up."

"You have not asked me if I care, Peter."

Peter looked at her. She was very near to tears, very sad, very beautiful.

"I'm afraid to ask," said Peter, and picking up his hat he made for the door. There he turned, looked back, was lost.

"My sweetest heart!" he cried, and took her in his hungry arms. But even then, with her arms about his neck at last, with her slender body held to him, her head on his shoulder, his lips to her soft throat, Peter put her from him as a starving man might put away food.

He held her off and looked at her.

"I'm a fool and a weakling," he said gravely. "I love you so much that I would sacrifice you. You are very lovely, my girl, my girl! As long as I live I shall carry your image in my heart."

Ah, what the little Georgiev had said on his way to the death that waited down the staircase. Peter, not daring to look at her again, put away her detaining hand, squared his shoulders, went to the door.

"Good-bye, Harmony," he said steadily. "Always in my heart!"

Very near the end now: the little Marie on the way to America, with the recording angel opening a new page in life's ledger for her and a red-ink line erasing the other; with Jimmy and his daddy wandering through the heaven of

148

friendly adventure and green fields, hand in hand; with the carrier resting after its labors in the pigeon house by the rose-fields of Sofia; with the sentry casting martial shadows through the barred windows of the hospital; and the little Georgiev, about to die, dividing his heart, as a heritage, between his country and a young girl.

Very near the end, with the morning light of the next day shining into the salon of Maria Theresa and on to Peter's open trunk and shabby wardrobe spread over chairs. An end of trunks and departure, as was the beginning.

Early morning at the Gottesacker, or God's acre, whence little Jimmy had started on his comfortable journey. Early morning on the frost-covered grass, the frozen roads, the snap and sparkle of the Donau. Harmony had taken her problem there, in the early hour before Monia would summon her to labor—took her problem and found her answer.

The great cemetery was still and deserted. Harmony, none too warmly clad, walked briskly, a bunch of flowers in oiled paper against the cold. Already the air carried a hint of spring; there was a feeling of resurrection and promise. The dead earth felt alive under-foot.

Harmony knelt by the grave and said the little prayer the child had repeated at night and morning. And, because he had loved it, with some vague feeling of giving him comfort, she recited the little verse:—

"Ah well! For us all some sweet hope lies Deeply buried from human eyes: And in the hereafter, angels may Roll the stone from its grave away."

When she looked up Le Grande was standing beside her.

There was no scene, hardly any tears. She had brought out a great bunch of roses that bore only too clearly the stamp of whence they came. One of the pickaninnies had carried the box and stood impassively by, gazing at Harmony.

Le Grande placed her flowers on the grave. They almost covered it, quite eclipsed Harmony's.

"I come here every morning," she said simply.

She had a cab waiting, and offered to drive Harmony back to the city. Her quiet almost irritated Harmony, until she had looked once into the woman's eyes. After that she knew. It was on the drive back, with the little darky on the box beside the driver, that Harmony got her answer.

Le Grande put a hand over Harmony's.

"I tried to tell you before how good I know you were to him."

"We loved him."

"And I resented it. But Dr. Byrne was right—I was not a fit person to—to have him."

"It was not that—not only that—"

"Did he ever ask for me? But of course not."

"No, he had no remembrance."

Silence for a moment. The loose windows of the cab clattered.

"I loved him very much when he came," said Le Grande, "although I did not want him. I had been told I could have a career on the stage. Ah, my dear, I chose

149

the career—and look at me! What have I? A grave in the cemetery back there, and on it roses sent me by a man I loathe! If I could live it over again!"

The answer was very close now:—

"Would you stay at home?"

"Who knows, I being I? And my husband did not love me. It was the boy always. There is only one thing worth while—the love of a good man. I have lived, lived hard. And I know."

"But supposing that one has real ability—I mean some achievement already, and a promise—"

Le Grande turned and looked at Harmony shrewdly.

"I see. You are a musician, I believe?"

"Yes."

"And—it is Dr. Byrne?"

"Yes."

Le Grande bent forward earnestly.

"My child," she said, "if one man in all the world looked at me as your doctor looks at you, I—I would be a better woman."

"And my music?"

"Play for your children, as you played for my little boy."

Peter was packing: wrapping medical books in old coats, putting clean collars next to boots, folding pajamas and such-like negligible garments with great care and putting in his dresscoat in a roll. His pipes took time, and the wooden sentry he packed with great care and a bit of healthy emotion. Once or twice he came across trifles of Harmony's, and he put them carefully aside—the sweater coat, a folded handkerchief, a bow she had worn at her throat. The bow brought back the night before and that reckless kiss on her white throat. Well for Peter to get away if he is to keep his resolution, when the sight of a ribbon bow can bring that look of suffering into his eyes.

The Portier below was polishing floors, right foot, left foot, any foot at all. And as he polished he sang in a throaty tenor.

"Kennst du das Land wo die Citronen bluhen," he sang at the top of his voice, and coughed, a bit of floor wax having got into the air. The antlers of the deer from the wild-game shop hung now in his bedroom. When the wildgame seller came over for coffee there would be a discussion probably. But were not the antlers of all deer similar?

The Portier's wife came to the doorway with a cooking fork in her hand.

"A cab," she announced, "with a devil's imp on the box. Perhaps it is that American dancer. Run and pretty thyself!"

It was too late for more than an upward twist of a mustache. Harmony was at the door, but not the sad-eyed Harmony of a week before or the undecided and troubled girl of before that. A radiant Harmony, this, who stood in the doorway, who wished them good-morning, and ran up the old staircase with glowing eyes and a heart that leaped and throbbed. A woman now, this Harmony, one who had looked on life and learned; one who had chosen her fate and was running to meet it; one who feared only death, not life or anything that life could offer.

The door was not locked. Perhaps Peter was not up—not dressed. What did that matter? What did anything matter but Peter himself?

Peter, sorting out lectures on McBurney's Point, had come across a bit of paper that did not belong there, and was sitting by his open trunk, staring blindly at it:—

"You are very kind to me. Yes, indeed.

"H. W."

Quite the end now, with Harmony running across the room and dropping down on her knees among a riot of garments—down on her knees, with one arm round Peter's neck, drawing his tired head lower until she could kiss him.

"Oh, Peter, Peter, dear!" she cried. "I'll love you all my life if only you'll love me, and never, never let me go!"

Peter was dazed at first. He put his arms about her rather unsteadily, because he had given her up and had expected to go through the rest of life empty of arm and heart. And when one has one's arms set, as one may say, for loneliness and relinquishment it is rather difficult—Ah, but Peter got the way of it swiftly.

"Always," he said incoherently; "forever the two of us. Whatever comes, Harmony?"

"Whatever comes."

"And you'll not be sorry?"

"Not if you love me."

Peter kissed her on the eyes very solemnly.

"God helping me, I'll be good to you always. And I'll always love you."

He tried to hold her away from him for a moment after that, to tell her what she was doing, what she was giving up. She would not be reasoned with.

"I love you," was her answer to every line. And it was no divided allegiance she promised him. "Career? I shall have a career. Yours!"

"And your music?"

She colored, held him closer.

"Some day," she whispered, "I shall tell you about that."

Late winter morning in Vienna, with the school-children hurrying home, the Alserstrasse alive with humanity—soldiers and chimney-sweeps, housewives and beggars. Before the hospital the crowd lines up along the curb; the head waiter from the coffee-house across comes to the doorway and looks out. The sentry in front of the hospital ceases pacing and stands at attention.

In the street a small procession comes at the double quick—a handful of troopers, a black van with tiny, high-barred windows, more troopers.

Inside the van a Bulgarian spy going out to death—a swarthy little man with black eyes and short, thick hands, going out like a gentleman and a soldier to meet the God of patriots and lovers.

The sentry, who was only a soldier from Salzburg with one lung, was also a gentleman and a patriot. He uncovered his head.

151

Printed in Poland
by Amazon Fulfillment
Poland Sp. z o.o., Wrocław